She was being watched

Somewhere out there in the dark night, somebody stood poised above her, probably on a hill, looking at her through binoculars. She'd sensed it for so long that not only could she picture the scene, but her breathing had gone shallow, and all of her joints had liquefied.

Part of her wanted to turn around. Part of her could envision the scenario if she did. She'd turn. A bullet would fly through the night. The glass behind her would splinter into a million-piece spray. And she'd crumple to the floor, as her companions dove under the table.

She shook her head as if to clear the haze but she couldn't. She was sinking into a fog of desperate fear, the kind of fear that kept you up all night because you didn't dare close your eyes. And if she didn't do something soon, she'd never come out....

ABOUT THE AUTHOR

Suzanne Mayer is a busy and happy mother of three children who has been married for twelve years and works full-time as an executive secretary at a company that designs landfills. She loves the challenge of writing mysteries, dropping clues without giving away the resolution of the puzzle.

In for Life
Suzanne Mayer

𝓗𝓪𝓻𝓵𝓮𝓺𝓾𝓲𝓷 𝓑𝓸𝓸𝓴𝓼

TORONTO • NEW YORK • LONDON
AMSTERDAM • PARIS • SYDNEY • HAMBURG
STOCKHOLM • ATHENS • TOKYO • MILAN

Harlequin Intrigue edition published June 1990

ISBN 0-373-22139-8

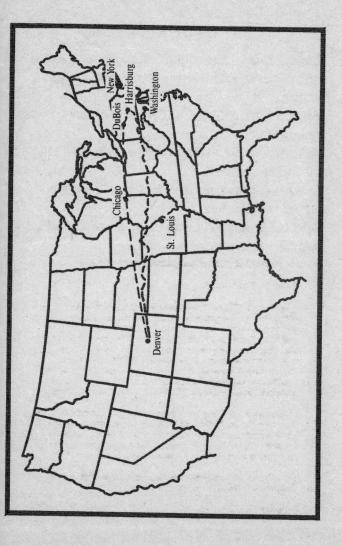

CAST OF CHARACTERS

Linda Miller—She couldn't stop running for her life, not even after the murderer was brought to justice.

John Santos, Sr.—An underworld boss who was caught in the act.

John Santos, Jr.—He vowed to get revenge in his father's name.

Simon—The mysterious right-hand man who served two masters.

Michael Rosen—He had an old score to settle, and he was determined to win.

Chapter One

"Thanks," Linda Miller called, waving goodbye to her unwanted police escort, looking as if she were about to turn and walk into the old stone house that served as the offices for Bingham and Bingham, Attorneys-at-Law. But as the cruiser's red taillights faded into the hot August night, she glanced sideways at the Mercedes that was parked in her space, automatically memorizing the license number even though Senator Bingham's car was parked right beside it. Nine chances out of ten the car belonged to the individual with whom her boss was conferring, but if it didn't, it would have to be towed.

She wouldn't hang around this parking lot after midnight on a Friday under the best of circumstances, but she definitely wasn't coming back outside for a license number when two policemen were threatening to drive her home if her boss couldn't.

The front door was unlocked, but that didn't really surprise her since Mr. Bingham's car would not be in the parking lot unless he was here. But when she opened the door and found a dark, quiet reception room, she froze. The only thing she could see was the shadowy outline of the desk, and once she closed the door even the outline disappeared.

She turned her head and saw a light at the end of the hall. One of those long, thin lines on the wall that indicated the door of a lighted room was cracked open. It didn't light the hall. It didn't light her way. But it did prove she was right. Dark reception room notwithstanding, Mr. Bingham was in his office. He wasn't the kind to leave a light burning in his room unless he was in it and, thinking about it, she decided his frugality also explained the darkness around her.

She took two faltering steps, then sighed. Her heels were high, her purse was bulky and clumsy, and the room was darker than a forest on a moonless midnight. Still, she wasn't going to turn on a light. In the right frame of mind Mr. Bingham might chuckle about this mess she'd gotten herself into, so she wasn't going to rile him by wasting electricity. She swallowed her pride, tightened her grip on her shoulder bag and walked around the desk. If she ever got divorced again, she wasn't going to let her friends talk her into celebrating.

When she reached the senator's office, she stopped. As she'd suspected, the door wasn't completely closed, and through the three-inch opening she could see a short man, a man no taller than a preteen. His coffee-brown hair was straight and hung boyishly to his forehead, but the thick growth of his black beard forestalled any notion that this man was a youth. He had dark, penetrating eyes, eyes that showed he was thinking, concentrating on his surroundings. But they didn't move. Not one of his muscles even twitched. His lips were nothing but a thin pink line, his jaw a block of bearded granite.

For a second Linda debated turning and running, if only because the man was positively scary, but she didn't. She couldn't. Those policemen had promised to come back and make sure Mr. Bingham was here and willing to take her home, and she wasn't about to gamble that they might have been bluffing.

After a light push, the heavy wood silently moved three more inches and Linda's eyes widened. The senator was seated in his buttery-brown leather chair, but his arms were held back by two enormous oafs who were dressed in suits. Each sported enough muscles and facial scars to categorize them as thugs. A fourth man, another very short man, walked behind the desk and pointed a shiny, wicked-looking knife under the third button of the senator's shirt. Even before she could scream, the blade was thrust into Bob Bingham's barrel chest.

"Oh, my Lord," Linda whispered. Fear and revulsion galvanized her muscles and she stood frozen, just staring in disbelief.

Four pairs of eyes turned in her direction, and for the first time, Linda saw that the murderer wore clear surgical gloves. Slowly, almost casually, he began to peel them off. "Get her," he said, jerking his chin toward the door.

Linda whirled and ran down the dark hall. On instinct, she skirted the desk in the reception room, but someone behind her slammed right into it and cursed profusely. Still she didn't get time to recognize her good fortune, because her spike heel fell the wrong way on the shiny tile and she slid the remaining four feet to the door. Just as she righted herself, someone seized her upper arm and she lost her balance again, but her jumbo purse swung around and landed in the stomach of her assailant, which resulted in a deep grunt of pain and a loosened grip on her arm.

Taking full advantage, Linda jerked free and slid out from under the strap of her heavy bag, letting it fall to the floor. She grabbed the doorknob, but as she turned it, five fat fingers wrapped around her wrist. Without as much as a second thought, she slammed her heel on her captor's foot, then gave a mighty pull on the door and zipped out of the building.

Down the steps she went, mindless of where she was going. She took off like a shot, not remembering her car or the bright streetlights that snatched away the cloak of darkness and made her an easy target. Every breath she drew shivered in her chest. She didn't hear the heavy thud of footsteps behind her, but that scared her even more. If they weren't behind her, they could have taken a shortcut, which would put them in front of her. She could be running into their waiting arms. Even worse, they were probably smart enough to get their car. One way or another, they were going to catch her. And once she was caught, she'd be killed.

She heard the sound of feet then—the tap, tap, tap of leather hitting the cement steps of the office—and the bones of her legs turned to lead. Her knees banged together like a magnet and steel even as her ankles turned to Jell-O, and she fell to the ground, scared to the point of shivering. In the distance she heard a car door slam, then the first sounds of an engine, but they hardly registered. Her heart thumped so hard it hurt, and she couldn't get any air even though she was breathing fast and hard.

Twin beams of headlights enveloped her and she screamed, scrambling to her feet again. "Oh, help me," she moaned, forcing her rubbery legs to run. Fear might have rendered her temporarily helpless, but imminent death put the fire in her blood again. She swallowed her shuddering breath and commanded herself to run. *Run!* her mind screamed. *Run!*

Like a lobster claw, two giant arms closed around her from behind, fastening her elbows to her waist. She kicked and clawed like a madwoman. "No! No!" she shrieked. "Get away from me!"

"Darn it! You crazy woman! You asked for this!"

Linda barely had enough time to realize she recognized the voice before she was bodily lifted from the pavement. The man carrying her swung around and began to stride to the police cruiser angled halfway on the sidewalk. Once there, he threw her onto the hood, grabbed her nape and shoved her face against the cool metal.

"Take it easy, George!"

The gruff voice sounded from above as Linda panted uncontrollably, unable to get her bearings.

"Would you look at this?" the young trooper commanded. "The idiot bit me!"

"Oh, quit your griping."

Linda turned her cheek to the car hood and felt strangely disembodied from the whole scene. Two minutes ago she had been running for her life, now she was lying across a car hood listening to her rescuers quibble. For a second she wondered if she was dreaming, but there was cool metal against her skin and white heat that seared her brain, then slowly rolled down to her toes. Just under the surface of her skin, it skimmed muscle and flesh, like a soul seeking escape from its mortal prison.

"All right, but the next time she tries to run, you chase her!"

"Not on your life," the other man replied through a guffaw of laughter. "You're the one who wanted to stop her," he emphatically pointed out. "I thought she was driving just fine . . . a little slow. But there's no law against that."

Linda closed her eyes as they argued, but she plainly saw Bob Bingham's face contorted with pain. She saw his blood as it soaked his shirt. She remembered the triumphant look in the eyes of the man who pulled a knife through the senator's body with the practiced precision of a sadistic fiend. And the white heat began to move again. This time from her toes, tingling up her legs, dancing through her middle and landing in her brain. There was a pause, then the liquid heat tumbled to her feet.

Realizing she was about to faint, Linda drew three deep gulps of air. She couldn't pass out, the murderer would escape. "My boss," she said, choking on her words because her tongue felt as though it had tripled in size. "My boss..."

"Your boss what?" her captor demanded, once again tightening his grip on her neck.

"He...he...oh...he's..." *Dead.* She couldn't say it. It was too hard to believe, too horrible. And again she considered that she might only be dreaming, but the cold metal below her cheek was a solid testimonial that all of this was very real.

"Let her go, George," the gruff voice ordered.

George's hand left her neck, but even though she was free, Linda stayed sprawled on the car hood. "Hmp... hmp...hmp..." She listened to her own breathing as the white heat traveled through her again. Top to bottom, bottom to top, and then down to her toes again. The warmth was taking her, pulling her away to a quiet place where she wouldn't have to think or talk.

"Come on, miss. Let me help you up."

Gentle nudging accompanied the coaxing sympathy, and Linda opened her eyes to see that the owner of the gruff voice was a tall, skinny man of about sixty. Hazel eyes worriedly passed their gaze over her face. "Come on, now. There's nothing to worry about. We just want to make sure you're okay."

Even as he spoke, he pulled her off the hood of the car. The younger policeman stood to the side, watching her warily.

Rubbing her hands over her face, she leaned against the fender of the cruiser. Her black paisley skirt was twisted around her hips and her white blouse gaped open, but she didn't notice or care. Drugged with fear and confusion, she ran a hand through her ash-blond hair. She wanted to talk, but the words were frozen in her brain, trapped in the fluffy clouds of the white heat as it tried to seduce her into unconsciousness.

George clicked his tongue. "Come on, Bill. Let's just take her home!"

"No!" Linda screamed. "You can't!" She grabbed Bill's bony arm before he could turn to respond to his partner. "My boss, Senator Bingham...I...I..." Her shaking started again. Even her teeth chattered. She clamped her mouth shut and willed away the white heat that wanted to envelope her. "I saw him get k-k-k-killed... murdered," she whispered, then followed the sound of the word as it echoed around her, pulling her into the tunnel of the white heat.

"What!"

Bill caught her as she began to slide down the fender. Holding her upper arms, he gave her a light shake to keep her from fainting. "Senator Bingham murdered? Are you sure?" he gasped, stunned.

"Forget the stupid questions! Just go!" George roared, grabbing his gun as he spun away and began running down the street.

"Wait!" Bill yelled. "George! Wait!" He looked directly into Linda's eyes. "Who's in there?"

Her eyes widened with fear. "I don't know." The fear enveloped her again, and her teeth began chattering. It hurt to breathe. Her limbs shook uncontrollably.

"How many? Do they have guns?"

"No...no...a knife!" She stopped, panting air into her lungs as she thought. "Four men," she said, then closed her eyes to picture the scene. "Two short...oh, and two really huge!"

George took off anyway, pounding down the pavement like a bull elephant in heat. Bill opened the back door of the cruiser and shoved her inside. "You stay here."

"No! Oh, no!" she yelped, grabbing his arm and jumping out again. "You're not leaving me out here by myself!"

Bill didn't waste time arguing. He threw his arm around her waist and dragged her with him, hiding them both in the shadows of trees and shrubs, being cautious enough to protect them in case Bob Bingham's attacker hadn't left the scene. Before they even got a block away from the cruiser, George was running toward them.

"The house is empty...I even checked the closets," he announced, holstering his gun. "But I found the senator. He's dead as a doornail."

Senator Bingham dead.

She might have said it out loud, she didn't know. At that point she didn't care. The white heat wasn't really clear and shiny, it was dark, dark and cold. She felt herself being lifted. Heard the mumbled sounds of sympathy.

"Call it in," Bill said quietly, then Linda didn't hear anything at all.

As MICHAEL ROSEN JOGGED up the steps of the Harrisburg police station, he glanced at the rising sun. Already the air was heavy with humidity, intensifying the earthy scent of the Susquehanna River, but Michael didn't mind. In fact, he liked the smell, and he drew a deep draft of air to savor just before he pulled open the glass door. This day promised to be the best of his life, and despite the tragedy that precipitated his happiness, he couldn't stop a smug smile.

He strode to the sergeant's counter without stopping to take in the scene. Police stations were the same all over the country. The haughty and the humble carried an air of tiredness, despair and desperation. He didn't need to look around to feel it, smell it. He knew it all too well.

"Michael Rosen," he announced, passing his identification card to the round-faced sergeant.

After careful inspection, the sergeant handed it back. "Last door on the right."

The directions were hardly more than an agonized whisper, and Michael's brows rose as he pivoted away from the tall wooden counter. Senator Bingham was well loved, no one could dispute that, and Michael knew his death would touch many deeply. However, when one was murdered by the most ruthless underworld boss on the East Coast, sorrow got shoved aside and realistic questions replaced it.

Heels clicking in the silent hall, Michael steadily approached the door, once again smiling at his good fortune. Not only did he have a witness, but that witness—whatever her reasons—had taken a license plate number that put John Santos, his son, and two of his closest aides at the scene of the crime. Michael nearly laughed. After ten years of investigation, fate had simply handed him Santos on a silver platter. It was almost too good to be true.

He pushed open the door and saw a small woman sitting on a wooden bench. Two exhausted policemen bumbled to comfort her. The thin one held coffee. The young one held her. The corners of Michael's mouth lifted. Undoubtedly this was the secretary, the woman who'd actually witnessed John Santos committing murder. She was perfect! Small enough to look weak. Weak enough to evoke sympathy. Sympathetic enough to be believable. And believable enough to convict a man who'd eluded investigators for half a century. He had a witness, a license plate number and a ghastly crime that would put Santos behind bars for the rest of his life. Michael's smile grew until the ends of his mouth almost touched his ears.

"Gentlemen," he said, entering the room with the air of a pirate boarding a captured ship. "I'll take over from here." He flashed his ID again. "Go home and get some rest."

The little blonde clutched the arm of the younger policeman, but when she spoke, her voice was surprisingly calm. "Do they have to go?" she asked, turning round sapphire eyes in Michael's direction. She seemed young, twenty-five, maybe twenty-six, but the haunted look in those big blue eyes made Michael realize she was much older, if only in experience. But that was so much the better. If there could be such a thing as informed vulnerability, it was in her eyes. Her expression shouted *innocent victim* but in such a way that you didn't pity her, you respected her, and that would manifest itself to any jury. That vulnerability was every bit as valuable as her testimony.

Even as he pictured himself tossing John Santos behind bars and throwing away the key, he cleared his throat. "They don't have to go, but I'm sure they're tired...."

"I'm staying," the younger policeman said, patting her hand.

"And so am I," his partner assured.

Great! Michael thought, and resisted the urge to roll his eyes in disgust. He'd forgotten how beautiful maidens drew all kinds of chivalrous knights out of the woodwork, even when that maiden didn't really need anybody's help. And this woman didn't. He could tell that just by looking at her.

"Fine," he said, smiling tightly. "Let's go over your statement."

Confused, the blonde glanced at her two knights, and even though Michael's irritation grew, so did his respect for her. It wasn't fear he saw in her eyes, it was the positive questioning of a careful person. She wasn't saying anything to anybody, unless or until she knew it was the right thing to do. And though that was smart, they didn't have time for this.

The older officer rose from the bench and approached Michael. "It's been a long night, Mr . . ."

"Rosen," Michael informed with another forced smile. "Michael Rosen."

The officer extended his hand. "Bill Washington," he said, pumping Michael's arm. "That's George Downing with Linda."

"You two were the officers at the scene, right?" He couldn't believe this. He was supposed to come here, verify her statement and then whisk her out of town before Santos marshaled his forces. Instead, he was shaking hands and exchanging how-do-ya-dos like an old lady at a tea.

"Yes," George proudly confirmed as Michael took a seat at the long, narrow table. "I charged the premises after Linda told us what she saw. I thought we'd nab that bozo before he got away, but no such luck."

"Uh-huh," Michael said, rubbing his fingers across his chin. The way Michael heard the story, the only reason this woman was alive was because she'd literally run into the police. And the only reason the police were still alive was the smattering of traffic normal for Friday nights. But instead of counting their blessings, they were recounting events as if this were a typical crime, which it wasn't. John Santos hadn't just escaped capture at the scene, he'd bought time to find out who Linda Miller was and get rid of her. Even it if meant committing another murder—and it did—he wouldn't spend ten minutes in jail. But Michael wasn't quite sure how he was going to explain that without sending his witness into cardiac arrest. He placed his elbows on the table and put his hands together, steepling them under his chin. When he spoke, it was quietly. "Either of you two get a look at Santos?"

Bill looked up sharply. "No."

"You didn't see the car?"

This time George shook his head.

"But Linda was in the doorway of the senator's office when Santos…the John Santos…pushed a knife into his chest."

The already quiet room seemed to turn to stone. Linda Miller stared at Michael with a very confused expression, her breath coming out in short panting gasps between her lips. The two officers, however, had caught his meaning very clearly. "That's why she's here and not at her apartment," Bill said slowly, cautiously, as though he too wished to protect the sensibilities of the witness.

"Uh-huh," Michael said again, finally understanding. What they were doing—or thought they were going to be doing—was protecting her themselves. Admirable. Naive, but admirable. "And what about tonight?"

Bill cleared his throat. "George's couch opens out into a bed. We were gonna talk to you about that."

"Uh-huh," Michael said again. They were either horribly misinformed or absolutely crazy, but he wasn't going to argue this issue in front of the witness, because if they'd already prepared her to sleep on George's couch, then he'd probably need their assistance to convince her that wasn't such a smart idea.

"Gentlemen, if one of you would take me to your captain, I think we could clear this up, and then I'll verify her statement."

George glanced up at Bill. Bill looked down at George. With only their eyes, they held a discussion, then Bill turned to Michael. "I'll go."

Michael unfolded his long frame from the chair and followed Bill to the captain's office, where his security clearance awaited. As the captain not only confirmed Michael's identity but explained that Linda Miller's situation warranted more than spending the night on George's couch, Bill swallowed and studied Michael so carefully Michael had to hold back an exasperated groan. Through the course of the grueling night, these officers had grown quite protective of Linda Miller, and though that was understandable to a point, Michael was beginning to think these two had watched one too many police programs. Even so, he maintained his calm when he defended himself.

"Spent two years in Vietnam," Michael announced, spreading his hands like an innocent. "Been with the FBI since the day I got out of the marines. I've devoted the last ten years of my life to catching John Santos.... If you can't trust me to take Ms. Miller into hiding, then you can't trust anybody."

"Bill?"

When the captain spoke, Bill spun to face his superior.

"I've checked this myself... every angle..."

As Captain Harris explained a procedure Bill Washington should already know, Michael thrust his hands into his trouser pockets and paced to the window, well aware that Bill followed him with his eyes.

"Where are you takin' her?"

For that, Michael turned to face Bill Washington, a seasoned policeman who'd become personally involved with a witness in less than eight hours. It couldn't have been a bonding from the crime. Bill hadn't seen the murder, only Linda Miller had.

He let a minute pass in silence, then smiled grimly. It could be that all this sympathy and caring was a cover. It could be that Bill Washington was only pretending to protect Linda Miller until he got the right opportunity to turn her over to Santos or get rid of her himself.

"Did it ever cross your mind that, perhaps, I don't trust you?"

Bill's eyes seemed to double in size. The flecks of amber in their hazel base intensified until they fairly sparkled with suppressed fury. His arms tensed, his lips thinned, and every atom of his being poised to lunge across the room. "Yeah, well, George and I aren't exactly sure we trust *you* either. It's pretty darned convenient that they sent you, one guy, to take her. How do we know you won't kill her? Your ID might check out. You may really be with the FBI and you might be the best darned agent they ever had, but how do we know you're not on the take? How do we check up on you?"

So that was it. The reason for the delays. The vague conversations in front of the witness. At least it made sense. And was something he could deal with. To get someone to trust you, sometimes you had to trust them first. "I'm taking her to my house," he answered simply.

"Your house!" The words exploded from Bill as if they'd been fired from a cannon.

"Maybe *retreat* is a better word," Michael decided, walking away from the window. "I have a cabin in the mountains in Colorado. Very few people know about

it...in fact, it's titled in my commanding officer's name."
He stopped and smiled. "It's a well-known fact that I hate
that man. No one would ever dream we'd share a piece of
property. In fact, Colonel Roberts doesn't even know he's
the proud owner of twenty acres of mountain."

Bill didn't respond with words, but his face betrayed his
understanding that a cabin in the mountains would be
isolated and therefore secure. His gaze continued to follow Michael around the room. "Has Santos been picked
up yet?" he asked quietly.

Michael turned away, fingering the dusty drapes. He
considered lying, but once again, he chose the truth.
"No."

Bill's breath came out in a hiss, and, furious, Michael
pivoted. Four monster strides took him across the room.
He didn't like answering to small-city cops, but more than
that, he hated wasting time.

"That's why I have to take her now. Now," he repeated, poking his index finger into Bill's chest. "I don't
need your permission, and I don't have time to baby you
just because you feel you have a prior claim on the
case...or the lady."

The captain leaned back in his chair. Michael let his
finger nest in the empty button hole of Bill's worn shirt.
Bill sucked in his breath but nonetheless considered his
options. For a full thirty seconds silence reigned, then Bill
spun around, strode to the door and left the room without another word.

Chapter Two

By twisting her arm, Linda tried to subtly manipulate the FBI agent's fingers in the hope of loosening his grip on her bicep, but it was useless. The hold he had on her could have kept a rhinoceros from charging, and he wasn't letting up.

"Where are we going?" she asked as he pulled her away from the sergeant's counter and began to lead her through the common area, toward the hall. She watched as his gaze automatically ran the length and width of the room, then stopped on Bill and George, who stood in the corner by the glass door. She hadn't missed, nor had she liked, the looks he'd been giving Bill and George all morning. She also hadn't liked him. But she realized he was only doing his job. They'd explained about protective custody, and she knew this man would be guarding her until after the trial, so she had to get used to his less than charming personality and the abrupt, almost insulting way he treated everybody, including her. But the way Linda saw it, there was only an hour or so of real trouble left. If she kept her mouth shut until he drove them to a hotel or wherever they were staying, then she'd lose him just by going into the bathroom. He might not trust her to go to the ladies' room here, but in their hideaway, a place he'd secured, he wouldn't dare follow her into the bathroom, and that's where she'd find her peace and quiet. And for more reasons than retreat, she hoped it was soon.

She glanced at her protector and saw that even as they walked, he scanned the room. Watching. Waiting. For what, she didn't know, but his preoccupation with doors and windows was starting to make her nervous. He wouldn't let her go to the ladies' room, he wouldn't let go of her arm, and now he was watching the door and counting the windows as if she were about to let out with a war cry and fling herself through the glass.

Following a pattern of motion, his intense brown eyes swung in her direction, and he caught her staring at him. For a few seconds they just looked at each other, and in that fraction of a minute he seemed bigger and more imposing than he had all morning.

She quickly looked away.

"Where are we going?" she asked again, hoping the hotel was very close, wishing he was a foot shorter, fifty pounds lighter or a lot nicer.

"DuBois."

Puzzled, she quit walking and looked up at him again. "DuBois? What's DuBois?"

He went another step, but stopped with a jolt because she wasn't moving. "It's a little city," he answered, then took a step, but she didn't budge from her spot, and rather than get into a tug-of-war, he backpedaled.

"A little city?" She'd never heard of it. "Where?"

He sighed. "About a five-hour drive away."

Five hours before she saw the inside of a ladies' room? No way! "We can't go to DuBois!"

He caught her off guard and began to walk again. She stumbled behind him as he glanced at the desk and received a nod that Linda perceived to indicate all was in readiness. Just from the messages he'd received while questioning her, Linda knew his original rental car had been exchanged for another and the state police had been alerted.

What she didn't know was that every five miles an unmarked car would check their progress. A private plane would take them from DuBois to Minneapolis, where an air force jet awaited to take them to Kansas. In Kansas, they'd charter another plane that would take them to Arizona. In Arizona, another air force jet would take them to Omaha. And in Omaha, Michael would get his own plane and fly them to safety. She didn't know the trip would take days, because no one knew that. No one knew any more about this journey than they had to know to complete their end of the mission. It had taken Michael years to mastermind this complicated, expensive, foolproof plan, and no one or nothing could change his mind about even the tiniest detail. Linda didn't know that, either.

"Don't worry, you're not staying," Michael replied, totally unmoved by her outburst. "If you're afraid of running into somebody you don't want to see while we're there, you can put your fears to rest. We're not even going into town." He stopped Linda by tightening his hold on her upper arm. "Go say goodbye to Mr. Salty and the Staypuff Marshmallow Man," he commanded, motioning toward Bill and George. "I'll come over to get you in a minute." He turned her in the right direction and pointed at Bill and George again.

For a second Linda stayed rooted to her spot, feeling more disoriented than angry. But she didn't get the chance to puzzle it out, because he flipped his hand for her to get going and she automatically began to move.

When she was two steps away from the officers, Bill reached for her hands. "Are you okay?" he asked anxiously. "Your hands are like ice."

"I'm fine," Linda assured, forcing a smile. Bill and George had stood by her all night, and she figured it was about time to let them off the hook. By rights they should have gotten to go home when Michael Rosen arrived, and she was beginning to feel guilty that she'd needed them to help her get through the long night. "Just a little nervous."

"Well, there's no need to be concerned about a thing," George said. He glanced at Bill and Bill nodded once. "Bill said this guy's an ex-marine. Decorated in Vietnam and everything. You couldn't be in better hands."

"Do you know where you're going?" Bill asked as he squeezed her fingers.

She laughed airily, trying to lighten the mood so they'd realize she'd regained her composure, her ability to think and her stamina, things she'd lost the night before. "I thought I was going home. At least to pack—"

"No such luck," George interrupted. "Until after the trial, you'll be in protective custody."

She knew that. She didn't like it, she was beginning to sense that everything was more complicated than she'd first imagined, but she knew what he was telling her. She wouldn't see the outside world until after the trial. She smiled at George to ease her own mounting fears. "We're going to some place called DuBois. But he told me not to worry, that we wouldn't be staying...."

Saying the sentence aloud conjured vivid images that made her blood run cold because she started to get a realistic perspective of what she'd unwittingly agreed to do. They had to use her statement to put John Santos in jail. In other words, there'd be a public announcement that she'd seen an underworld figure commit murder. That announcement put her own life in jeopardy, so she'd have to hide out. But she couldn't hide out alone. The government wanted the opportunity to keep her alive long enough to testify at an actual trial, so Michael Rosen was taking her to DuBois.

Which meant she was going to a place she'd never heard of with a man she didn't know, and while they waited for the trial, a mobster would try to kill her. Suddenly she realized there was a good possibility she wouldn't survive the next six weeks if she let the district attorney's office go ahead with their announcement that she'd agreed to testify.

Panicking, she glanced around. She couldn't do this, but she couldn't very well come right out and say that...could she? Well, there was only one way to find out. She faced Bill. "I don't like this. But I guess I don't have a choice, do I?"

"You could choose not to testify," Michael put in from her right, and she gasped and actually felt herself jump off the floor. He had the feet of a panther and the sensitivity of a bull moose, and the combination was likely to drive her crazy. Not only that, but he was big. Tall, very muscular, very masculine.

"But you still witnessed John Santos committing murder. Not testifying doesn't necessarily mean he'll let you live.... Actually, whether you like it or not, you're the safest with me."

Even as her heart galloped from the shock of his sneaking up on her, the rest of her body went perfectly still as she stared at him. Safest with him? Maybe it was just a matter of perspective, but he made her more nervous than she'd ever been in her life.

"He's right," George said. Searching Linda's face with a harrowed expression, he sighed heavily. "I wish I could go with you, but I can't."

"No, you can't," Michael agreed, his words coming out in a fashion that made Linda shiver. There was no way that she could go through with this. Oh, she knew she had to testify and she understood his logic. The problem was she couldn't spend five or six weeks with Michael Rosen. His hard-line police attitude would make her crazy. She had enough to worry about with running from John Santos, she didn't need the added pressures of living day and night with Robocop. At the very least, she wanted another FBI agent . . . maybe a woman . . . that was it. She wanted a female agent to live with her while she waited for the trial. She was the boss here. That's what they'd told her. You testify and we'll do whatever you want. Hadn't they brought her breakfast?

Michael caught Linda's upper arm again. "Come on. Let's go."

"Oh, no!" she said, raising her right hand, index finger extended, ready to stop this before it went any further. But before she got the chance, all hell broke loose on the street. At least ten cars screeched to a halt directly in front of the police station—they actually parked in the street and on the sidewalk—and people just swarmed out. Some in suits and ties. Some in jeans and T-shirts. Some in shorts. One guy wore nothing but cutoffs, and there was a woman hopping into her shoes. Nearly everybody had a notebook and of those who didn't, ninety percent held television cameras.

"Great! Just great!" Michael said. He dropped Linda's arm and bounded to the wall of windows for a better look. "Darn it anyway! He's got Santos!"

Bill was right behind Michael. "Would ya look at that! It's Pierson."

George shoved Bill out of his way. "That son of a bee. He musta heard us call in the license number and then drove around the county until he found the car."

Everybody in the room ran to the window as Michael glanced around, obviously seeking an escape route. Watching her jailer, who for once wasn't watching her, Linda slipped behind a wide policeman. She wasn't quite sure what she was doing, but she was away from Michael Rosen, and at the moment, that was the goal.

Using people as shields to keep her hidden, she nosed her way to the huge window by the glass door. She positioned herself in front of a woman twice her size, and, confident that Michael Rosen couldn't see her, she prepared herself to stay right where she was for as long as the crowd gathered at the door. Once Santos was in, she'd slip out. And after she'd had a good night's sleep and a decent cup of coffee, then she'd call the DA and tell him she'd testify if she could hide out with a female FBI agent . . . or maybe a nicer FBI agent. She wasn't going to be picky about this, but she wasn't going anywhere with Michael Rosen. She was tired, grief stricken and just plain scared. She wanted a friend or companion, someone she could relax with while she awaited her destiny.

Squeezed between a fat woman and a wall of windows, Linda felt ridiculously safe until she actually saw the scene beyond the glass. Immediately her eyes widened in disbelief. No fewer than twenty reporters scrambled after two uniformed policemen who hustled an old man up the cement steps. Even though she recognized him as the man who killed the senator, he didn't look like a criminal, just a small, silent man being led up the steps by two proud-as-a-peacock policemen.

Then she remembered the blood. She saw Bob Bingham's face contorted with pain. She felt fingers skimming her flesh as men lunged across the desk to grab her arms. She remembered the sound of breath so close she could feel the hot moisture pelleting her cheeks.

White heat traveled from her skull, just under the surface of her skin, down to her toes, and her breathing got heavy, but she didn't think she was going to faint. She was too scared to faint. Or maybe too keyed up to faint. She was remembering with the clarity of second sight, almost as if she were reliving her feelings, picking up her emotions of the last second before Bill and George rescued her. Except she didn't want to run. She wanted to stay. She wanted to see what happened next, because she knew she wasn't in danger anymore. She felt safe, protected. Not by the crowd, not by Michael Rosen, but by some mystical force, an eerie air of fantasy that seemed to swirl around her, feeding her curiosity, silencing her fear.

From a distance she could hear George. "I shoulda known! That brownnose. I'll bet ya fifty dollars he sleeps with his radio!"

"You do," Bill returned mildly as Linda stood frozen, watching reporters who scrambled up the steps like a wall of flesh and blood, hoping to muscle their way through the crowd and be the one in the door right behind John Santos...*the* John Santos, mob boss, murderer, celebrity in his own right.

Someone grabbed her arm. She felt the bruising pressure of five meaty fingers as they sank into her flesh, then Michael Rosen took command again. "Let's go!" he ordered, trying to move her, but she looped her fingers around a waist-high wooden rail and stayed right where she was. This man had changed her life. This quiet little man who looked like he couldn't hurt a flea had pushed a knife into the chest of the man she considered her best friend.

She tightened her hold on the window guard and refused to budge, except to turn slightly to get a good look at the man who so casually murdered in cold blood.

He was an ugly little man, and Linda felt no guilt or shame in rendering that verdict. He was short and pudgy, and he had a big, fat nose that made his eyes look tiny and beady. His white hair was thinning and plastered in place.

She studied him. She wouldn't even have to see him kill to know he was evil. Gucci shoes and Brooks Brothers suits couldn't hide it, and on closer inspection Linda realized his clothes weren't meant to hide it, or even cover it. The display of good taste and money just made him socially acceptable.

A tall, good-looking policeman held the door for Santos, and Linda stepped closer, still gripping the railing. Michael tried to grab her arm, but once again she eluded him. She slid her hands down the railing, taking slow, cautious steps toward the door. She'd never seen a murder before. Never seen a murderer. Never hated anybody...not like this. Never like this. There was a deep anger, mixed in with the dead pain of loss, and a sickening fascination. The kind of fascination that overrode all your normal inhibitions and pushed you to do things you wouldn't normally do. She took another step toward the door.

Michael Rosen was furious now, cursing as she avoided him by keeping the breathless crowd between them. But she heard him from a distance, as if he were in a vacuum, and she saw everything around her happen in slow motion, as if fate wanted to give her the opportunity to get to the door before Santos was surrounded by reporters. She took another step. This time Santos saw her.

He shrugged off his police escort, and the press of the crowd separated him completely. He took one step that put accuser and accused nose to nose, because he was no taller than she was. Linda looked into his beady steel-gray eyes, and she swore she could see evil—not hate, not desire for revenge, no passion, no emotion—just evil.

There was no softness in him, even his leatherlike skin bore no sign of vulnerability. Up close, his very expensive attire was like a mockery of human values. Fancy fabrics and designer labels couldn't hide the evil. And once again she very strongly sensed that he didn't want to. The look in his eyes was a very clear advertisement of what he would do, what he could do, for the right price.

He said something to her in a language Linda couldn't understand. She just stared at him. His eyes narrowed and his tone changed as his words came out with the velocity of a tornado. She knew he was cursing her and tilted her head as she watched him, the same way one watched a monkey in a zoo.

There was noise. There were flashes from cameras. There was a very angry, very forceful FBI agent tugging on her arm. She yanked free of him, and before he could grab her arm again, two people stepped between them.

"And I vow, you'll not see this night!"

For this threat Santos reverted to English, as though he wanted to be sure she understood her fate. She didn't flinch, blink or move a muscle. He wasn't real. He couldn't be real. Nobody could be that cold, cruel and calculating and think they were right.

His face grew red as anger overtook him. He sputtered again and spit on her shoes. First one, then the other. Very slowly, very carefully. Symbolically, it seemed.

She looked down at her shoes, then looked up at him just as his captors yanked him away and Michael Rosen scooped her off her feet and began running.

But she couldn't stop staring at that beady-eyed man. Twisting in Michael's arms, she watched as he was led down the hall to the room where she'd given her accounting of last night's brutal stabbing. He was evil. He personified all the things she'd experienced in other forms. Hate, death, anger, prejudice, violence. He was all of them rolled into one ugly leather-faced man. He stopped before he entered the door, glanced around until he found her in the crowd and smiled, then blew her a kiss.

It was the slap of reality that killed the fantasy, and suddenly it was all real again. She buried her face in Michael's shoulder, willing herself not to break down.

"Very interesting way of hanging on to your witness, Mr. Rosen."

The comment came from behind Michael, but he didn't even pause. He bounded down the hall, fast and furious, like a man running for a train that was already chugging away from the station.

"You know it's useless," the man shouted as Michael continued to ignore him. "No matter where you go, we'll find you. Probably tonight."

Michael stepped into a waiting elevator, and Linda lifted her head to discover they were flanked by two uniformed officers. As the doors swished closed, Linda saw Bill and George holding back the crowd. In the last second before the doors connected, she caught a glimpse of another of the men from the night before. Not the thugs, but the bearded man, the one who looked no bigger than a teenager. He was casually milling in the throng with his hands thrust into the pockets of his tan corduroy trousers, but he was watching them. Not in a curious way as everyone else was. No, this guy seemed to be waiting. When she caught his eye, he saluted. Michael cursed fluently and the doors slammed closed. The elevator jerked to a start.

"You could have gotten yourself killed!" he thundered, and slid her to the floor. "For that matter, you could have gotten both of us killed."

Linda just looked at him. Last night she witnessed a murder. Two minutes ago she stood face-to-face with the killer, because she had to, even though she wasn't sure why. Now she was being screamed at in the presence of two policemen, who, to their credit, stayed face-foward and didn't do anything but breathe and watch the elevator doors. If she closed her eyes, she knew she'd see silver dots and probably faint dead away. But she couldn't do that. She wouldn't give Michael Rosen the satisfaction.

She busied herself with straightening her rumpled paisley skirt to give herself a minute to regain her composure. "Who was that?" she asked quietly.

"That was the one and only John Guido Santos."

The lilt in his voice caused her to glance up at him. He was smiling a strange triumphant smile that scared her silly even as it answered a hundred questions. Jailing Santos was a Michael Rosen victory. To him, this was more than a human chess game; it was personal, and she was more than a blue-eyed pawn.

Now she knew why he wouldn't let her go to the ladies' room in the police station. Now she knew why he kept such a tight hold on her arm. The only thing she didn't know was what made it personal. Why did this particular case mean so much to this particular man that he always had to hold her arm or, at the very least, keep her in view? "I knew who he was," she said, staring at him with round sapphire eyes full of confusion. But who are you? she wanted to ask. Who the devil are you, and why does this seem to be so personal to you? With her luck she was probably in the middle of some mob vendetta, and before this was all over with she'd be the one to pay the price. "Who was the man who said he'd find us?" She surprised herself with how steady her voice sounded, considering the fact that her bodyguard scared her as much as her pursuers.

The elevator jerked to a stop. Michael Rosen grabbed her upper arm and gave one tug before he walked between the two uniformed officers. "His son."

"Whose son?" Linda asked, almost skipping to keep up with him. They were in a parking garage, obviously the basement of the police station. There were all makes and models of cars, but cruisers were predominant. Where the sun as much as peeked in a crack, a uniformed officer stood poised with a shotgun. She looked around in awe. So many policemen to protect one five-foot-four, hundred-and-fifteen pound woman? Now these people were acting every bit as crazy as Michael Rosen was.

"John Santos's son," Michael impatiently answered. "That's Johnny, Jr. or Johnny-jump-up...whatever. He goes by a couple of names."

He pushed her into a late-model, midsize wine-colored car. It looked like fifty million others she saw on the streets of Harrisburg every day. He slammed the door behind her, and she sank into the plush accommodations. The car was cool and dark and the soft seat felt like heaven. She closed her eyes and her sandy lids scratched over her tired irises, but after being awake for twenty-eight hours, even that felt good. Suddenly a five-hour drive didn't seem all that terrible anymore.

He slid in beside her and slammed the door. "Put your seat belt on."

She heard him, knew she should do as he said, but couldn't get her hands to move. Even scared, or maybe because she was scared, sleep didn't have to do much to seduce her.

He started the engine. "Fasten your seat belt."

That time he used the annoying tone she hated, but she barely heard it. Her body was sinking slowly, irrevocably into a warm, soft cloud of sleep and her mind saw no reason to stop it.

"Darn it."

She heard the mumble. She heard the deep breath he drew and the way he expelled it in exasperation. She felt his fingers fumbling with her seat belt and then the lungelike movement of the car as it surged forward.

"Princess," he called as he shook her arm.

"Princess!"

Her head snapped up. "What?"

"You can sleep all you want once we're on the main highway, but until we get out of the city I want you awake and alert."

"Why?" she moaned miserably. "I'm so tired I can't even see straight."

"You don't need to see anything. Just sit there and look normal."

"Couldn't I lie down in the back seat?"

He laughed heartily. "Are you kidding? From the right angle, if the person was in the right spot, say waiting at a stoplight, they'd get a perfect bead on your back, or your head, and that's it for you."

She looked at him as if he were from Mars. "What are you talking about?"

As he manipulated the vehicle through the rows of cars in the parking garage, he concentrated on driving. In the silence, she glanced around in amazement at the number of policemen hovering discreetly on the street. To any on-looker it might appear they were trying to control the crowd that had amassed because of John Santos's appearance. But they had guns, wore bulletproof vests and solemn faces, and seemed to be looking all ways at once. Suddenly Michael Rosen didn't have to answer her question, she knew why she couldn't lie down in the back seat. John Santos might be behind bars, but he had powerful friends and deadly companions, and they were all roaming the streets looking for her. They weren't waiting for the day before the trial or even a week before the trial; John Santos wanted her dead now. The hunt had already started. In fact, it probably never stopped from the night before.

The beginnings of a panic attack fluttered in her stomach, but Michael Rosen cleared his throat as she nipped it in the bud. There was no way she'd panic in front of this guy. She closed her eyes and got comfortable. Just as soon as she was alone, she'd let go, have a good cry, maybe even beat her pillow because her friend was dead. But for now, she'd just take deep breaths and pretend she was in Oregon or France . . . or maybe Moscow. . . .

"Hey, eyes open," Michael commanded, and this time he nudged her arm. "I want us to look like a perfectly normal couple driving through town. . . . We could be carpooling to work. That's it. Sit there and act like we're on our way to work."

"It's Saturday."

"Okay. Then pretend we're on our way to the mall to do a little shopping."

She glanced at her watch. "The mall doesn't open till ten."

"Okay," he said, sounding as though he were getting exasperated with her, but the highway ramps were upon them. "Oh," he mumbled, then pressed the gas pedal. The car picked up speed, joined a row of automobiles already cruising down the highway and left the city behind. "Okay, pretend I'm an FBI agent trying to hustle a witness to safety. You be the witness."

"Ha ha. Very funny," Linda muttered. "I guess that means I can close my eyes."

"Yep. I didn't realize how close we were to the highway."

"That's one of the reasons I liked working for Bingham and Bingham. At five o'clock, you'd get into your car, pull onto Front Street, go through two lights and presto, the highway was right there." She turned sideways and snuggled into her seat. In another minute and a half she was asleep.

When her breathing leveled, Michael relaxed his grip on the steering wheel. He'd forgotten she missed her sleep, until they got into the car and she snuggled into the seat as if it were a pillow. But once he remembered, it explained a lot of her idiotic behavior. He knew some women lacked common sense, but this one went beyond all understanding. She was now the worst enemy of a man who killed for sport, and instead of running for a trench coat and dark glasses, she stood in front of a wall of windows, talked too much and too loud, and didn't seem to realize decisions had already been made for her. From this point forward she either did as she was told, or she died. It was that simple.

"SHE'S A PRETTY LITTLE THING, isn't she, Simon?"

"Yes, Mr. Santos. That she is."

"All that red hair...and eyes so green I can tell their color the whole way across the lawn... What's her name?"

"Amanda." Simon answered, then he laughed. "A-manda-Lynn."

Johnny laughed, too. "She'll probably be a musical child." He set one foot on the fence railing and watched the toddlers throw sand at each other. "Are you sure the other one didn't have a girlfriend? A sister?"

"Positive, sir. He's as unattached as the girl. The only link we have right now is Bill Washington's granddaughter."

Johnny rarely cursed. When he did, it was softly. "Damn." He set his foot on the ground and dusted off his hands. "Well, then I hope Rosen told Bill Washington where he was taking his witness."

"That's highly unlikely," Simon noted quietly.

"You're right," Johnny conceded. "But nonetheless it's our only hope." He started walking away, but stopped and took another look at the red-haired three-year-old. "Don't take her," he decided suddenly. "Let's see if we can't just scare the old man into telling what he knows. We'll take her only if he doesn't cooperate."

Too stunned to respond, Simon didn't move a muscle. Then slowly everything began to fall into place and he smiled. Many things would be different with the old man gone. Many things.

"OKAY," MICHAEL CALLED. "Sleepy time's over."

"Already?" Linda groaned as she turned around on her seat. She groaned again when her muscles protested.

"Five hours twenty-seven minutes…" He glanced at her and grinned. "I stopped for breakfast. I was told you'd already eaten, so I let you sleep while I ate."

"Wow!" she gasped. "A whole twenty-seven minutes. You left me alone all that time."

"Nope," he very quickly contradicted her, because her tone of voice just confirmed a very ugly suspicion he'd formed while she was sleeping. "I had two uniforms guard the car while I ate.... You really don't know how much trouble you're in, do you?"

"You had two strange men watching me sleep?"

"I only met you this morning and I watched you sleep for five hours...."

She groaned. "Just shut up, okay? I don't think I want to be reminded.... I don't think I want to think at all."

"That's a problem," Michael said, glancing at her again. They were in the wilds of Pennsylvania, more appropriately, the backwoods. Any minute now the airport would just appear out of nowhere, so he took this last chance to look at her to see if he could confirm his suspicions. "I know that's a problem." He turned his attention to the road again and sighed heavily. "Look, kid, I'm getting the impression that you don't understand what's going on here. I didn't kidnap you, I'm hiding you from the underworld."

"I know that!" she mumbled, clearly annoyed—whether it was with him or the topic, Michael couldn't tell.

"Okay, so you know that part," he said, sighing again. Why me? he asked the heavens. Then he took another deep breath and continued. "Have you figured out yet that John Santos is going to try to keep you from testifying? In other words, have you figured out yet that you're an endangered species and that a big part of my problem is keeping you alive?"

She remembered the policemen in the parking garage and on the street. In her mind's eye she saw their bulletproof vests and their shotguns. "Yeah."

"Okay, then. I need some cooperation from you...."

"You're getting lots of cooperation from me, Bud! I saw a murder, I ran right to the police...."

"You ran right into the police, you mean...."

"Whatever!" she said, and tossed her hands. "I gave a statement, stayed up all night giving a statement," she corrected angrily. "Then spent a grueling hour repeating everything to you, as if you couldn't read it for yourself. I am cooperating!"

He pulled the car off the road and turned on his seat until he faced her. "No, dear," he said, "you're still missing the boat, and I'm not quite sure why. But I do know that unless you and I get a few things straight, we're not going to attain our objective. That objective is to keep you alive, safe, happy, well fed, until the trial. Now, things will go a lot smoother if we work together. For instance, when I tell you to do something, you should do it."

"Oh, baloney," she scoffed. "I think you're on some kind of a power trip."

Laying his arm on the steering wheel, Michael raised his eyes toward the ceiling and prayed for strength. "You're not hearing what I'm telling you."

"No, you're not listening to what I'm telling you. I'm," she said, pointing at her chest, "your—" she pointed at his chest "—witness. I'm the only reason John Santos is in jail. And I know that. I know what I've done and I know what I'm doing.... And I am really tired of you pushing me around and treating me like a two-year-old."

"Then stop acting like one," he suggested. "And listen to reason. I—"

"Did it ever occur to you that I don't want to listen to reason?" she interrupted, shouting. "Because what you think is reasonable and what I think is reasonable are two different things." She stopped and sighed. "Look, I'm going to level with you. I'm not even sure I'm going through with this. I don't think I can handle testifying.... I watched my boss...my friend...get murdered last night...."

"Put away the violin, Stradivarius. I don't wanna hear it." He started the car again and began inching off the shoulder and onto the road. "Here's the facts, ma'am," he mocked as the car picked up speed and the airport popped up on the horizon. "You don't have time to get adjusted. You don't even have fifteen minutes to feel sorry for yourself. For the next six weeks, as everyone prepares for the trial, each and every member of John Santos's staff and a few hundred people who'd like to be on John Santos's staff, and a couple of hundred thrill seekers and nuts will try to get rid of you before you get rid of Santos. And as for not testifying—it won't do you a damned bit of good. You're still a threat. And even after the trial, after he's convicted, executed or put away for the rest of his life, you're still in danger. We still have to hide you, protect you. Whether or not you know it, you're in for life."

She looked at him. For the next twenty seconds she wore a hole in his cheek with her hot gaze. Then she turned away in a huff. "I don't believe you."

Exasperated to the point of giddiness, he started to chuckle.

"I mean I believe you and I know I'm in big trouble and I know I'm under the federal witness protection thing.... But I think right now, at this minute, you're exaggerating. Either that, or you have a very vivid imagination."

Even as she spoke, a bullet hit the strip of chrome around the windshield. Instinctively Michael Rosen cupped his hand over her head and shoved her down as he pressed the gas pedal to the floor.

"How's that for a vivid imagination?" he muttered in disgust. "Get down and stay down!"

Another bullet hit somewhere in the vicinity of the trunk. "Damn! They're aiming for the gas tank." He slapped the steering wheel with the heel of his hand. "Damn!"

Michael thought with morbid humor that the misaimed bullets sounded like rocks hitting a tuna can, because distance disconnected the sound of the bullets from the crack of the rifle, which Michael heard seconds after each and every ping.

"The local help must be poor shots," Michael said, looking around at the open field. "They do that, you know," he told Linda even as his mind was working full speed trying to think of a way to get them the hell out of here.

To turn around was to go back into a deep forest, which would be dangerous.

"If they don't have the time to ship their payroll killers to where you are, they'll check the yellow pages and hire a local."

But he'd never been any farther north, so that was unknown territory. Another problem...

"Somebody who'll know the location and terrain, even the people involved. Such as which pilots will turn in the other direction and which pilots will run for the police if somebody starts shooting up the hangar or chasing strangers on the runway."

His only hope was the airport. Beside the hangars, he saw several planes, but he didn't have keys or time to ask permission. On a good day somebody would be taxiing to a runway, and he'd pull an Indiana Jones-type stunt to force them out of their plane long enough that he could commandeer it, but not so today. What started out as the best day of his life had gone so far downhill, he'd have to look up to see rock bottom.

The crack of the rifles echoed around them, but the bullets weren't hitting close enough that Michael heard the strikes. Still he couldn't afford to take chances. Any minute now somebody could get lucky. Frantically he scanned the area, still hoping for that two-seater taxiing out of a hangar. No such luck. He was just about to dub this the worst day of his entire life when he saw the blades of a helicopter spin once, then twice, then begin the slow rhythmic progression that indicated the craft was getting ready for flight.

A quick right turn put them on the grass and in the path of the chopper, but the closer they got, the more Michael wanted to groan with frustration. From a distance you couldn't see the rusty body of the old monstrosity, but up close that condition was more than apparent, and the noise was atrocious. Michael pounded his hand on the steering wheel. The darned thing couldn't be flight ready. In all probability it was just being transferred to another hangar, and if that was the case, it wouldn't do him one damned bit—

Suddenly two bullets hit the car, one in the right front fender and one in the left rear. He was surrounded, and they were getting lucky.... Either that or these were new people who were better shots or people stationed closer to the hangar. Michael jammed his foot on the gas pedal. He didn't have a choice. Fate was handing him a chopper. He'd take the darn chopper.

He jerked his car to a stop in front of the noisy craft and shoved open his door. A bullet hit the dirt in front of him. Nonetheless, he pulled Linda across the front seat, face-down and prone. Using the car door as a shield, he stretched until he could reach the helicopter door, which he yanked open. A young, stunned pilot gaped at him.

"Sorry, guy," he yelled, but the pilot couldn't hear him. Over the deafening roar of his aging craft, the pilot hadn't even heard Michael's car approaching, which accounted for why Michael had the advantage of the element of surprise. He grabbed the unsuspecting man by his shirt with one hand, even as his other hand pulled the earphones from the pilot's ears. Dust swirled not more than a foot away, and Michael knew another bullet just missed the car. "Run for cover," he shouted to the pilot, but once again knew he hadn't been heard. Just as he knew the pilot didn't know a bullet had stirred the dust around him, because the kid punched him a good one in the chin.

Michael cursed, spit blood and grabbed the man by his jacket collar, holding him while he grabbed his wallet to flash his ID. The pilot looked at it, then glanced at Michael as Michael released his collar. The noise of the helicopter precluded an explanation that Michael was commandeering his vehicle, but an explanation didn't seem to be necessary. The pilot backed away slowly, taking a new interest in the swirls of dust that continued to materialize around the noisy helicopter. He licked his lips, then spun and ran into the hangar.

Michael ducked on instinct, realizing he'd been an open invitation for a bullet the whole time he was upright. Still crouched, he slid Linda across the seat, threw her over his shoulder and then dumped her into the copter, rolling her to the other side. He jumped in, letting the door slam behind him. A quick glance at the instruments made him breathe a sigh of relief. He tapped the gas gauge and sighed again before he moved the lever and swung the craft into the air.

THEY WATCHED the helicopter take flight from the privacy of their limo. For several minutes neither said a word.

Then John, Jr. leaned his head back and sighed. "My guess is Johnstown. It's small, private, and he knows the airport because he keeps his own plane there."

Simon shook his head. "I say Pittsburgh."

John turned to face him. "Pittsburgh? In Johnstown he's got friends, connections. Pittsburgh's too big. How's he going to explain a stolen helicopter?"

"He's not. He's probably on the radio right now arranging for his superiors to do the explaining."

John tapped his fingers on the armrest. "I'm still calling my people in Johnstown."

"I think I'll phone our Pittsburgh contingent."

"They can't do anything. It'll be too crowded. Someone will see them." He shifted uncomfortably. "I was across the desk from my father when he eliminated Bingham, but Ms. Miller must not be able to make a positive identification or I'd be sitting beside my dad in a jail cell right now. I can't risk that somebody will make a stupid move, get his tail thrown in jail and then sing like a bird about who hired him."

Simon smiled. He liked a man who put reason ahead of revenge. He liked a man who thought with his head, not his gun . . . or knife as the case may be. "I'll do the hiring. You'll be protected."

"Not enough." He tapped his fingers again, then sighed. "Send somebody, but just to follow them, unless Rosen and his witness slip into a dark corner, then your employee can use his discretion." Rubbing his newly grown beard, he turned to Simon. "And his discretion had better be above reproach."

"Don't worry," Simon replied. "I'll choose my game piece very carefully." He shifted, took a close look at John, Jr. and smiled. "And in the meantime, I think you should consider shaving. I know you think the beard makes you look older, but if you go to trial with that hair on your chin, you're going to end up sharing a cell with your dad after all."

John, Jr. snorted a laugh. "The beard makes me look like a criminal?"

Chuckling, Simon settled back on the soft leather seat. "Not really. But I think it makes you identifiable. My guess is she remembers only two things from last night— your dad's face and your beard. Your new beard. The beard that probably hasn't made it yet into your FBI folder. I think if you shave, your condemning evidence will slide down the drain and you'll be off the hook."

Chapter Three

"Welcome to the Greater Pittsburgh international airport."

"It's lovely." Being shot at was the ultimate fear, getting motion sickness in your rescue craft was the ultimate humiliation, having your bodyguard laugh about it was the ultimate insult. They hadn't spoken two words since she'd lost her breakfast into an air bag, and she had no intention of being friendly now.

"We like to think so," he said, then jumped to the pavement. He started walking around the vehicle, and Linda quickly glanced around for a door handle. There was no way he was going to pick her up and put her anywhere again. She was tired of him treating her as if she were a package not a person, and she was standing on her own two feet from here on out. He wasn't touching her again. Not to push her out of the way of a bullet, not to hand her out of the helicopter.

Just as he rounded to her side of the chopper, she jumped to the pavement. "Who's gonna pay for all this?" she asked, shielding her eyes from the sun as she looked up at him. "I don't even have enough money to reimburse the pilot for the gas we used."

"Don't worry about it," he said, taking her arm. Immediately she jerked free, but he merely took her arm in a firmer grip and began striding into a nearby hangar. "From here on out you're part of the federal deficit."

"Great," she muttered, sighing heavily. Not only was he touching her again, but he had such a tight hold on her arm that the circulation had crawled to a halt. And she was getting the impression that even if he did notice her arm was turning blue, he wouldn't care. "Will you stop!"

"What? Stop protecting you? Stop walking? Stop talking? What? Stop what?"

"Stop hurting my arm!" She jerked on it one more time and he tightened his hold.

"Listen, kid, I haven't got the time or the patience to deal with you...personally, that is. I have to get you somewhere. And the sooner I get you there the better."

"Wouldn't it be nice if I got there in one piece?"

"Oh, don't worry, you'll be in one piece."

"Yeah, one scraped, scratched and bruised piece."

"Could you stop being a pain for a minute? I can't think with you squawking in my ear."

"And what do I do while you think? Stand here and watch my arm turn blue?"

He looked down then, saw how his fingers were making deadly white indentations in her rather frail-looking arm. When he glanced up at her, she raised both brows in silent reprimand.

He sighed and loosened his grip, but not much. "Happy now?"

She nodded, but was smart enough not to show a self-satisfied smirk.

"Now behave," he commanded, and began walking again. "We've got a serious situation here and I really do have to think."

"Couldn't we think from that bench over there? I've been walking, driving, flying, moving for the past six hours and I—"

"Look, I know motion isn't your strong suit, but we don't have time to sit. I had a positively brilliant plan and they cracked it. I don't know how or why, but they cracked it. So here we are in Pittsburgh, when we're supposed to be on our way to Minneapolis." He stopped, looked around, then pulled her along in a different direction. "To make matters worse, we're kind of on our own. I don't know who I can trust and who I can't trust, so I don't trust anybody. Santos didn't just change our course, he eliminated everybody but you and me when he broke the codes of my plan. From this point forward, we don't talk to a soul. But," he continued, still striding along with Linda scurrying to keep up with him, "more important than maintaining silence, my next move will have to be totally unpredictable."

"Okay, fine, 007, but how about if I sit while you march around the hangar thinking?"

"No. I want to have a hold on at least some part of you, so that if I need to I can push you down, kick you out of the way, or sit on you so they can't get to you, unless they go through me."

She watched his face while he spoke, heard the subtle insinuation in the tone of his voice. They might be fighting for her life, but to him there seemed to be fun in the challenge. She'd suspected it was personal, and that was bad enough, but fun? Being shot at—fun? Running from the mob—fun? A cold shiver of fear scurried down her spine. "If I didn't know better, I'd think you were enjoying this."

They reached a pay phone and he stopped. When he dropped her arm, she rubbed her sore flesh. He reached into his pocket for change.

"What can I say? I love my work."

He wasn't kidding. His tone was dry and he was sort of smiling, but Linda knew he wasn't kidding. On some odd level he was enjoying this. Right then and there she decided she didn't want to hear any more. She looked around as he dropped his money into the pay phone and began punching out numbers.

"Hi, it's me."

She pivoted and stared at him. *Hi, it's me?* She assumed the one person exempt from their vigil of silence would be his commander, and that was the person he was running to phone, but one didn't say "Hi, it's me," to their commander, did they?

"I've got about three hundred in cash and I have a few credit cards, but I need my plane. Can you . . ."

He saw her looking at him and turned away, placing his hand over the phone so she couldn't hear him.

"Well, I'll be darned," she muttered, realizing he might be talking with someone about her destiny, but she wasn't going to be privy to the conversation, even though she was supposed to stand right beside him. She felt like sighing and stalking away, finding a seat somewhere. Unfortunately, he hooked a piece of her arm again.

She couldn't do any stalking, but she did sigh and turn away from him in the only show of disapproval she could use. With her nose in the air, she glanced around the surprisingly clean and orderly hangar, but suddenly all the hair on the back of her neck went poker straight and boinged to attention as if someone had poured ice water down her spine.

They were being watched. She'd drawn male attention since the day she hit twelve, so she knew when she was being watched, and she was definitely being watched right now.

Before she made an idiot of herself by panicking and screaming like a banshee, she looked at Michael Rosen. He casually leaned against the wall, holding the phone receiver in one hand and the fleshy part of her arm in the other. Once he chuckled. Twice he smiled. Obviously he didn't sense anything unusual.

"I have twelve hours, tops, before the entire country will recognize her from newspaper pictures, but instead of using back roads and fleabag motels, I'm just buzzing right across the country, first class all the way. I'm going with quick, not quiet. Otherwise, every two-bit hood from here to Hong Kong will have time to take a crack at her. But that's what's going to throw them off. By the time they get to where we've been spotted, we won't be there anymore...."

She shivered, half from relief that his plan sounded good to her and half from cold fear. Somebody was actually trying to kill her. She was the one he was talking about. She was the one he was trying to protect. It was her life that was in so much jeopardy. And though he'd dragged her through a spray of bullets and then forced her to ride in a vehicle that was so rocky she vomited, she suddenly realized she'd now be dead if he hadn't. Her already taut neck began to ache then tingle. Somebody was watching her again.

Trying to be calm, inconspicuous, she looked around. A dusty breeze danced in from the long, flat plain that surrounded the hangar. The sound of someone pounding on metal mixed with the steady hum of distant engines, while people went about airport business as usual. She saw no guns, no knives, no suspicious-looking characters and decided she was probably imagining things because she was scared. Then she got the sensation of a million tiny bugs crawling on her hairline, and she knew she wasn't imagining anything.

"That's just it. He won't get out. He'll die in prison. That's the motivation . . . look, forget the plane. Just pour some money into my account so I can use my bank card. No, No . . ."

Michael Rosen was so busy planning their future that he didn't seem to realize he should be worried about their present. Linda slowly glanced around again, this time with big eyes and an open mind for creative weaponry. Three men clustered by a small plane and stared at her with open admiration. One even pointed. But she sensed only appreciation and speculation about who she was or maybe why she'd be in their hangar, and she managed a shaky smile. No threat there. And she knew what the threat of danger felt like. She'd lived with a drunken mother all her life. Not only had she learned to divine when someone was watching her, but she'd also developed the skill of sniffing trouble in the air. She hadn't been able to risk actually seeing her mother to read her facial expression, so she had to feel danger before it hit her. It got to the point where all she had to do was walk into the house and she'd know whether to turn around and walk back out again because she'd be beaten if she stayed. And though she knew the men across the hangar weren't a threat, she couldn't shake the feeling that the person watching her would kill her if he got a chance. Which meant she was safe in a way, otherwise she'd already be dead. The man could obviously see her. She was standing in an open building with no protection, nothing to jump behind except Michael Rosen, who was yakking on the phone as if he'd just called his wife to say hello. But the hangar was bustling with activity and that's probably what saved her. This busy place, this place full of witnesses, wasn't what her observer considered an opportunity to kill her.

Michael Rosen was still talking on the phone, huddled away from her, defying interruption, and the hair on the back of her neck was still standing at attention while those million bugs crawled along her flesh. She might be safe for the moment, but that was all she could count on. The minute she was alone or in a quiet corner or behind something that would shield her assailant, he'd stab her, choke her or shoot her through a pillow. Her breathing grew shallow, but her chest grew heavier and heavier because her heart was pounding, expanding like a beach ball with every breath she drew, as she stared at the people around her, wondering who plotted to kill her.

A mechanic walked away from a plane toward a side entrance where several men pushed an ancient vehicle through the door. Across the room a young kid who had been polishing the outside of a small white craft that looked like a glider, rose, stretched and headed for the door on his side of the room. Her brow furrowed and for a minute she forgot the heavy thudding of her heart. This had to be a private hangar or a rented hangar...

"I need my plane," Michael Rosen had said. She remembered hearing that. She already knew he was a pilot. He flew the helicopter. It almost didn't surprise her that he'd have his own plane. So, all things considered, it wasn't unusual that he knew his way around a private hangar. He probably left his plane here periodically....

And that was the problem. That was why her heart began to thump again. Why her hands got clammy. Why her legs trembled like two weak reeds in rippling water. Why her subconscious had warned her she wasn't safe here.

If Michael Rosen knew enough about John Santos that he knew where to hide her so that Santos couldn't find her, then couldn't it be true that Santos knew Rosen? In fact, he could be as much a Rosen expert as Rosen claimed to be a Santos expert, if only because they'd spent so much time pursuing and dodging each other. That being the case, it was very possible that someone from the Santos organization either followed them here or knew to look here to find them. In fact, the Santos people might have planted an assassin just in case Michael Rosen was forced to resort to his own hangar for sanctuary. And that person might even be targeting her with a gun right now, because the room that had been full of men in coveralls was now empty, empty and quiet, except for the sound of the commercial planes. A sound that would easily cover the sound of a gun.

She tugged on Michael's sleeve.

"Let's go."

Her voice was deep and breathless. The hangar was getting hot and seemed to be closing in on her. She had to get out of here. Someone was about to shoot her. She'd bet her life on it.

"Let's go," she said again, pulling on his arm.

He cradled the receiver of the phone on his shoulder. "Look, Dad, set everything up the way we discussed. The more money you can put into that account, the better. I'll keep you posted."

Linda jerked on his arm again as he hooked the receiver. "Someone's watching me," she whispered, staring at him with round blue eyes full of fear. "We have to get out of here!"

"No," he said, dusting off his suit coat before taking her hand and again starting off with her in tow. "We have to get a rental car."

His calm only fed her fear, but two laughing men entered the hangar, and she breathed a sigh of relief. "You don't understand. Since the day I hit puberty, people have looked at me, watched me. I've learned to sense it."

"Are you bragging or complaining?"

They went down a ramp and she saw the door to a tunnel. Her eyes grew even wider and her mouth fell open. They were walking out of the frying pan and right into the fire. She yanked on his arm until he stopped. "I'm not bragging or complaining. And I'm also not going into a tunnel where someone can shoot me and then scramble out and I'll bleed to death on the concrete floor."

"And you had nerve enough to tell me I had a vivid imagination," he said and began to walk again.

She had no choice but to follow. He was bigger and stronger and not above using both to his advantage.

"Please," she said, simultaneously struggling to keep up with him and get free. "I know when someone is watching me, and I can also tell whether it's good watching or bad watching.... My mother—"

"Will you stop!"

"No!" He wasn't paying one bit of attention to her, and the door kept getting closer and closer. Her every breath shivered in her chest and set off a chain reaction of trembling through her entire body, but her mind seemed to grow sharper and her will stronger. There was no way she was getting into that tunnel. "I heard part of your phone conversation. You own a plane."

"So?"

Behind her she heard the click-click-click of heels hitting the cement. Someone was following them. The tunnel door loomed like the grim reaper, portal to a passage where a murder would take place. Those who saw them go in wouldn't realize only the killer would come out. And those who saw the killer come out wouldn't realize he'd left victims behind.

Weak-kneed and sick in the stomach, she caught a great gulp of air to keep from throwing up again. "So, you're supposed to be a Santos expert, and yet you haven't caught him. Did you ever stop to think that maybe the reason you never caught Santos is that Santos is also a Rosen expert?"

He stopped walking and faced her. "I've thought of that," he said, then grinned. "Many times, in fact."

"Okay, then, that explains why it feels to me as though someone's watching us."

"I personally feel you were right the first time," he said and began to walk again.

"What first time?"

"When you said men had been watching you since you hit puberty. You're darned good-looking. You probably knocked everybody's eyes out when we walked into that hangar. There, is your ego satisfied?"

"You imbecile!" she screamed, totally exasperated with him. "This is not about my ego. It's about my life—saving my life. Your job, remember? I think someone knows you well enough to suspect that you'd turn up here and I'm not going into that tunnel."

He opened the door. "I've never used this hangar, this runway, this tunnel before in my entire life. In fact, I've never landed in this airport, except when I took commercial flights. If Santos's men are at this airport, they made a lucky guess. If they honed in on this hangar, they're clairvoyant."

The tunnel was cool, quiet and smelled musty. It was also short and filled with people. Linda didn't even have enough time to get really scared before they were opening a door that took them to the baggage claim center of the airport. In two minutes they were lost in a crowd, and in ten minutes they were standing in line for a rental car.

"Keep your vivid imagination in check," Michael ordered, pocketing the paperwork from his car transaction. "I don't want to hear a peep out of you again." He took her by the shoulders, and the way he looked at her would have scared Rambo. "Especially not in a public place. I never want to hear you say that family's name where even a dog can pick up on it. And I'm the pro here. You're something like the tennis ball. You're in the game, but you have no control over what happens to you. Them's the rules, ma'am," he said then grabbed her arm to start walking again. "And I have no intention of changing them. Especially since your sixth sense is woefully inaccurate."

He was right, Linda knew he was right. She'd gone through life like a sniveling coward, afraid of her own shadow and why? Because she believed she had a nose for danger. More than once it had occurred to her that she made mountains out of molehills, but a sixteen-year-old kid didn't go into a house where she suspected a drunk, angry mother waited.

"Look," he said as they entered the car. It was a late-model, flame-colored Chrysler. "I know you're scared, but don't confuse a rush of fear with intuition. It isn't that I don't want to listen to you. It's more that I can't." With that he slammed his door and she slammed hers. In another two minutes he was fighting traffic, and she was staring petulantly out the window.

He was right again, Linda thought, but that didn't make it any easier to swallow. Even worse, the whole experience had dredged up childhood memories that made her feel young and scared . . . not just scared. And she knew that if she tried to explain what she felt, he'd either reassure her with hollow words, as her father always had, or else he'd brush the whole thing aside as ancient history, as her ex-husband always had. Her fear was a living, breathing part of her, very real and very much in the present, but her father never believed the former, and her ex-husband never understood the latter.

"I think from here on out, the best way to handle this would be to pretend we're married."

Grateful to come out of her morbid thoughts, she turned and gave him a puzzled frown. "What?"

"We should pretend we're married," he repeated, braking for a red light.

As they waited for the signal, Linda stared at him. He wasn't what anyone would call a perfect male specimen, but he certainly had sex appeal by the bushel. His six feet of flesh and muscle was finely honed symmetry. But his nose had been broken and he presently needed a shave, so he wasn't really handsome—not storybook, movie-star handsome anyway—though he was sexy, appealing, male. That was it. He was male. His lack of pretty-boy features actually made him more, not less, attractive, because his ruggedness made him more masculine.

Considering his suggestion, she tilted her head. If her ex-husband was anything to go by, unapologetic masculinity was her downfall. And he'd already admitted he found her attractive, too.

"I don't think so."

"You don't get to think, remember?"

Mentally counting to ten, she rolled her eyes then looked out the window. She didn't have a temper. Generally she didn't even talk back, never argued and usually did as she was told without question. But if she didn't argue with this particular man, he'd get her killed in the process of protecting her; and if he didn't get her killed, he'd make her life miserable because she had a sneaking suspicion he kept forgetting she was human.

"All right then," she said, taking a deep breath. "I don't want to pretend I'm married to you. There are—"

"You don't get choices either, Cinderella."

She tapped her fingers on the armrest of her door. The beginnings of a headache snaked through her brain in a silent warning of things to come.

"Look," he said, making an unexpected left turn that almost rolled her to his side. "I can't leave you alone for six or eight hours while you sleep. Stop and think. You'd be totally unprotected."

She didn't say anything, just stared out the window.

He sighed heavily. "Do you think I want it this way? Do you think I'll get some kind of big kick out of being by your side twenty-four hours a day? The only time I'll get a break is when I go into the men's room, and I'm still not convinced I shouldn't take you in with me."

"Don't do me any favors."

At that he laughed. Then he made a right turn and a left turn and screeched the car to a stop at a rinky-dink used car dealer. "Your instructions are these," he said as he turned off the engine and rested his arm across the back of the seat. "Keep a low profile. Look normal. Don't do anything that brings undue attention and we'll be fine."

"You should practice what you preach," she said, and opened her car door. "For a person who doesn't want to attract attention, you drive like a moron."

He pushed open his door and bounded after her, grabbing her arm when he reached her. "I'd also suggest you refrain from name-calling. It—"

"What's the matter? Can't take a little constructive criticism?"

"My driving isn't at issue here. If you—"

"Huh! That's not how I see it. If you want me to keep a low profile, then you should, too. I'll pretend we're married, but only if you watch your driving."

A salesman materialized from a glass-walled office and waved at them as he smiled broadly in welcome.

"I told you, no compromises. I—"

"You," she said, trying to jerk her arm out of his grasp, but he wouldn't let go, "better make up your mind in about thirty seconds, because here comes Carl Car Salesman. You promise to watch your driving and I'll be Mrs. Michael Rosen. I'll even pretend we have three kids. Otherwise, I'll stay as silent as a mouse and let this man draw his own conclusions. And with the way you're holding my arm, I'd bet my last nickel he calls the police to report a possible abduction the minute we leave."

He dropped her arm and smiled tightly. "Mrs. Rosen, you're a pain."

"Coming from you, Mr. Rosen, that's a compliment."

"Not Rosen," Michael decided in a whisper. "Let's just be Mr. and Mrs. Johnson."

"How creative," she muttered as the car salesman approached them. His long, loping strides reminded her of a giraffe. "Johnson and Johnson. Someone ought to name a company after us."

"Hi," Michael said and extended his hand. "Sam Johnson and this is my wife, Lorraine."

"Bill Brown," the salesman replied, taking Michael's hand and pumping vigorously. "How can I help you?"

"I'm buying my husband a car," Linda jumped in. "We just found out that we're expecting our first child and I'm thanking him for the privilege."

Still smiling at Bill Brown, Michael stepped on her foot, lightly, but enough that she'd realize he'd finish the job if she didn't shut up. "My wife's such a kidder," he said, and looped his arm around her shoulders, almost crushing her bones in a bear hug. "That's why I love her, but I'm here on business. You should have received a call from Matthew Rosen of Rosen Foods," he said, motioning with his free arm for the salesman to lead them to the little office. "I'm a purchasing agent for his company, and we're looking for a good buy on a Jeep."

"We've got lots of Jeeps," Bill Brown assured.

"Fine. As soon as we clear up the payment issue, we'll take a look."

They turned and began walking toward the glass office, and a breeze kicked up. It blew dry dust around their ankles and tossed Linda's skirt into the air. She caught it just as a cool tingle ran down her spine, and she stopped walking. Her upper arms froze. Her breaths had weight and measure again.

They'd been followed.

Michael realized she wasn't beside him, and he stopped and pivoted. "Aren't you coming, dear?"

Her breath shivered out. She glanced behind her, but saw nothing except a normal stream of traffic. The wind ballooned her skirt again. If she mentioned this to Michael in front of Bill Brown, he'd never forgive her. If she mentioned this to him later, he'd tell her she'd imagined it.

Maybe she had.

She pushed her skirt down again. "I'm coming."

Chapter Four

Linda never thought the day would come when she'd miss Molly Benson's nonstop chatter, but after hours and hours of riding next to a stony and silent Michael Rosen, she'd pay someone to talk to her right now.

They filled the tank of the Jeep with gas and headed west on I-70. For the first half hour or so, Michael Rosen fiddled with the radio but couldn't seem to pick up a station, so with a heavy sigh, he snapped it off.

Hours passed with Linda watching trees go by and looking at houses and truck stops and trying to imagine the kinds of people who inhabited or frequented such places, and then, she supposed, because of watching the scenery, she got a severe case of motion sickness. She took a deep breath and closed her eyes, knowing she had to think of something, anything, to get her mind off her rolling stomach, and that's when she started thinking about Molly Benson.

Molly was a divorced mother of three who was desperately trying to keep her family together. Not just in the conventional sense of the word. Oh, no. Molly wanted a good, close-knit family, and she did everything in her power to be a good mother, a good housekeeper, a den mother, a breadwinner and one-fifth of a car pool. The only thing that Molly never accounted for in her life was herself, and as a result, she used the office as entertainment of sorts. She made coffee, chatted with everybody about their families, took her problems to the attorneys, had luncheon engagements, shopped when the attorneys were in court and in general neglected her job responsibilities, which Linda eventually assumed.

But Linda never minded. If anything, Molly intrigued her. She'd never met anybody who could talk as much or as long or as fast, and because she found Molly entertaining, Linda gladly helped her. Keeping up with Molly's work as well as her own became second nature for Linda. As did going to Little League games, lending Molly her car, lending Molly money, buying gifts for Biff, Marcie and Brian—Molly's adorable kids.

She took another deep breath to try to stop her sad thoughts but once again became aware of the movement of the car, and she realized she had to think, about everything, so she'd forget about the fact that she was moving and her stomach wasn't a traveler....

She was going to miss Biff and Marcie and Brian. She was going to miss Molly. She was going to miss Polly Bingham, Mr. Bingham's tall, skinny niece who couldn't spell. She was going to miss Graham and Alexandra... Lord, there was a pair.

Graham Bingham was Polly Bingham's workaholic dad and Alexandra was his devoted secretary. Linda once found out they'd worked around the clock, twenty-four straight hours, to get a brief to federal court... they were crazy.

Craziness notwithstanding, Graham and Alexandra would take Mr. Bingham's death very hard. The people who were a part of Bingham and Bingham, Attorneys-at-Law, were a mixture of relatives and friends who intermingled to the point that everybody became family, with Bob Bingham acting as dad....

She stopped again. That was another touchy subject. She couldn't think of Molly and her kids. She couldn't think of Mr. Bingham. She didn't want to think of how Alexandra would sob and sob and probably forget to eat or how Graham would sit in his office and stare at the Susquehanna River.

"Hungry?"

"Huh?"

"I asked if you were hungry."

She wasn't. Not really. But she desperately wanted to quit moving. "I'd love something to drink."

He rolled the Jeep to a halt in the parking lot of a truck stop, and despite the fact that it was a little after seven o'clock in the evening, the pavement was sizzling hot. The air was heavy with dead-of-summer humidity.

All the same, Linda was glad to get out of the car. She stepped onto the hot blacktop of the parking lot and took a deep breath of the heavy air, waiting for Michael Rosen to give her instructions. He didn't say a word, just motioned for her to walk to the front of the Jeep and she did, but she paused again, waiting for him to catch up to her.

Once he was beside her, he motioned for her to precede him to the door of the small low-roofed establishment. The paint on the outside walls was peeling, and there was a hole in the screen door.

She pushed open the door and the sounds of the juke box assaulted her, but it was the scent of greasy food that made her stop short.

"I can't go in there."

"What?"

She took a deep breath, and when the smell hit her nostrils, she regretted it. "I said, I can't go in there."

"Why the hell not?"

"The smell," she said, and almost choked because she couldn't hold her breath when she talked.

He sniffed. "Smell's fine to me."

"It may smell fine to you," she said, pushing past him to get out the door. "But it's making me gag."

Michael Rosen followed her outside. She leaned on the wall and began taking slow, deep breaths to calm her stomach.

"What in the devil is the matter with you?" he asked, so exasperated with her he didn't even bother to hide it.

"Didn't you learn anything from our helicopter ride this morning?" she asked, rubbing her fingers along her temples because now she was getting a headache, too.

"Yeah, I learned not to judge a book by its cover. That old beast we took might have looked like it was going to fall apart any second, but it got us to Pittsburgh in record time and safely, too."

"But it shook and rattled and just about killed me."

He looked at her. "If you're telling me you get sick because of being tossed around, I already understood that much. But you're losing me with the rest of it. That Jeep rides as smooth as silk. There's no reason for you to be sick now."

She sighed, the horrible queasy feeling making her shaky and weak. "Just because I didn't get tossed around, it doesn't mean I'm not sick."

He heaved a persecuted sigh. "And you're sick now."

"Horribly, disgustingly, deathly sick."

"Doggone it!" he muttered, and slapped his thigh as he paced away from her. Then he walked back with his hands open, palms up, and he said, "Look, you can't do this."

She stared at him. "Believe me, if there were a way around it, I wouldn't do it."

He rubbed his hand across his forehead, thinking. "Okay," he said, trying to sound reasonable and failing. "This really doesn't have to be a problem. We'll just look for a drugstore and get some over-the-counter remedy. How does that sound?"

She sighed. "We can't."

"What do you mean we can't?" he asked, stupefied.

"Most motion sickness pills put me to sleep."

"Right now, that might not be such a bad idea." He gripped her arm and began leading her to the Jeep. "Come on, let's find that drugstore."

"But I thought you wanted me awake and alert," she argued, again struggling to keep up with him.

"Right now, the thought of you being sound asleep is actually a very pleasant one."

"And what if somebody tries to kill me and you need me to jump out of the way or duck or something."

"I'm just about certain nobody's figured out where we are yet."

"But you're not a hundred percent certain."

He stopped, sighed and said, "Look, you're fine. You're safe." He waved his hands in a gesture of dismissal. "Okay."

"You contradict yourself all the time," she mumbled as he took her arm again.

"No, I don't."

"Yes, you do."

He stopped again. "What is bugging you now?"

"These pills put me out cold. Even if you try to shake me awake, I won't be able to get up. But if that doesn't bother you, then it doesn't bother me, either."

He hooked her arm again, walked her to the door of the Jeep, then pulled it open. "We're getting the pills."

"Fine," she said sarcastically. "If you want me to sit beside you and snore, that's fine with me."

"It's better than hearing you sigh for two hundred miles."

"Just what's that supposed to mean?"

"Nothing," he said, slammed her door and strode around the Jeep. As he pulled open his door, he said, "Not another word. I don't want you to throw up. I don't want to hear you complain. But most of all I don't want to feel like I have to entertain you."

"Entertain me!" she gasped. "You haven't said two words—"

"And I don't intend to."

He started the engine of the Jeep and Linda glared at him, then turned away. "You are not going to be able to wake me up."

"I already said that was fine."

"Fine."

"Fine."

After fifteen minutes of driving around the little city, they found a drugstore. They walked in silently and, without a word, Linda picked out the medicine. She broke their vigil of silence to suggest they buy a bottle of water so she could take the pills in the car and they wouldn't have to stop at all anymore.

He seemed infuriatingly pleased with her suggestion and headed back down the aisle to the bottled water, not even realizing she was being sarcastic.

Before they reached the checkout counter, Michael picked up a small cooler. "We'll grab some ice and a few cans of cola, too."

"Fine," she said, wondering why he'd bothered to consult her but somewhat pleased that he had, because it clued her in about their plans. Just from the way he'd bought that cooler, albeit a disposable one, Linda knew they were in for a long, difficult journey. She wasn't pleased to be making a long trip, but she was glad to be oriented, because it helped to understand that they would be driving for days. At least now she could prepare herself, if only emotionally.

They drove onto the highway again, and Linda settled down to get comfortable. Just as she predicted, she fell into an immediate sleep. It wasn't deep and it wasn't comfortable, but it was enough that she wasn't aware of the whine of the tires or the passing of scenery. As the night descended and the air cooled, the evening almost became pleasant. She'd drift to sleep and then float back to consciousness long enough to see a road sign or some other marker to let her know how far they'd traveled. Then she'd let herself fall asleep again.

When the moon was high and a million stars twinkled overhead, Michael shook her shoulder. "Come on, kid. We're going inside."

She sniffed a breath of air. "What?"

"Inside," he said, pointing at the door of a hotel belonging to a well-known chain.

"Oh, okay," she said, and turned toward her door. She fumbled for a minute, groggily searching for the door handle but couldn't find it. When she did, she sprung it so quickly she nearly rolled out of the Jeep.

Just in the nick of time, Michael ran over and caught her before she fell on the ground. "Wake up," he said, sighing. "At least a little bit so I can get us checked in."

"Okay," she said, leaning on him.

"Come on, I mean it. Wake up."

"I can't," she mumbled. "I told you, I can't."

"Sure you can," he said, walking her toward the door. "One foot in front of the other. That's it. Good girl."

She took a deep breath. "Where are we?"

"At a hotel."

"No, I mean, like, where are we?"

"You mean, what city?"

She sniffed again as he pulled open the glass doors. "Yeah."

"Now, what possible reason would you have for wanting to know where we are?"

Bleary-eyed, she looked at him. "I don't know."

"Okay, see? It's no big deal then if I don't tell you where we are. Right?"

"I guess," she said as he continued to help her walk to the counter in the lobby.

"Frank and JoAnna Burnside. We have reservations," Michael Rosen announced as he leaned Linda against the counter. "My wife gets carsick and I gave her some medicine. Puts her right to sleep," he explained as Linda began sliding down the counter. He hoisted her up again and, holding her with one arm, he reached into his back trouser pocket for his wallet.

"I'm sorry, Mr. Burnside," the counter attendant said. "But I can't seem to find your reservations."

"Oh, my mistake," Michael said as he handed the young woman his credit card. Even bleary-eyed Linda could see the name on the card was Burnside. "The reservation is probably in the name of my company—Rosen Foods."

The counter attendant typed the company name into the computer. "You're right. Here it is." She typed some more as Linda took deep, long breaths to keep herself awake. "That's Room 214, Mr. Burnside. Do you need help with your luggage?"

"In fact, I do," Michael said, handing the woman the keys to the Jeep. "There's just one bag in the Jeep, but it looks like I'm going to have my hands full getting my wife to our room.''

"No problem,'' the attendant said, then smiled. "We'll have your bag in your room in about fifteen minutes.''

"Great,'' Michael said, turning away from the counter. He took Linda by the arm, pulled her tightly against him and then put his arm around her. "Are you okay?'' he asked solicitously.

"I'm fine. Just sleepy,'' Linda answered, snuggling into his side.

"Yeah, well, we'll have you in bed in about ten minutes.''

"Good,'' she said, then took another deep breath and nestled against him.

They waited for the elevator in silence, and when it came, Michael helped her inside. In a matter of seconds they were at their floor, and in another minute Michael had their room door open.

"What is your problem?'' he asked as he sat her down on the bed.

She collapsed onto her back. "Sleepy. I told you pills make me sleepy.''

"You took that pill six hours ago!'' he said, and stormed to the bathroom, slamming the door.

Linda opened one eye. Hadn't he just been nice, even sweet to her a minute ago? Or had she dreamed that?

The porter knocked on the door, announcing that he had Michael's bag, and Linda sucked in more air, assuming that she'd have to get up and answer the door, but Michael came charging out of the bathroom.

When he opened the door, though, he was smiling happily. "Thank you so much!'' he said, and handed the young man a dollar as he took his duffel bag and the Jeep keys.

He closed the door and with the eye she could keep open, Linda watched him storm to the second of the two double beds in the room. He tossed his duffel bag down and rummaged through until he came upon a white T-shirt that he threw to the bed on which she lay. It landed beside her.

"Sleep in that," he said, his tone tired and disgruntled. "I don't want you to get your clothes wrinkled."

With every ounce of energy she could muster, she sat up, glancing at the shirt.

He rummaged for more supplies, which he carried to the dresser by the bathroom door. "There's a comb, toothbrush and deodorant. I don't want us to look out of place, so if we keep our appearance up, no one will suspect a thing."

She looked at him, then glanced at the things he'd laid out for her. Stifling a yawn, she said, "Okay."

He sighed. "Do you want the bathroom first? Or may I use it."

"I—I—"

He sighed again. "Look, why don't you just go first. You're going to fall asleep again and then you won't get a shower. Maybe you won't even get out of your clothes—"

Stopping him with a wave of her hand, Linda nodded and headed for the bathroom. She stripped, careful to lay her blouse and skirt on the closed lid of the commode. Even semicomatose, she knew what he was telling her, and she was smart enough to accept his counsel without question. They were not to look in any way out of the ordinary, and wearing the same clothes for a few days would present obvious problems.

She frowned thoughtfully, then threw her underwear, her panty hose and her bra into the sink and washed them. They were working toward the same goal, keeping her alive, and even if Michael Rosen wasn't smart enough to let her be a part of the decision making about her own destiny, she wasn't so stubborn that she'd ignore the obvious.

After her shower, she slipped into the enormous white undershirt and then put a bath towel over her shoulders because she didn't have a robe. When she entered the bedroom, Michael Rosen was watching TV. She cleared her throat.

"I was thinking that maybe if we took the top off the Jeep, you know, let the wind blow in and around me, maybe I wouldn't get sick."

He sighed as he rose from the bed. "I guess it's worth a try." He reached into his bag, which was laying open at the foot of the bed. There were at least four cotton shirts and two pair of jeans. Obviously he was a simple dresser, and her white blouse and shiny paisley skirt with the spike heels were going to look a little silly.

She cleared her throat again and backed away from him as he approached the dresser where she had placed the toiletries he'd given her. "Another thing..."

"Will you stop acting as if I'm going to slap you or something!"

"Will you stop yelling at me!"

He sighed heavily. "All right. What now?"

"This skirt," she said, holding it up for him to see, "is pretty fancy, because I was out with my friends before I... anyway, it's a little too fancy, and I was thinking that if we had time, maybe we could stop...."

"We don't have time to stop."

"One quick trip to a five-and-dime and I could get a pair of shorts and tennis shoes."

He didn't say anything, just began assembling his own toiletries for his shower.

"All right. All right. Fine. I'll ride around in a satin skirt and you wear your blue jeans and Nikes, and we'll stick out like two sore thumbs. It's fine with me."

"Will you get a hold of yourself. I was thinking about your suggestion and I happen to think you're right." He sighed again. "Look, I live by myself and usually work alone. I'm not used to having somebody tag along. I'm going to be a little slow to answer your questions and not very talkative. I'm sorry, but that's just the way it is."

With that he walked into the bathroom, and Linda went to the closet where she hung her skirt and blouse. Now that she'd slept for six hours and had had a reviving shower, she wasn't very sleepy. But Michael Rosen obviously was or he wouldn't have stopped for the night.

She crawled under the covers and turned away from the second bed in the room. At least now she knew it was his nature to be nasty, she hadn't done anything wrong. She only hoped she could survive several weeks of not communicating with anybody.

Lord, how she missed Molly Benson.

Chapter Five

The cabin was nothing like what she'd expected. Clean, it would have been the perfect weekend hideaway. As it was, dust marred one's ability to appreciate its perfection as a retreat. When the door opened, she saw the dust first, then the cathedral ceilings, a galley kitchen and two men playing cards in the game area set up in the back corner.

"Al, Jonesy, this is Linda Miller."

As Michael closed the cabin door, Jonesy rose. He was fiftyish, chewing tobacco and hugging his cards. "How do you do, Ms. Miller?"

Al sat with his back to the door and seemed more concerned about placing his bet than meeting the newcomer, but when he finally turned and saw Linda, he almost tripped himself, scrambling from his seat. Tops, Al was thirty. He was handsome as the devil and twice as cocky. "Nice to meet you," he said, and then gave his most charming grin.

Michael casually stole a look at his albatross witness. He knew she was pretty. A blind man could see that. But they'd just traveled across the country in a Jeep, and she shouldn't look good enough to bring Al off his duff and make him stutter. However, even after all their traveling, Linda looked about as good as a woman could look. Her feathery hair wasn't quite straight but sort of curled toward her face, with a sun-bleached golden color. Her T-shirt, the one he'd bought at the five-and-dime, was neat and tidy, but her shorts were what attracted the most attention because of her long, shapely legs.

"Are you hungry?" Michael asked, and didn't wait for a reply. Instead he took the few strides necessary to get him past the counter that separated the sitting room space from the kitchen area and served as the place where you ate your food, unless you wanted to take it to the table in the gaming ground.

Linda sat on one of the four stools on the sitting room side of the counter. "I'm starved."

"Well, there's sausage or bacon to go with eggs and toast," he said, peering into the refrigerator.

"Can't we eat something normal like macaroni and cheese?"

He twisted his head away from the refrigerator and stared at her. "Normal?"

"Eggs and sausage are for breakfast. It's after four. I'm hungry for real food."

"Yeah, Rosen," Al chided as he slid onto the stool beside Linda. "You might think the world revolves around eggs and bacon...and sometimes sausage, but the rest of us eat regular food." He turned to Linda. "Can you imagine what this guy's cholesterol level is?" Even as he asked the question, he lit a cigarette.

"I'd imagine his cholesterol level is no worse than the condition of your lungs."

Opening a cabinet door, Michael smiled wryly. *Go for it, Casanova,* he thought, just barely stifling a laugh. *It will give me great pleasure to watch her tear somebody else to shreds for a change.*

"Bad habit," Al agreed, and immediately put out his cigarette. "I've been trying to quit for months." He gave Linda another charming smile.

Michael caught a loud groan of frustration just before it passed his lips and then had to stop himself from slamming the cupboard door. It was bad enough that Al was being a two-bit sucker for a pretty face, but there wasn't a scrap of food in this place, save the usual fare of breakfast entrées, which were quick, easy and generally satisfactory to him.

"I smoked," Linda said, pushing the ashtray as far away from her as she could get it. "And to be honest," she added sheepishly, "I only quit a few months ago."

"Really?" Al asked, sliding his elbow along the bar to get closer. His green eyes sparkled and so did his pearly-white teeth. Linda returned his smile shyly, happily, and Michael slammed a cupboard door then bent to search the few shelves beneath the counter.

"Yeah, I...well, you know the hype about smoking isn't really hype. It's true. I came face-to-face with the damage smoking could do and I said, hey, dummy, just quit."

"That's great," Al said.

"Thanks. I'm very proud of myself," Linda said, again sheepishly, shyly, and Michael couldn't help it, he turned from his quest for food and stared at her. He couldn't remember her ever speaking nicely to him, let alone thanking him. To his recollection, she hadn't even thanked him for the T-shirt, shorts and tennis shoes he bought her. Come to think of it, she never thanked him for saving her life. And there she was, thanking some two-bit Casanova for a worthless compliment.

"I quit twenty years ago," Jonesy announced, taking the stool on the other side of Linda. "Never been sorry, but I have to admit, there are days when I still crave a smoke. Especially when I work with somebody who smokes like a chimney." He gave Al a withering look over Linda's head.

Clearly insulted, Al's mouth dropped open. "Hey, I don't smoke that much," he said. "There are people who smoke packs and packs of cigarettes every day. I have a cigarette or two. That's all."

"Huh!" Jonesy jeered. He tapped Linda's arm and pointed toward the card table. "Go check that ashtray and then tell me what you think."

"That ashtray hasn't been emptied since we got here." Al had bypassed indignant and gone right to ripsnorting mad.

"Now, boys," Linda said, and touched both of their wrists. "Don't fight," she said, then she laughed, actually laughed. "I feel like your mother."

Michael couldn't believe what he was hearing. Pivoting away from them, he took a deep breath, counted to ten, then turned around again. Al was taking a good look at Linda, who was laughing at Jonesy, who was saying something about a card trick.

"There's nothing here but the eggs and stuff," Michael said as he crossed his arms on his chest and leaned against the white stove. "I can go shopping now, or we can eat what we have and I'll go in the morning."

"Whatever," Linda said, then shrugged. She turned to Al. "I think Jonesy and I should reform you."

"Yeah," Jonesy agreed, grinning maliciously.

"Well, if anybody could," Al said, taking Linda's hand, "I think it would be you."

Michael slammed the frying pan onto the steel frame of the gas burner. Out of the corner of his eye, he watched Linda glance around at the cabin again, but noticed she hadn't jerked her hand away from Al.

"This is nice," she said.

At her words, Al and Jonesy looked around as though seeing the place for the first time.

"A little dusty," Al said, frowning.

"Yeah, dusty," Jonesy said. Both obviously had begun to see the cabin through Linda's eyes, and neither appeared to be pleased.

"But nice," Linda prompted.

"Yeah, nice," Jonesy said.

"Nice," Al agreed, though not enthusiastically.

"You just don't see the potential."

When she said that, Michael looked around. He remembered the cabin empty, the way it looked when he bought it. It was new then. Built as a hunting retreat by an industrialist who died before he set a fishing rod onto the front porch. The man's wife had no use for it, and Michael got it for a song. He remembered seeing the beamed ceilings, the empty bookshelves, the neat and shiny row that was a kitchen unit and immediately falling in love with the place. He remembered envisioning cozy furniture and neat rows of books. He saw an afghan on the wooden rocker and fat feather comforters on the beds. He even imagined red-and-white curtains and dish towels. He'd never envisioned secondhand furniture, old dish towels and worn-to-threads blankets. He'd seen then what Linda saw now. He broke an egg into the hot pan.

"Do you have a vacuum cleaner?"

Michael glanced over. He thought for a second, then shrugged. "Don't think so."

"You should get one when you go shopping tomorrow," Linda said, leaning her elbows on the counter. "We could give this place a thorough going-over from top to bottom."

"It's fine the way it is," Michael said, even though he knew it wasn't.

"It's dusty," Linda said, and Al and Jonesy said things that sounded like halfhearted agreement. They had to admit the place was dirty, but there was a definite lack of enthusiasm about cleaning. "Heaven knows how long we have to live here," Linda continued, accenting the live. "So, while we do, it would be nice if it were clean."

"I don't want to clean," Michael said, flipping the first of the three eggs in the pan. "I hate to clean."

"All right, I'll do it," Linda said.

He sighed heavily. "I don't want anybody to do it."

"Why?"

"Why?" he mocked. "Did you ever notice you have an irritating tendency to question every decision I make?"

"Why shouldn't I?" Linda demanded. "You don't volunteer anything. The only way I find out even the smallest detail of what you're planning to do with my life is if I question you."

"Well, stop it. It bugs me."

"Yeah?" Linda challenged, and both Al and Jonesy gaped at her. Michael understood perfectly well why. She was small and soft and pale...innocent looking. When her sharp tongue got going, it was almost hard to believe.

"Well, it bugs me that I have only one pair of underwear," she said, putting her hands on her hips. "But I don't say anything. I don't even have a dollar twenty-nine to buy another pair. And that bugs me, too. But have I complained? And I'd like to sleep in something other than your stinky old shirt. I haven't had a hot bath or a decent meal in a week, and just from the look of this place, I'm not going to get them here, either."

At the end of her last sentence her voice began to shake. She was mad, but it wasn't just anger trembling through her words, it was a scary jumble of emotions that could mean just about anything. Every nerve ending in Michael's body quivered in anticipation. Al and Jonesy got wide-eyed then leaned away from the impending storm. Linda took a deep breath.

"So, you stop it!"

She jumped off her stool, and before anyone gathered their wits to utter a response, she ran to the back of the cabin, swung open the first of two bedroom doors and jumped through the portal, slamming the door behind her.

"Nice goin', Rosen."

"Yeah, Rosen."

"Just shut up, okay?" Michael said, running his hand over his mouth. A small billow of stinky smoke hit him, and he cursed as he grabbed the hot handle of the cast-iron skillet and threw it into the empty sink. The crisp eggs and smoldering grease hissed when they hit the wet porcelain, the skin of his fingers just melted against the hot iron. Biting back another curse, he turned on the tap and rinsed his singed flesh. Jonesy and Al were looking at him as if he'd just committed a crime.

"You make her sleep in your shirt?" Al asked in disbelief. "Couldn't you even buy her a nightie? You get reimbursed, you know. It's not as if the money's coming out of your own pocket."

Jonesy shook his head sadly. "One pair of underwear?"

Michael took a deep breath and grabbed an old jacket from the hook by the door. It was hot now, but by the time he got back from the city, if you could call a strip shopping center, a gas station and about a hundred homes a city, it would be dark. After dark, it got cold. Sometimes freezing cold. He jumped into the Jeep, turned the key and jammed the gas pedal to the floor. She wanted underwear; he'd get her underwear. Contrary to popular belief, he wasn't a tightwad or even impersonal to the point of being cruel. He was just so preoccupied with keeping her alive; he hadn't thought about her underwear. Which, he decided, might be considered admirable behavior by some people.

As his anger abated, Michael leaned back on the seat and relaxed. He'd never really been mad, just disgusted, and, if truth be known, he was sort of ashamed of himself for not realizing how uncomfortable and unhappy she must have been over the past week. But, dammit, not only was he trying to think ahead, he'd also been forced to backtrack.

It baffled the devil out of him how anybody had found out about DuBois. He couldn't think of a single soul he'd told except Linda. He was realistic enough to know she'd probably told Bill and George, but they really weren't a threat. And the links in the initial chain of people who were to get them to DuBois were above reproach. So he was stumped, had been stumped to the point of going crazy trying to figure it out . . . until now.

Driving through the peace and quiet of the tree-covered mountains, noting the way his Jeep engine was a deafening roar in the solitude, Michael realized he'd missed an angle. It wasn't just who she told that had to be considered, but who might have overheard, as well. Just like the sound of his Jeep in the forest, Linda had one of those clear, resonant voices that rode right through the air as crisp and clean as if she were using a microphone. Even if there hadn't been a Santos spy in the police station, any of the street types would have recognized Linda for an outsider, not a police woman, not a reporter, not an attorney; and once Santos got the word on the street of what he needed, twenty bucks could have bought the word Du-Bois, if nothing else.

Michael slapped his hand on the steering wheel, then relaxed in his seat again. There really hadn't been any harm done, and a lesson had been learned. He now knew he couldn't risk telling Linda anything. Not only had she very easily trusted Bill and George—to the point that she confided without thought—but she liked to make small talk with waitresses and gas station attendants, and though they may be harmless, the walls always had ears. So, considering her penchant for trusting strangers, and considering that her voice traveled well, and considering that perhaps she might be lonely enough or scared enough to want a friendly face to tell her not to worry, then Michael's only recourse was to keep her hidden. And that's why they were here.

Which left him with only one problem...

Michael took a deep breath and glanced around. The foliage was thick and forestlike, dense with trees and therefore dark even at five o'clock in the afternoon. The nearest city, town, village, whatever it was, was forty miles away. The cabin didn't have a phone, because if you had a phone, you existed, if only on a list, so in the interest of keeping the cabin private, he'd taken great pains to isolate it even more than it was naturally. And, dammit, Bill Washington knew where it was.

At the time he had considered it the lesser of two evils. Now, he had to call it a security leak, if only because there was some question about the DuBois foul-up. In all probability, someone had overheard Linda in the police station, but if Michael was wrong about that, it could be a deadly mistake.

It was funny, he thought, looking around at the uncut weeds, some as tall as two feet, and the thick growth of trees. The isolation that made this the perfect hideaway, also made it a rather dangerous place. Particularly since it wasn't really a secret anymore. If Bill Washington told Santos's men about this cabin, they could hike up any one of a hundred trails and do so unnoticed, because they could duck down in the grass, slip behind a tree or just wear brown and green and blend right in. And Michael wouldn't be any the wiser, because nobody could watch a whole mountain unless he had a small army, and if he ordered that many assistants, then he might as well drop Santos a line and invite him to dinner.

Still, Michael didn't think Bill Washington had told Santos anything. Not because Mr. Salty was disgustingly honest and loyal, but because normally the local authorities wouldn't know anything, so Santos wouldn't waste his time browbeating a policeman who shouldn't have been involved any further than Linda's initial statement. If there was a security leak here, if there was a problem, it was Linda Miller herself. Her fear, her crystal-clear voice, her trusting personality all added up to trouble as far as Michael was concerned.

As he reached his destination an hour later, Michael concluded that Linda was safest right where she was. The cabin was invisible by air, difficult to reach and contained three agents who'd be keeping watch. Even if Santos thought to question Bill Washington, that didn't mean Washington would remember the state let alone the deeded name of the property. And even if Santos got the deeded name and located the place on the map, that didn't necessarily mean he'd find it in the forest. And even if he found it in the forest, that didn't mean his hired guns could get Linda before Michael, Al and Jonesy got them. The way he saw it, no place was really perfect, and the way the scales were tipping, it was better to keep her hidden than it was to keep her moving. A moving target might be harder to hit, but a silent target was usually harder to find. And you can't hit something you can't find.

He jumped out of his Jeep, checked his dwindling cash reserves and strode into a Safeway. Up and down the aisles he went, buying everything he didn't like or usually didn't buy. He bought steaks—something he only ate in a restaurant. He bought bags and boxes and cans of prepared things that just needed to be popped into an oven or boiled in their bags. He bought potatoes, rice, lots of butter, flour, sugar and a case of cola. And then he went on a quest for macaroni. Specifically, macaroni and cheese. He found it, sighed with disgust and threw it into his heaping cart, then headed for the checkout.

He exhausted most of his money, argued with a kid about who'd push his cart to his vehicle, then loaded his supplies into the back of the Jeep. Returning the cart to the lineup along the wall, he realized that next door to the supermarket was one of those multipurpose stores that sold everything from hardware to underwear. He thanked God for what he considered his first piece of luck and then went inside where he purchased the necessary clothes for his witness's comfort. He left the department store with a two hundred-dollar charge on his credit card and two jumbo bags, and as he was about to cross the informal traffic lane, a car pulled out of nowhere. He jumped out of the way and wasn't even scratched, but three things happened. First, he got that feeling in the pit of his stomach again—the one that was cold, dead fear caused by running from ruthless killers, who might have just tried to eliminate him disguised as a mother with three children. Second, his instincts started humming that he'd made a bad choice no matter how logical. And third, he flattened himself against the display window of a store called Teddy's.

Regardless of the pounding of his heart, he still chose logic over instinct, because the real mob would have driven right through the building to get him. They wouldn't have gasped and swerved away. That mother with three kids really was a mother with three kids, she was just a poor driver or maybe a preoccupied driver. And his imagination was working overtime because his stress level had hit its limit. What he needed was some rest or maybe just a good laugh or two.

He pushed himself away from the glass, and his gaze collided with a black lace garment that looked to be just about the size of Linda Miller. The thing was trimmed with red ribbon, and the mannequin wore a red ribbon choker with an old-fashioned pendent around her neck and a similarly fashioned garter belt around her thigh. A little sign at the mannequin's knee assured the prospective purchaser that this little number would give any lady sweet dreams. He didn't doubt it for a second.

Michael grinned at the black lace nothing, then grinned again because he had forgotten to buy his good friend Linda pajamas.

"HE CRACKED, MR. SANTOS."

John, Jr. sat back in his chair and sighed with relief, closing his eyes as he listened to Simon.

"We didn't get much out of him, just a lead, but I'm positive that's all he knows. We put Amanda on the phone and when she spoke, he broke down and cried."

John, Jr. sighed again. "Excellent work, Simon. How good's the lead?"

"Actually, it's paper-thin, but we'll work it."

"I know you will," John said, then smiled. Simon had been his father's right-hand man for years, more years than John, Jr. could remember, and if Simon said they'd work this lead, they'd work it. "How should we return the child?"

"I'll take her to a shopping mall," Simon answered without hesitation. "I, personally, will see that she doesn't run off before her grandfather gets there to pick her up. And when he gets there, I'll blend into the crowd."

"Good man," John said, then cradled the receiver of the phone.

MICHAEL ENTERED THE CABIN cautiously, half-afraid of the reception he was about to get. All three of his roommates were playing cards. Nobody even looked up from the game. He heaved a sigh, not quite sure if that was good or bad, and took his first two grocery bags into the galley kitchen. He made two more trips to the car for groceries, then leaned across the counter.

"I...uh...brought macaroni and cheese," he said, and wasn't even quite sure why. He supposed it was as close to an apology as he was going to make, especially considering the fact that he hadn't done anything wrong...hadn't deliberately done anything wrong, anyway.

Linda looked up from her cards. "Is it Kraft?"

"Kraft?"

"You know, Kraft macaroni and cheese," Al explained in exasperation.

Michael glanced into the bag beside him. No macaroni. He searched through the second bag, but didn't spot the blue-and-white box until he looked into the third. "Yeah. It's Kraft."

She smiled slowly, and across the room their gazes met. "When somebody buys me macaroni, I can forgive them just about anything."

For some absurd reason, that pleased him enormously. Not that he felt he needed forgiveness, he quickly assured himself. It was more that a happy project was a quiet, easily managed project. And he now knew that one of the ways to calm this one down was with the right food.

"Do you like ice cream?" he asked as he walked to the door of the cabin again.

Her eyes widened with happy disbelief. "Did you buy me some?"

"No," he said, grabbing the doorknob. "But I'll try to remember it the next time I'm shopping. How about one of you guys starting the macaroni? I'm starved."

"I'll do it," Linda said, and jumped from her seat.

When he reentered the door, carrying her lingerie, her jeans, her sweater, her blouses...her underwear, she was breaking apart a head of lettuce while Al and Jonesy stashed the groceries.

"Come here," he said, motioning toward the couch and chair arranged by the cold stone fireplace.

"What?" she asked, then saw he was carrying three enormous bags.

"Just come here, okay?" He walked to the couch and tossed her new wardrobe onto it, then sat on the chair. Sheepishly she sat on the couch. "Go ahead," he said, this time waving his hand in the direction of the three bags. "I had every intention of getting you some things once we got settled in. Our little argument sort of forced me to go today...and alone," he added deliberately in case she criticized his choices.

"Sorry," she mumbled.

"Don't do that again," he said, finally feeling that he was regaining the upper hand he needed to keep everyone safe. "I've got a job to do, a very serious job. I'm doing it the best way I know how."

"I'm sorry," she said, not venturing even a peek at him or the bags beside her. She just stared at her hands.

Michael almost sighed with disgust. He'd wanted to make her understand their predicament, not totally cow her. It seemed he would never figure out how to deal with this woman. Then he remembered the teddy.

"Why don't you open that last bag first?"

She glanced up. "Which?"

"The one from Teddy's," he said, and settled back in the overstuffed dusty-blue chair.

Hesitantly she took the indicated bag and pulled apart the two ends. She looked inside, looked up at him and looked inside again. He burst out laughing. She peered at him again, peeked into the bag again, then burst out laughing, too.

"Well, you said you wanted something to sleep in other than my old shirt. I figured that meant you wanted something more feminine."

She blushed scarlet and felt hot enough to faint. "This isn't feminine. It's bordello."

"Oh." He shrugged, teasing her and enjoying it. "I wouldn't know the difference."

She gave him a shrewd look. "No, I don't suppose you would."

He laughed again. "Dig a little deeper in the bag," he suggested, pointing.

Without removing the black teddy from the bag, Linda did as she was told and gasped. "Oooooh."

"Yeah, I told the salesgirl you were the pink-lace-and-satin-slippers type. She insisted all women liked black lace and garters...."

"What garter?"

Her eyes got big and water blue, and for a second Michael felt he could drown in them. Instead he rose and ruffled her hair. "That was humor," he said, and walked away. "I'll finish the macaroni. You go unpack your bags." He walked away laughing and feeling better than he had in days.

The peace wouldn't last, couldn't last, not with four people living in a three-room cabin, but he decided to worry about tomorrow, tomorrow.

Chapter Six

She was being watched.

Somewhere out there in the dark night, somebody stood poised above her, probably on a hill, and they were looking at her through binoculars. She'd sensed it for so long that not only could she picture the scene, but her breathing had gone shallow, her back felt warm, and all of her joints had liquified.

"I'm gonna see your Tootsie Roll and raise a pack of Smarties."

Part of her wanted to turn around. Part of her could envision the scenario if she did. She'd turn. A bullet would fly through the cricket-filled night. The glass behind her would splinter into a million-piece spray. And she'd crumple to the floor as her card-playing companions dove under the table.

"It's a Tootsie Roll and a pack of Smarties to stay, Linda."

She wished they would have closed the drapes. Then there wouldn't be a black wall of night behind her. Maybe she should have asked to sit somewhere else.... No, then she'd be looking into a black wall of night. Then she'd be seeing eyeballs in the darkness. Every time a leaf rustled, she'd hyperventilate.

Michael Rosen snapped his fingers under her nose. "Earth to Linda. Earth to Linda. Come in, Linda."

She shook her head as if to clear the haze, but she couldn't. She was sinking into a fog of desperate fear, the kind of fear that brought each of your nerve endings to life until they crackled like electricity in water; the kind of fear that kept you up all night because you didn't dare close your eyes. And if she didn't soon do something, albeit only speak, she'd never come out. "I'm sorry," she said, glancing at her cards. Her hand was trembling. Her stomach was rolling. She knew that if she tried, she wouldn't be able to stand.

"One Tootsie Roll. One pack of Smarties. You in or out?"

She fingered her supply of penny candy. If she stayed in, she stayed in this chair. If she folded, she could calmly get up and go...where? To her room where she'd be all alone? Across the common area to the sitting spot, where she would imagine someone falling down the stone fireplace just like Santa, except this guy would have a machine gun? Did she want to stand in the kitchen where a long thin window ran the length of the countertop that housed the sink?

"One Tootsie Roll." Michael Rosen was clearly exasperated. "One pack of Smarties. In or out?"

"In," she decided, tossing the ante into the pot, but when she moved her arm, a shiver ran from one shoulder blade to the other, because moving made her conspicuous, obvious, a living, breathing target. She felt her hunter stalking her, planning his moves as he sat in the darkness behind her, watching her, rubbing his hands together in victorious anticipation. Sweat beaded on her forehead and her chest began to hurt. She could see him just as clearly as if she were standing right beside him.

"Two pair."

"Uh-uh-uh. Don't take the pot. I've got three aces."

Their voices sounded like the echoings from the bottom of a deep metal pot, or maybe words through a megaphone, and she knew she was losing the battle. The longer she sat with her back to the wall of windows, the more frightened she got. That fear induced premonitions, which grew more and more realistic, until her senses were so distorted she couldn't tell what was real, what was panic. She took three deep, measured breaths, still feeling the movement of someone creeping up behind her. Hearing his breathing. Sensing his arms as they circled her from behind and then seeing in her mind's eye as her black-gloved assailant flattened his hands on her face and smothered her.

"So, what d'ya got?"

She looked up. All three men were staring at her. She tried to talk but couldn't. Every breath she drew burned from her nose to her lungs, outlining passages, then expanding her ribs.

"Oh, for crying out loud," Michael said, grabbing her cards to see for himself, but her grip was so tight he couldn't pry them loose. Her fingers hurt, and the breaths that she took had a sound now.

"You okay?" Al rose.

"Linda?" Jonesy pushed his chair away from the table.

"Now what?" Michael growled.

Now what? she repeated in her head, feeling like an idiot. She was literally and figuratively frozen with fear. And though anxiety attacks from intuitive fear were normal for her, she hadn't had one in years. She couldn't remember how to deal with it, and she didn't want to explain it, because these men would simply think she was crazy.

By sheer dint of will, she rose and laid her cards facedown on the table. "I think I'm just going to go to bed."

"Get back here," Michael commanded. "Four-handed poker is bad enough, but three's a drag!"

"No," she said, just barely controlling her horrible trembling and knowing she'd brought on this attack herself. She was protected, isolated, just like when she hid under the expressway bridge, knowing her mother wouldn't look in the tall grass to find her. But hiding in the dark is sometimes worse than facing the enemy. Especially when you could hear the crickets, smell the river, know snakes were crawling all around you. "I'm tired."

"You slept until ten," Michael reminded. He rose and folded his arms across his chest. "It's only nine-thirty. So sit."

"No," she said, and started shaking uncontrollably. Snakes. Tall grass. The scent of humidity mingling with grass and foliage. The sound of crickets. The sight of darkness and the taste of fear. It had been twelve years since she sat under that expressway and waited. Cold and scared. Usually hungry. Praying her mother wouldn't find her...

Her mother. She never thought about her mother, and now she couldn't stop thinking about her mother. About being alone. About a husband who never understood and a dad who didn't want to...

And she couldn't stop shaking, while three different men—three strangers—stared at her because they didn't know why she was acting like a fool and she couldn't tell them. She wouldn't tell them! She'd never tell anybody again.

She turned and ran into her room, slamming the door behind her.

Stupefied, Michael stared at the door. Al lit a cigarette. Jonesy sat back in his chair.

"You sure got some way with women, Rosen."

Al spit a piece of tobacco off his tongue. "Yeah, you sure do."

"Just shut up, all right?"

"Sure," Al said. "Anything you want."

"That's right," Jonesy agreed sarcastically. "You're the boss. If you want to be nasty to a scared young woman, that's your prerogative."

"I wasn't being nasty," Michael grumbled, and flopped to his chair again.

"You weren't being nice," Al pointed out.

"I'm not supposed to be nice."

"Why not?" Jonesy asked, and gathered the cards from the table. Slowly, rhythmically, he shuffled them.

Why not? Michael asked himself, then couldn't believe he had. He wasn't supposed to be nice, he wasn't supposed to be soft...but he knew she was young and he knew she was scared; and because he could see a future she hadn't contemplated yet, he knew this wasn't the worst of it. And in a certain sense he felt responsible, because it was him, Michael Rosen, who wanted Santos at any cost. He'd just never thought the cost would be somebody else's life.

"It couldn't hurt to go in there and apologize," Jonesy pointed out casually.

"I think she just needs a shoulder to cry on," Al said, rising. "Why don't I go in there and talk to her?"

Instantly Michael was on his feet. The last thing Linda Miller needed right now was that blond charmer sitting on the edge of her bed. "I'll do it."

He tapped on her door, two light knocks. For a minute it appeared she wasn't going to answer. He almost wished she wouldn't.

"Yes? What is it?"

Her voice couldn't have been any softer. He only heard it because he was straining. He cleared his throat. "It's Michael. You okay in there?"

There was a long pause. Finally she said, "Yeah."

She was either crying or right on the verge of tears. The tight, constrained tone of her voice could mean nothing else. With any other witness he would just walk away, give her some space, some privacy. With this one he couldn't. Not just because she sounded as if she needed comfort, but because he was beginning to feel guilty. For the first time in ten years, he wondered if stopping Santos was worth the cost. Not because there was a price to be paid, but because of the person paying it. She was too young, too innocent, too pretty to ruin her life for a cause that wasn't even her own.

He pushed open the bedroom door. She was huddled under her covers even though it was sweltering hot. All five feet four inches of Linda Miller was rolled in a ball that shivered beneath a scratchy gray wool blanket. Guilt hit him again, this time in a crashing wave. He took two cautious steps into the room.

"You don't sound okay. You sound like you're just about to cry."

"Really?" she asked sarcastically. "I wonder why that is?"

He took another three steps, each one got a little bolder. He might not be at fault for the fact that she had witnessed a murder, that she was the one paying the price, but he was directly responsible for her being upset tonight. She was justifiably scared, and considering the person and the circumstances, he should be a little more sensitive. "I'm not exactly the nicest guy in the world and I know that."

Still burrowed in her covers, she sniffed. "That's an understatement."

"But I'm only trying to protect you." He was by the bed now and hooked one arm around the post as a drunk would a street lamp. "I know I get carried away, but you see I—"

"You're a bully," she interrupted. She rubbed her face in her pillow, and her breath came out as a shuddering sigh. "I witnessed a crime and now have three-quarters of the underworld looking for me. But there are times when I think I'd much rather take my chances with the underworld than spend the next six weeks with you. You're a chauvinistic, inconsiderate, self-righteous bully who doesn't think of anyone's feelings, anyone's comfort but his own. Now get out of here. I'm scared, I'm tired, I think I'm just going to close my eyes and pretend the rest of the world doesn't exist."

She could yell at him forever and it wouldn't affect him. He was trained to expect hysterics. But when her voice wavered, when she sounded young and scared, all his training went out the window and he got the strangest urge to take her away and hide her from everybody. From Santos, the press, the DA, the FBI, everybody. He had to swallow a lump in his throat before he could speak. "I wish you wouldn't do that."

"What? Be scared? I think you've gone out of your way to make sure I was."

"I didn't want you to be scared, I wanted you to realize the seriousness of your predicament."

"I did. Never for one minute have I forgotten that it took only thirty seconds for that man to kill Bob Bingham. Never for one minute have I forgotten the trouble I'm in," she said, then buried her face in her pillow, ignoring him.

He sat on the edge of the bed, put his elbows on his knees and his chin on his steepled fingers. "I really wish you wouldn't do that."

"And I really wish you'd get out of here."

"I'm not leaving until I'm sure you're okay."

"Don't pull that on me," she mumbled. "I'm too tired to lie here and listen while you pretend you care about me. You don't. You've yelled at me, argued with me and tossed me around like a sack of potatoes, and now you're feeling guilty. Well, I'm not going to kiss and make up. You deserve to feel good and guilty. Now, get lost."

"You know, you're not exactly blameless here. I'm supposed to be protecting you, yet you never listened to a word I said. You're lucky to be alive. Every time I gave an order, you questioned it. Every time I made a plan, you mocked it. You've got the sharpest tongue of any woman I've ever met."

"Well, you and my ex-husband should start a club then, because you're the only two people in the world who feel that way. But don't despair, there's a good reason. You see, Mr. Rosen, the only people who ever hear my sharp tongue are those who push me into a corner. The rest of the world—the people who treat other people decently—know me as rather soft-spoken. My ex-husband—"

"What was his name?" Michael interrupted because she was back in character, feisty and defensive again, and he realized this argument was actually calming her down. Which meant something else had upset her. Not him. Not cards. Maybe not even the mob. In fact, he had the damnedest, strangest, oddest feeling that somehow or another her ex-husband, or maybe thinking about her ex-husband, fit in.

"What difference does it make?"

"Well, none really. But if I'm going to form a club with him I'll have to call him and if I want to call him, I'll need to know his name."

She twisted in bed, dragging the covers with her, and gave him the most puzzled expression Michael had ever seen. "What are you talking about?"

"The club...the one your ex and I are going to start. The Linda Miller Sharp, Sarcastic Tongue Club."

With her hands braced beside her hips, Linda pushed herself up until she was sitting. The covers fell and Michael noticed she was wearing the teddy. The black lacy teddy. The garment chosen as a joke, not real nightwear. And she knew that, so why the devil was she wearing it?

"His name is David Anderson and he's right in the Harrisburg phone book. You can't miss him. So why don't you just jump in your Jeep and go find a pay phone and give him a call."

"Can't," Michael said, trying desperately to keep his eyes fixed on her face, but he knew there was a milk-white shoulder exposed, and he knew that if he looked farther down he'd see the satiny smooth swell of her breast beneath black lace. He thanked the heavens he hadn't let Al come in, then wondered if he was actually any better. "We're not supposed to make contact with anybody, remember?"

"And here I thought you just didn't want to run up a big phone bill."

Struggling with a grin, Michael shook his head. "You just can't quit, can you?"

"Didn't you ever hear anybody say they had to laugh because as soon as they stopped laughing, they'd cry?"

"No, but I guess it makes sense. Especially now. Linda, I am sorry," he apologized sincerely, because this was the opening he'd been waiting for. "But you have to understand that I am only doing my job."

"I do understand that you have a job to do. And heaven knows I understand the significance of that job. But half the time I feel like we're fighting one another. I thought we were supposed to be a team."

"We're not supposed to fight, but we're not really a team, either. We're something in between."

"I don't see why," she challenged, getting indignant. "Darn it! Stop and think about this a minute. I'm your witness! I'm doing you a big favor! Yes, I understand how much I need you. But I think our problems stem from the fact that you haven't yet realized how much you need me."

He didn't say anything. For a long time he just stared at the braided rug beneath his feet, wondering if he dared to say what popped into his mind and yet realizing if he didn't, if they didn't talk about this, there wouldn't be peace between them. Finally he asked, "Is that the connection?"

"Connection for what?"

"Well, right off the bat you associated me with your ex-husband. Now I understand why. I must remind you of him—maybe not in looks, but actions. You think I'm using you and you must have thought he used you, took from you and didn't appreciate you. And so you're upset tonight because you're thinking about him and remembering how he used you."

"No, not really." She sighed and fell to her pillow again. "I had a very simple marriage, only the divorce was complicated. My ex-husband never used me. He never needed me."

Michael winced and glanced away. He'd been right, he just phrased it wrong but he wasn't going to argue the point. "How long have you been divorced?"

She sort of laughed. "How long have we been together?"

He peered at her. "A little over a week..." Then he groaned. "Don't tell me..."

"You guessed it. My divorce became final, I went out and celebrated with my friends and got stopped by the police officers Bill and George, who forced me to find someone to take me home. So I went to the office to call somebody, but Mr. Bingham was already there. As they say, the rest is history."

They were quiet for another couple of minutes while Michael squirmed inwardly, thinking about the past ten days. She got divorced, she witnessed a murder, and she was running for her life. It was no wonder she lashed out at him. He was the only constant in her life. And he was a bossy, insensitive lout. A man who often called her "the project," as if she didn't have a name.

He sighed heavily, then slid to the top of the bed so he could lean against the headboard. After he was comfortable, he reached down and gathered Linda up in his arms, resting her head on his shoulder. "We're not really a team. I'm not trained to use you as part of the team. I'm trained to see you as the project. Do you understand?"

"Sort of."

"I guess what I'm trying to say is that I'm sorry if you misunderstood, but I didn't deliberately treat you cruelly, I suppose I was treating you impersonally. Does that make sense?"

"Yeah."

"And since we are going to be together for a while, I'll lighten up."

She swallowed and he could feel the way her entire body responded to the simple movement. It didn't surprise him that she'd so casually accepted his embrace, because he realized how badly in need of comfort she was to snuggle in the arms of a bully.

"I'd appreciate it."

"So tell me, how does one have a simple marriage and a complicated divorce?"

"It's not something you plan, I'll tell you that."

"Feel like talking?"

She waited a minute before she answered, "Do you feel like listening?"

"What else do we have to do out here?" he mocked one of her prior tirades and she laughed. She was soft and warm and so small he could feel her breathing. "Tell me about your simple marriage first. We'll hit the complicated divorce some night when we're really bored."

She laughed again, then sighed and nestled more snugly against him, and Michael had to stifle the urge to kiss her hair. Never had he felt someone's personality, but with Linda it was easy. She was small and soft and innocent. Totally vulnerable. Just like a child. It was amazing.

"The simple marriage was actually a miracle."

"Oh," he said, resting his chin on the crown of her head. All he had to do was listen, nod and occasionally agree verbally while he enjoyed the scent of her hair, the smoothness of her skin. It really wasn't such a bad proposition.

"My father ran off. I can't really say that I blame him. My mother drank day and night. I don't remember her sober."

"So you married your husband to get away from your mother."

"Sort of," she agreed. "David and I grew up together. When we were kids our parents lived side by side. Then right when I got to high school, my dad got a promotion and we moved away. David and I never saw each other again until right after my dad left. It was funny," she said, and squirmed to get more comfortable. "I graduated from high school and the next day my dad left. My mother wasn't sober enough to realize either had happened. So, I packed a bag—and I do mean a brown paper bag—and left."

"And you ran into your husband and he married you to get you off the streets."

"No, I ran into my husband and he gave me a place to stay for a few days. He'd always fought with his dad, so when he graduated from high school, he left home, too. He was still on good terms with his family, he just couldn't live with them. Anyway, his place was a mess. And it ended up that instead of finding a job, I just kept his house clean and did his laundry. It was funny, we sort of got married right then and there."

"The arrangement worked out, so one day you made it legal."

"Well, not exactly."

"For a simple marriage, this is getting complicated."

She laughed against his chest. "We lived together two years, just like a brother and sister. Then one night, there was a storm, a violent thing that scared me so badly I could hardly breathe. So I crawled into bed with David." She stopped and sighed. "I shouldn't tell you this, but I seduced him. He was asleep and I was curious."

"I get the picture," Michael laughed. "So then you made it legal."

"Yes, and it was wonderful. Five years," she said. "Five years of living together and working together, and it all fell apart the first time we came to a controversy, because there was no love to bind us together. But we're saving the divorce for another night."

"No, no, tonight's fine," he insisted, finding that he really was interested. Or maybe confused. It sure sounded to him as though they loved each other. Heaven knows if he was married to a sweet little thing like Linda Miller, he wouldn't let her go. And he wanted to know how or why somebody could and did. "You can't start an intriguing topic like that and then just drop it."

"Well, I guess the best way to explain is to say that all the years we were married, I considered myself the luckiest woman in the world. David had a wonderful job in construction and made great money. We didn't want kids yet, both of us knew we had to grow up first ourselves. So we thought it would be good for me to get a job and I started working. I job-hopped for a while, but David didn't care. We agreed about everything. Talked about everything. Didn't make any emotional, irrational decisions, because our relationship was based on need. It was very generic. And I used to think that love was a highly overrated commodity. David and I did not love each other—not romantically. We were not passionately, desperately in love. We were committed to each other because of need."

"It makes sense to me," Michael interjected, agreeing wholeheartedly.

"It does," Linda said, leaning so she could look up at him. "Many times I thought about writing a book about marriage. I had a perfect one. Because our goals were so focused, and our roles so well-defined, we were the happiest two people in the world. And then I got pregnant and everything fell apart."

Michael stiffened. "Nobody told me you had a child."

"I don't. I had a miscarriage."

He visibly relaxed. "Sorry, but a child is the best way to get to a witness. If you had one, or a niece or a nephew, or favorite neighbor even, they'd find that kid and that'd be the end of you."

"Well, I'm childless," Linda said, then nestled into his side again. "Kids weren't even allowed in my apartment building."

He'd upset her. Just the tone of her voice was enough for him to see he'd upset her. "Finish your story," Michael prodded softly.

For a long time she said nothing. Finally she sighed. "I wasn't sure I was ready for a child yet. David didn't want the baby at all. To him it was a simple matter of an abortion. I couldn't do it."

A sudden gust of wind rattled the cabin, then rain pattered against the window. Michael rubbed his hands up and down her arms. "Good for you."

"David took it very hard. I think he was scared. He's only twenty-seven, you know? I don't think he wanted the responsibility. Anyway, the senator talked me into leaving him. Just temporarily, he'd said. He got me an apartment, and it was such a relief to be away from David that I knew I'd never go back. My marriage was over."

"It must have been a terrible blow."

"It was and it wasn't," Linda responded. "I was rid of David's constant nagging, and the senator was with me every step of the way. He'd even found a couple to adopt the baby. I wasn't even showing yet, and already he'd found parents and a home for the baby. Because at that point, as a single parent, making a secretary's salary, I knew I couldn't keep the baby. I filed for divorce, custody wasn't even discussed. David was ignoring 'the pregnancy,' as he'd called it. And at that point I really didn't give a darn, because I knew what I was going to do." Her voice had risen with conviction so that when she paused, the room seemed eerily quiet. The only sound in the world was the light patter of rain against the glass.

When she spoke, it was slowly, hesitantly and very, very softly. "And then I miscarried and my whole world came crashing down."

"I'm sorry," he whispered, feeling her grief as a living, breathing thing in the room. There was guilt, too, but she wouldn't talk about that with him. Not yet. He stroked her hair. "I'm really sorry."

"I never felt so alone in my life...."

She looked up just as he looked down, and it was at that point that she stopped talking. They'd shifted and squirmed enough that their faces were only an inch apart. If he took a deep breath, he knew he'd smell the salt from the tears she'd just shed for the loss of her child, and if he only lifted his hand, he could trace the shiny tracks of wetness on her peachy skin. She didn't look young anymore. She looked timeless and ageless and wise beyond her years—wise beyond anything he'd ever achieve. She was mature, intelligent and beautiful. Soft and warm. Satiny smooth. With the bluest eyes in the whole world.

Still it wasn't physical temptation that lured him to bridge the gap and brush his lips over hers. She was soft and now he knew she was sweet, but more than that, they'd developed a bond of trust he didn't quite understand. It was a force that urged you to touch, implored that you taste, not for physical pleasure but for emotional completion. And he did so lightly, carefully. All this was very new to him. But it was also very nice.

He pressed his lips to hers again. This time the lids closed over her big blue eyes, and when they did, he had to fight to keep his own eyelids from following suit. The palms of his hands were itching to slide along her smooth,

smooth skin, and his legs wanted to scissor her close to him, but the consequences, he knew, would be disastrous.

He pulled away.

"Think you can sleep now?" he asked quietly, deliberately lifting her away from him and putting her onto the pillow where she belonged. He couldn't believe what had just happened. He'd just kissed a woman ten years his junior. A woman he was assigned to protect. A woman who thought he was a bully. A woman who had enough problems without having to worry about whether or not he'd kiss her again.

She stared at him. Her eyes were bright and confused. He wanted to kick himself.

"Yeah," she said, then cleared her throat.

He rubbed his hand along the back of his neck. "I'm sorry for that. I was trying to comfort you . . . no, that's bad. I sound like . . . well . . . never mind. It won't happen again." He walked to the door and then turned to face her again. "Good night, Linda."

She studied him for a minute, her wise eyes assessing him. She was uncanny. He'd never met anybody like her before. Cautious, deliberate, coolly intelligent. And yet naive enough that she didn't realize all that registered in her eyes. Including the fact that she forgave him and wouldn't hold a grudge.

"Good night . . . uh . . . uh . . ."

He smiled at her. "Michael. If nothing else, let's get on a first-name basis. Maybe that will ease the tension between us?"

She returned his smile. "It's worth a try. Good night, Michael."

BY THE STREAM it was hot and quiet. She sensed he was lost in private thoughts and said nothing, leaning back in the grass and closing her eyes. Michael had told her she was supposed to watch her fishing pole, but the longer she watched, the more her eyelids drooped, and she noticed his eyes were closing, too.

"I figured out last night that you sort of remind me of one of my sisters."

"Oh?" she said, breathing in the beautiful scent of nature. "Is that good or bad?"

"Well, let me put it to you this way, if you reminded me of my sister Helen, then we'd get along beautifully."

"Oh-oh."

She heard him draw in a deep breath. "Yeah. I think you're getting the picture."

"So, what's the sister like? The one I remind you of?"

He was slow to answer, and when he did, she could tell he chose his words carefully. But he didn't need to. She understood better than he realized. David never liked having feelings either. It was almost as if he felt having feelings made him weak, so he'd go out of his way to have a logical explanation for everything he did. In the same way, Michael Rosen was about to explain why he bullied her, then comforted her, then kissed her... and at one fell swoop. This would probably be good.

"She's very pretty. Very smart." He shrugged. "And she's about your age."

"Uh-huh," Linda said. It made sense to her. And it was easier for her, too. After all, she was the one scared to the point of acting like a fool. He was just the comforter. "So tell me more about your sisters. How many do you have?"

"Seven."

"Seven?" For that she sat up and gaped at him. "How many brothers?"

He grinned at her. "None."

"Oh, Lord, your house must have been crazy. Your mother should have drunk!"

"Nah! My parents handled it very well. I wouldn't have wanted the responsibility they had, but they took it on the chin. There were lots of things they gave up while we were growing up and lots of mistakes they made along the way, because raising eight kids isn't easy. But they kept their sense of humor. And basically, I think that's the bottom line."

"I guess so." She yanked on her line. He tapped her hand and frowned at her. "With eight kids your only recourse would be a sense of humor."

"It goes beyond what you're thinking," he said, then he chuckled. "Never mind. I won't bore you with family theories."

"No, no, tell me," she insisted. "I'd love to know."

He waved a hand as if to chase away the subject. "Nah."

"Oh, please. I have no idea of what normal is for a family and I'd love to know."

"That's what I'm talking about." He sat forward and grabbed his fishing rod even though he didn't move it, and Linda realized he was uncomfortable discussing his thoughts. Yet he kept going, sharing his secrets today instead of just listening to hers. It was nice. Odd, but nice. Maybe she really did remind him of his sister?

"The way I have this figured out, there is no perfect answer. Parenting is a matter of giving it your best shot and hoping for the best and then not dwelling on your mistakes."

"Is that all?" she giggled. "Here I thought you were going to tell me something neat about families and real parents and what it's like to have brothers and sisters, and all you tell me is the philosophy for living that's in just about any self-help book."

"It is?"

"Yes, it is."

"Oh." He seemed disappointed or disillusioned and said nothing more, merely lay on his side and studied the rippling water. He was quiet so long she thought their secret-sharing time was over, then he turned to her again. "You mean, everybody knows that?"

"Knows what? About giving life your best shot?"

"Yeah."

"I'm afraid so. Giving life your best shot, hoping for the best, and not dwelling on your mistakes is the same philosophy I've read in about six different books, said by six different authors. But your version's a little less wordy."

He chuckled, shaking his head. "How the mighty do fall. I thought I made that up myself."

"'Fraid not. About half the population of the English-speaking world knows that. Or has at least read it in one form or another."

"So, why don't people do that then? I mean, life could be so simple for everybody if people would just practice what they read."

"I don't know about everybody, but my mother could have certainly profited from that advice."

A silent minute passed, then two. Michael closed his eyes and Linda watched him almost fall asleep, lulled by the warmth of the morning sun. He wore his typical cotton shirt tucked into blue jeans, and she stared at his chest as his breathing raised and lowered it. He was such a normal, lucky person. And she'd bet he didn't even realize it.

"My mother couldn't admit she made mistakes," Linda announced softly. It startled her to hear she was talking out loud. It must have surprised Michael, too, because he opened his eyes and pushed himself up on his elbows, giving her his full attention.

"She didn't become an alcoholic overnight. Nobody does." She stopped and pulled a blade of grass from the dirt, not quite sure of how to explain or why she felt the need to. "Looking back, I realized that she and dad must have come from two different worlds." Staring at the grass she pulled between her fingers, Linda paused and smiled. "I saw her as beautiful and talented and sweet and wonderful...how all kids see their mother. And Dad was handsome and funny and just great to have around."

"So what happened?" Michael asked quietly.

"Nothing really," Linda answered in a soft but curious voice. "Everyday life seemed to chip away at my mother. For years and years I wondered how somebody who had it all could throw it away, then I realized she didn't think she had it all."

"Didn't know how good she had it, huh?"

"No, it was more like she was trying to impress everybody. It was more like...oh, I don't know...everybody had to agree with everything she said. Everybody had to love her dress, had to coo over her hair, had to...well, I think she wanted people to want what she had...I think she wanted people to envy her."

"And did they?"

Linda looked over at him. He was hanging on her every word, more than curious, more than concerned, more interested than anybody had ever been before. "Yeah. Lots of people did. But if even one person so much as looked at her crosswise, she went bananas."

"Paranoid?"

"No. She wanted to be perfect. I think she was dead for two years before I realized I didn't hate her, I felt sorry for her. She never understood that the only person you can please is yourself. She tried to please everybody but herself and ended up nuts...drunk...dead."

Overhead a bird squawked then swooped toward its prey. Michael sighed. "She beat you, didn't she?"

Linda looked down at the grass by her thigh. She smoothed her hands across the soft green tips. She wouldn't look at him.

"That's why you're afraid of the dark...why you got so scared last night. You were remembering, weren't you?"

She licked her lips. After David's reaction, she swore she'd never tell another soul...not another soul. Never. Not anybody.

"Weren't you?" he asked again, but softly, gently, in the tone of voice she had longed to hear from her father.

She took a deep breath. Another thirty seconds passed in silence. "I hid from her in tall grass, under an expressway. That's what I was remembering last night—being alone and scared. More afraid that she'd find me than afraid of the snakes..."

"She was a fool."

Swallowing, Linda glanced at him. "She was sick."

"You're kinder, more forgiving, than I'd be," he said, sounding angry and frustrated yet somehow comforting.

She smiled, then bit her lower lip. If she told him how much that one sentence meant to her, he'd probably brush it aside and ruin everything. She took a deep breath and faced him. "Just about anybody's kinder than you are," she said, then threw some grass at him. "You're a bully, remember?"

One side of his mouth lifted reflexively, then he began to laugh in earnest. "Yeah. I am, huh?"

They fished until it got too hot to stay in the sun, then Michael picked up the poles and began walking back to the cabin with Linda close at his heels. He didn't feel sorry for her, because she didn't feel sorry for herself. And he wasn't angry anymore, because she wasn't angry. And it took him an hour before he realized she'd manipulated him into laughing even as she changed the subject. She had the strangest darned effect on him.

"I suppose Al and Jonesy will be expecting fish for lunch."

Michael chuckled. "No. We've stayed here together before. Al and Jonesy are smart enough to make lunch." He looped his arm around her shoulders. Dressed as she was, looking scrub faced and natural, she could have been anywhere from fifteen to thirty. She was one of those timeless classic beauties who'd look every bit as good as she did now for the rest of her life. "How old are you?"

"Twenty-six, why?"

"Oh, I don't know. Just curious, I guess." They lapsed into one of those comfortable silences, which quickly became uncomfortable for Michael, if only because he was so comfortable with her. Getting friendly with a witness was generally unavoidable, but he honestly liked this one. And he'd never wanted to place a witness in a down-filled bed and make love to her until neither of them could move. He supposed that was the confusing part.

She ran ahead and jogged up the porch steps, but waited for him before opening the door.

"You're learning," he commented quietly. That made him even more uncomfortable, because maybe she wasn't learning to listen to him, but rather trying to please him. He carried their fishing poles to the hooks that were screwed into the log wall of the porch.

She took a deep breath. "Trying to be cooperative," she said, leaning against the wall by the door, waiting until he opened the door and motioned her inside. "Believe it or not," she said, stepping into the cabin. "This is closer to my normal personality. Generally, I'm cooperative, helpful and very cheerful. Hi, guys."

"Hi, guys," Michael echoed, and both walked through the front room to the kitchen. As they washed their hands, Linda glanced at the stove.

"Hey, you two, where's lunch?"

No answer.

"You've lived with me before," Michael chuckled. "You know better than to depend on me to bring back fish."

"Yeah," Linda agreed, then she giggled. "You should see him fish." She dried her hands and began walking toward the card table. "Do you know he can't even...oh, Lord!"

Al and Jonesy were seated at the card table, as though they were contemplating their next move, but a long thin red line ran across the neck of each one of them. A slow trickle of blood rolled down the crevice above Al's collarbone, and when she lowered her eyes to follow it, she saw his shirt was blood soaked. She grabbed the back of a chair and took a deep breath.

"Michael," she whispered. "Michael!" This time she screamed.

"Oh, no!" He grabbed her arm and began to run. "Where's my jacket? Damn! Damn!" With one hand securing Linda, he snagged his jacket from a peg by the door and then kicked it open. Now, he took a deep breath. "Stay," he commanded, looking into Linda's eyes. She nodded.

He poked his head out and scanned the forest. Nothing. Birds were singing and a breeze rippled through the trees. He pushed his hair out of his eyes and reached inside the doorway for Linda's hand.

"Michael."

"Shh-shhh."

"M-M-Michael, I think somebody's pointing a gun out the bathroom door."

The second he heard the word *gun*, he dove out of the cabin and yanked Linda with him. The pair flew over the porch and rolled down the steps. "Keep rolling," Michael yelled as he pushed himself up so he could look around. "If you can, get into the Jeep."

Puzzuit. Again the bullets disassociated themselves from the boom of their discharge. Every explosion of the rifle was heard but forgotten because the quiet sound of the bullet was more important.

Puzzuit . . . ping.

"Great! And I thought this was going to be easy," he muttered, shoving Linda under the Jeep. He scooted in after her and ran his hand through his hair. "Okay, here's the scoop. We've got to try to figure out how to start this thing." He looked up. All he saw was dusty metal.

"Where are your keys?" she asked breathlessly.

"In my jacket pocket, but we can't very well use them now, can we...."

Ping . . . ping . . . ping.

"Darn, this thing is tinny."

Somehow or another his jacket had ended up in front of the Jeep and she reached for it. Hooking a piece of the sleeve, she dragged it into their haven. While he inspected the underside of the Jeep, hoping for a clue of how to hot-wire it, she found the keys, rolled out from under the Jeep, rose to her knees, then fell in beside him again.

"What the devil are you doing?"

"We're going to start the Jeep," she said after taking a deep breath. "I saw this in a movie once. The bullets are only hitting from your side of the Jeep, so everybody with a gun must be in the house. That means I can use the Jeep for cover. I've already shoved the keys into the ignition without getting shot. So, now, I'll say one-two-three-go and you dive to push the gas pedal to the floor with your hand while I turn the key. Ready..."

He grabbed her arm. "You're crazy."

A bullet landed close enough to spray dust over his face.

She smiled triumphantly. "Your friends in the Santos organization may prefer knives to guns, but it looks like somebody's getting to be a pretty good shot."

He spit the sandy grime out of his mouth. "The answer's still no. The odds that we'll start the Jeep that way are pretty good, but the odds that we'll get shot are even better. If you think we can pull this off without getting a bullet in the back, you're crazy."

Three bullets hit the ground right beside him and raised enough dirt that he coughed.

"Then again, maybe not." He scrubbed his hand over his mouth. "Okay, we'll try this. Only, I say one-two-three-go. Got it?"

"Yeah, got it!" she mumbled, rolling her eyes.

Michael said the words and then he rolled, and she followed. Her head popped up. He dove for the gas pedal. She leaped for the key. In thirty seconds the vehicle purred to life. She crawled to the floor on the passenger side. He jumped in, jammed the pedal to the floor and sent them careening into the woods.

With the wind in his hair and laughing like a fool, he turned to her and shouted, "You know, I think you're finally catching on."

"Yeah," she yelled back, then fainted dead away.

MICHAEL CAME OUT of the bathroom, drying his face with the standard white terry-cloth towel found in all hotel bathrooms. He had another standard-issue towel around his waist. Linda was on her belly, sprawled sideways across the bed, her feet hooked over one side, her arms dangling from the other, staring at the worn indoor-outdoor carpeting.

"Next," he said, and tossed his wet towel onto her head.

She wasn't in the mood for smart remarks or fooling around or even talking. Without a sound, she took the towel off her head and let it fall to the floor in front of her.

The strip of white terry cloth bunched by his bare feet—his long, slender feet, which were connected to solid, sturdy, dependable ankles. Her gaze crawled up his big legs, past the towel that had him decently covered and traveled up his ultrahairy chest. He was one of those men who hadn't lost an ounce of their traditional masculinity to colognes, health clubs or fashion. Without his clothes, that was even more obvious than it was when he was fully dressed in one of his conservative plaid shirts and jeans. She wasn't in the mood for this, either.

She scooted off the bed and ducked into the bathroom, closing the door behind her. Coming across the country, they'd shared hotel rooms for at least a week. They'd snipped, bickered and irritated each other because they hated each other. This afternoon, retracing some of that same trip, they'd snipped, bickered and irritated each other because they were both upset about the deaths of their friends and they were unable to confide their feelings, share their feelings or even have feelings. Because that wasn't a part of the program.

He was hard-nosed again, a man with no feelings, no emotions. Even as she fell into a deep pit of depression, he went about business as usual and she wanted to smack him. But when she looked at him, she remembered what it was like to have him kiss her. How his lips felt brushing against hers. And she understood, forgave him, maybe even appreciated his objectivity in the face of her emotional weakness. That one little kiss linked them or perhaps changed her perspective, and she saw him as a male, a mate, a warrior in a savage land, not an insensitive grouch, and, heaven help her, she felt those old stirrings of femininity again. She wanted to smell flowery. She wanted to be small and soft and pretty for him. And she wanted to touch him. See what his chest hair felt like, if his arms were as solid as they looked. It was a magnetism, an instinct, a strong desire to touch and be touched. To be half of a whole.

She stepped into the shower and turned on the tap, reminding herself that she was lonely and desperate for comfort. Right now any friendly face would look good to her, but being consoled wouldn't bring back the men who had died. It wouldn't get her off the hook as far as testifying. And it would, without question, get out of hand and end up complicating things.

She scrubbed viciously, ridding herself of the dirt from their long journey, but was more concerned about the natural scents of pine and wildflowers, wind and water that lingered in her hair from their recent interlude by the stream. They had been so friendly out by that stream, and he had made her feel good, just like his buddy, but tonight she didn't want to be anybody's buddy. She wanted to sleep curled into some big strong guy who'd promise to protect her. And Michael Rosen was a big strong guy assigned to protect her. It was a dangerous situation all the way around, except he saw her as a sister, a little kid, a buddy.

She threw the plastic shampoo bottle at the wall, then held her head under the shower spray. *Control yourself. Control yourself,* she chanted as warm, soothing water cascaded all around her. *You're letting this make you* crazy. And you're stronger than this. You're smarter than this. Nobody, nothing, ever broke you before.

When she came out of the bathroom, she felt better. Michael, wet hair combed straight back to keep it out of his eyes, stood watching the television with the remote control box in his hand.

"Do you have a preference?" he asked, nodding toward the television as she stepped into the bedroom.

"Yeah," she decided, undesirably conscious of her braless state, uncontrollably conscious of his shirtlessness, and understandably tired of this whole mess. "I just want to curl up in bed."

She watched his eyes as they caught the fact that she was braless, then watched him school his features to control any reaction he might have had. She watched him shrug those beautiful bare shoulders. "Sounds fine."

She didn't breathe a sigh of relief, though she desperately wanted to. Instead, she licked her lips and said, "Good."

She crawled into bed. He took the extra blanket from the closet. She snuggled into her pillow. He settled down on the floor. She turned out the light but didn't close her eyes, even though she could see nothing in the darkness.

"Michael?" she called softly, after ten minutes of staring at nothing and realizing that was the rest of her life. "It's not going to end, is it?"

From his thirty-second silence, she knew he debated lying. "Everybody around you is in danger."

"Aren't you scared?"

"Not really."

She sat up, peering into the blackness. "Oh, come on," she chided. "After that episode today, you've got to be at least a little scared."

"They're not going to beat us," Michael said, and Linda could make out his form as he sat up on the floor. "They can't beat us. I won't let them beat us."

"Cute."

"No, just keeping a good mental attitude," Michael said, then sighed. "Linda, if I learned nothing else in the service, I learned that it doesn't do you any good to worry about possible problems, because they might not happen and you'll have scared yourself silly for nothing. But it does you a heck of a lot of good to see yourself achieving your goals."

"Positive imaging."

"What?"

"Positive imaging. It's another self-help theory. There's a book out about that, too."

"Oh, then, never mind."

"No. No," she said, leaning forward. His voice was a comfort in the darkness, the second best thing to curling up in his arms, and far less dangerous. "I'd like to hear your theories."

"Well," he said hesitantly, "I see us succeeding. I see us getting to that courtroom. I see you on the witness stand. I see the jury bringing back a guilty verdict."

"And because you see it, it'll happen?"

"No, because I see it, I won't waste time and energy worrying, and because I see it, I get a kind of power, maybe strength, sometimes ingenuity to make it happen. I don't know." She saw him shrug and lie down again. "Go to sleep."

She sighed. "It's hard to sleep in jeans."

"Take them off. Sleep in your shirt."

For a minute she stared at the ceiling, seeing it as only a square of blackness, a very small block, like a cell in a prison. "We start this again, don't we?"

"Start what?"

"All this—wearing the same clothes every day because we don't have any others, watching money because we don't know when we'll get any more, washing in gas station rest rooms and sleeping in the car when you don't want to risk stopping for the night."

"I'm sorry about that, but keep the positive picture in mind." He sat up again. "In fact, you imagine yourself testifying in some really snazzy outfit and I'll buy it for you when we get back home."

She laughed. "Snazzy? Snazzy makes me think of the Roaring Twenties . . . big feathers, rhinestones . . . satin."

"Think more practically. Rip off the rhinestones and get rid of the satin."

She laughed again. "What about the feather?"

"Toss that, too."

"Okay," she said, "but then all I'll have left is a black lace teddy." The second the words were out of her mouth she regretted them.

She had a black lace teddy, and though he'd bought it for her as a joke, it wasn't funny tonight, because she'd worn that garment on a night she needed comfort. On a night he'd given comfort. On a night he'd kissed her . . .

And it was almost as if she were daring him to remember. . . .

Her face flushed, and she was thankful it was dark and that he was far enough away that he wouldn't feel the heat from her embarrassment. She felt silly and awkward, like a teenager who'd thrown herself at a college boy. And heaven only knows what he was thinking.

There was a long silence.

Finally he said, "Think a little more practically than that. You never know who's going to be on a jury. We don't want to take any chances."

She sighed with relief, and they settled down again. But Linda didn't take off her jeans. She kept them on because she didn't want to make the sounds that would let him know she'd be just about naked under the covers. She wouldn't do anything that would look, sound or seem like an invitation. She wasn't going to embarrass herself again. But even more dangerous than embarrassing herself, in her frame of mind, if he heard the swishing of her removing her jeans and he sat up, maybe scooted closer to the bed, merely touched the corner of her cover...

Just thinking about him wanting her made her swallow, and she squeezed her eyes shut. She was wandering into dangerous territory, and it was the stupidest form of self-punishment she'd ever indulged. Not only was making love with him improbable, impractical and just plain idiotic, but it was a delusion of grandeur. A pointless meandering. It was, as he'd said, worrying about a problem that wasn't going to materialize. He didn't like her. He thought of her as worse than a kid.... He thought of her as a kid sister....

"Linda?"

"Yeah?"

"We could go back to the cabin."

"Oh?"

"You know," he said casually. "Get your clothes...and stuff. In fact, I can even call the home office tomorrow morning and tell them to have the cleanup crew bring the purse you left at Bingham's office. We do have to wait a day or two, but once the cleanup crew gets finished, there's no reason we can't go back. And then you'd have your wallet, and your makeup and...something to sleep in."

Her heart stopped. It could be that he was thinking of her comfort, being sensitive to her needs, that he'd learned his lesson from their trip cross-country. In all probability, when he said she'd get something to sleep in, he was talking about the pink nightgown, but she saw herself dressed in the teddy. The black lace teddy with the red ribbon and the curly, ruffled garter belt.

He saw her dressed in the teddy, too, but when he envisioned the garter belt he saw long, thin legs and curvy calves, trim ankles and her tiny feet in those darned spike heels of hers.

She saw him slide a strap from her shoulder.

He saw himself sliding a strap from her shoulder.

She saw his fingers gliding along her skin and she swallowed. "Do you think that's a good idea?"

He didn't miss a beat. He was lost somewhere between fantasy and reality, and part of him didn't even realize he was talking aloud. "Yeah."

She heard the smile in his voice, and she pulled the covers up to her chin. It was one thing to be uncontrollably attracted to him, it was quite another to know the feeling was mutual.

Chapter Seven

Waves of heat emanated from the sizzling pavement. Linda could swear she actually saw them. She leaned back, resting her head on the hot vinyl seat of the most recent rental car. This one smelled like cigarettes and didn't have air conditioning, both of which contributed heavily to her desire to throw up.

"How much farther until we stop?" she asked with a sigh. She now knew the real meaning of running for her life. They were always on the road because to put down roots was to become a target. So they kept going, kept moving, and she kept popping pills, but her system seemed to have grown immune to them, and even though they made her sleepy, they didn't quite put her to sleep. Worse, they had little to no effect on her nausea.

He tapped the gas gauge. Immediately the needle fell to the half-tank marker. "Oh, I'd say another fifty miles."

She flopped back to her seat again. "Great."

"Hey, it's the best I can do. People who are running from hired killers have to accept certain inconveniences."

She sighed heavily and leaned her head against the frame of the open window. Every time she breathed, it was like taking a hot brick into her stomach, and if she didn't stop thinking about it she would definitely become ill.

"You know," Michael said, biting the side of his mouth the way he did whenever he was thinking. "I'm really not supposed to talk about the case with you, but I can't help it. I have to know."

"Have to know what?" she asked, grateful for the diversion, particularly since he'd hardly spoken two words since they'd left the hotel in Colorado.

"What the devil was the beloved Mr. Bingham doing mixed up with a man like Santos?"

Linda shrugged. "Beats me."

"Oh, come on," Michael jeered. "Off the record, I swear. I have to know or I'll die of curiosity."

Resting her elbow on the back of the seat and her head on her closed fist, Linda faced him. "I really don't know."

"How could you not know? You were his secretary."

"I'd never seen John Santos or any of his men before. Whatever the senator was doing with or for Mr. Santos, it was personal."

"I'll buy that," Michael said, then bit the inside of his mouth again. His mind was working, she could see it in his eyes, and for the first time she wondered why he'd chosen this risky life when he could have been so many other things. He was intelligent, strong and persuasive...and he had a moneyed background. He never came right out and said it, but he didn't have to. There were clues all over the place. He owned the cabin they'd stayed in. Now his father's business was bankrolling most of their journey. It was set up so credit card receipts disappeared and rental cars were arranged, but nonetheless, the average American father and son couldn't have pulled this off. And Linda couldn't help but wonder why this particular team wanted to.

"Why do you do this?" she asked, even before she realized she was doing it.

"I make it a point not to talk about my personal life," he instantly replied, the same way he did every time she asked him anything.

Linda swallowed and looked away again. There were no more private conversations, no friendly gestures, no talk of teddies. There was only the whine of tires, perpetual motion and heat. Heavy heat that made her dizzy and weak.

She glanced out the window at the nameless trees, the heat-scorched grass, the summer sky.

"He was definitely into something illegal, and for Santos to have killed him he must have backed out of a deal or promised something he couldn't deliver. I'll bet that's it. I'll bet Santos did him a favor, maybe even when they were kids." He paused, pursed his lips and narrowed his eyes as he thought. "I know," he announced authoritatively. "Santos got Bingham elected."

Linda gasped, straightened up from her slouched position and spun to face him, one knee landing on her seat. "No way! The senator was a very popular man. He didn't need—"

"Nobody starts out popular. The senator's just like the rest. Come on, Linda, the man was killed by the mob. He owed them a favor and he didn't pay it."

"Okay, say he did owe them a favor," Linda said, pleased because she'd found the loophole in his theory. "And, just for the sake of argument, say Santos was the force that got Mr. Bingham elected. Why wait thirty years for repayment?"

"Good question."

The tires hummed along the pavement as Michael thought and Linda, satisfied, closed her eyes again.

"I've got it. Blackmail. Santos had something on Bingham, but Bingham wouldn't buckle under, so Santos—"

"Oh, baloney. Nobody had anything on the senator. He was honest. That's why he was so popular."

"Linda, the man was killed by John Santos himself. Santos only kills when he wants to make a statement. It's a warning to others of their punishment if they don't fall in line.... When Santos kills, there's a ceremony...."

"Could we drop this?"

"No. I want to pick your brain. This is driving me crazy."

"Well, I don't want to have my brain picked. I don't want to talk about this at all."

"Spoilsport."

"Spoilsport!"

"Yeah, spoilsport. All I'm trying to do is kill some time while I satisfy my curiosity, and you get all snippy and grumpy. You're always snippy and grumpy. Even when you're not tired and sick, you're snippy, grumpy, whiny."

"I get carsick! How the devil am I supposed to act when you're dragging me around the country—"

"For your own safety."

"Oh, I feel marvelously safe," she sarcastically retorted. "Since I've known you I've been spit at, shot at and seen two men murdered. You make me feel wonderfully safe."

"Did it ever occur to you," he asked patiently, "that your troubles started when you witnessed a murder, not when you met me?"

"No," she quickly responded, wiping sweat from her brow. "It wasn't all peaches and cream, but Bill and George were at least nice to me while they took my statement. You—"

"Have the wonderful pleasure of keeping you alive. I," he continued jeeringly, "have the delightful daily duty of listening to you grouch about your clothes, your food, your living conditions. A normal person—"

"A normal person would have run like the wind out of that office and not told anyone what she saw."

"You ran straight into the arms of the local authorities," Michael reminded in exasperation. "You had the choice of either admitting what you saw or going to jail for the crime yourself."

Linda bounced up straighter as her mouth fell open. "Me? That's a laugh!" she yelped. "Everybody was so anxious to put John Santos in jail, they never once considered I might be lying. They were too busy kissing my feet and praising me to high heaven."

"And you're mad about that, too."

"Yes!" she cried, for the first time realizing it was true. She was mad! Griping about inconveniences and motion sickness was just a cover for her real anger. And it was a deep anger. Almost a sting of betrayal. It had been eating at her since Al and Jonesy were murdered, but it was as hard to face as it was to ignore. So she'd buried it in her subconscious until now. "Yes! And do you know why? Because they sugarcoated a very bitter pill. Nobody warned me that Santos would kill anybody and everybody who tried to help me. I'm in danger. You're in danger. And I don't think it's necessary. They know who killed the senator. Not just because I'd told them, but because of the license number. And Bill and George even saw the Mercedes sitting in the parking lot when I pointed to Mr. Bingham's Lincoln to prove I had a ride home. I think that if the DA would have thought this through he could have come up with a way to convict John Santos without risking so many lives. I worked for attorneys. I know—"

"Will you stop?" Michael demanded. "There was no other way. Even if all you do is testify to seeing that license number, you still have to testify. So you might as well testify that you saw the murder."

"Baloney," she scoffed. "I think everybody just took the easy way out...at my expense...at Al and Jonesy's expense. Even you. Especially you. All you have to do is keep me alive until I give the testimony that convicts John Santos, and then it's all grapes and glory for you." She crossed her arms on her chest and flounced back on the seat again, slamming her eyes shut.

For a minute the only sound was the whine of the wheels along the pavement, then Michael burst out laughing. "What the hell's grapes and glory?"

"That, you twit, was an insult."

"So I gathered," Michael said, and he laughed again. "You know, Linda, you've been through a lot over the past couple of weeks, and I can understand that you'd be somewhat uptight—"

"Somewhat uptight!" she gasped. "I saw a horrible murder. Then got shot at. Then saw another two equally terrible murders. Then got shot at again. Now I'm trapped in a car with Attila the Hun. We eat when you want...stop to go to the bathroom when you want...most of the time you don't talk. You're about as much fun as Richard Simmons at a cake-eaters convention."

"Oh, and you're a real barrel of chuckles," Michael quickly countered. "You whine, you moan, you complain. Did it ever occur to you that I don't talk because I'm afraid of how you'll answer?"

She gasped. "Exactly what's that supposed to mean?"

"Well, for one thing, you very quickly, very easily told me—something of a stranger—your life story the other night. There isn't a thing I don't know about your ex-husband or your parents. And, quite frankly, even if there is more to tell, I don't want to know it."

"Well, pardon me," she snapped. "But I seem to recall you talking that night and the next day. In fact, while we were fishing, it was you who did all the talking."

"You see!" Michael said. "You see! This is exactly what I meant when I said I was afraid to talk with you. You just twisted the whole situation until it looked like I was pouring my heart out to you or something. I wasn't. I answered your questions. That's all. And now you're making a big deal out of it. I hope you have to go to the bathroom," he mocked. "Because I feel the need for some fresh air. So I'm going to stop, maybe for gas, maybe for food."

Linda bit her tongue as her fingers clenched into fists. She tried to swallow her anger, tried not to talk, but it was useless. The best she could accomplish was to lower her tone of voice so that she at least sounded rational when she sniped at him. She wasn't going to miss this chance to get her point across, but if she screamed like she wanted to, her point would get lost in the scuffle. "I know that I've been difficult to travel with, but you're not Prince Charming, either."

"I'm a much better host when my companion isn't a nag."

"Well, your companion wouldn't be a nag," she said, picking an imaginary piece of lint from her jeans, "if she knew where she was going, and if she could fall asleep one night knowing she'd wake up the next morning. I'm totally at your mercy for my food, my clothes, my everything, and I'm scared to death that I'm going to be shot, yet you won't even tell me where we're going. Why you've chosen one route over another. A little conversation could go a long way as reassurance."

"I'm not telling you things," he said as he whipped the car onto an exit ramp. The speed limit was twenty-five and he began braking. "For two reasons." He stopped and sighed. "You're going to hate this, but you do talk a lot. I never know what you're going to say to the waitress in a diner or the guy who pumps our gas. If Santos has a bead on our trail, and my guess is that he does, then anybody you talk to could be questioned. I can't trust that you won't slip something about our destination that some unsuspecting waitress would tell one of Santos's men while she's serving him coffee and he's feeding her a line about you being a missing heiress."

"Oh."

"You keep forgetting that Santos is tricky and has enough money to buy the information he needs."

"Like bribes?"

"No, like private detectives," he said for lack of better words. "My guess is that from Harrisburg to Hollywood money's been falling from the clouds like rain. And there are people greedy enough to want it and immoral enough not to ask questions about why you're being sought. Right now, your worst enemy isn't the mob, it's everybody and anybody who sees your face. And that's why your overzealous mouth is trouble. And that's why I can't tell you anything."

"Oh."

"Oh," he mocked, then caught sight of her sliding down in her seat. "I never mentioned that before because I was afraid that if I scared you, you'd start acting overcautious and do stupid things like slide down in your seat. Acting as if you're scared arouses suspicion. I thought, hoped, I could keep you under control and wouldn't have to explain to you that you have to watch yourself. Now, I'm wishing I wouldn't have said anything, because I can see you're not going to act normal anymore."

"Sorry," she mumbled, sitting up straight and trying not to look nervous. "You said you had two reasons. What's the other reason you don't tell me where we're going?"

They stopped at a traffic light. He rubbed his hands together. When the light turned red, he zipped through the intersection.

"What's the other reason?" she asked again, her own suspicions aroused.

He sighed heavily. "This is going to start one whopper of an argument. I can tell. So why not just save it for another day when you're less touchy?"

Staring at him with narrowed eyes, she ran her tongue along the back of her teeth and desperately prayed to keep her temper, even though she knew she wasn't going to. "Why do you keep doing this? Why do you keep insulting me today?"

"I didn't insult you, I spoke my mind," he said, making a quick left, then another. She wondered if he was deliberately losing them in the quiet little town and then realized he was probably looking for a place to stop.

"No. No. You spoke your mind the other night when we were getting along. You spoke your mind the day we were fishing. You're deliberately antagonizing me now. I'm smart enough to know the difference."

They came upon a strip of road that housed a combination gas station-restaurant, some businesses and a convenience store. A little off center with the rest of the street was an old Victorian house that had a "Rooms" sign in front of it.

"Look, we're going to stop for gas and then get back on the main highway. Do you think you could keep all this to yourself until we're away from civilization again?"

Hot, tired, sick of riding in a car while suffering from motion sickness, Linda asked, "Why don't we spend the night?"

He didn't answer, she didn't really expect him to. He drove them to the combination restaurant and gas station and got out. Five minutes later he returned to the car, pumped their gas and got back in. He started the engine, manipulated the vehicle through the traffic and pulled onto the main highway without a word.

"You know," she said, studying her fingernails. "You could have at least addressed the issue of spending the night."

He was chewing gum and didn't answer until after he'd twisted it between his front teeth. "We can't."

"Just that simple?"

"Just that simple."

She continued to examine her fingernails, ignoring the fact that he was chomping on his gum as if his life—or maybe holding his temper—depended on it. "What if I had a really good reason for wanting to stop now?"

"You don't. There isn't a reason good enough."

"Michael?" she beckoned, still not looking at him. "You, having seven sisters, should be more than a tad familiar with the fact that women are different from men . . . and maybe there were personal, private, woman things I needed."

"Don't start." He stopped her with a short command. "Because if my memory serves me, your personal, private, woman reason for wanting to stop every hour was last week."

"Darn it!" Frustrated, she pounded her fist on the back of the seat.

"Mind's like a steel trap," he said, tapping his index finger against his temple as he cracked his gum. "Besides, cut me a break, I can remember what happened last week.''

"I don't care!" She pouted. "I'm hot, tired and sticky. I want a bath. I want a nap."

"It really doesn't matter," he said through a long-suffering sigh. "We're broke—I'm broke. We can't afford another motel. And we really shouldn't use one of the credit cards until—"

"And I really don't give a darn. It's not my fault you bought enough gas to become a member of OPEC. I didn't ask to be taken halfway around the world. All I wanted was protection until the trial." She stopped and her eyes narrowed dangerously. "In fact, I didn't even ask for protection," she said, her voice rising as her temper grew. "Because I didn't remember agreeing to testify. And I don't want to. I want to go home and forget any of this happened." She faced him, crossed her arms on her chest and said, "Take me home."

All of a sudden, Michael began to laugh. "You've said a lot of stupid things in the last two weeks, but that about takes the cake. Mostly because I've explained, and I know you understand, that you'll last about a minute and a half on your own...."

"Oh, really? And just whose idea started the Jeep?"

"One lucky idea—one lucky break—and you think you're Wonder Woman." He sighed, steered the car to the shoulder of the road and slowly rolled it to a stop. Without preamble, he stretched over and opened her door. "Well, Wonder Woman, if you're not going to testify, I don't have to take you anywhere. So, it's been nice knowing you." He reached into the glove compartment and took out a business card. "Here's the number of my supervisor. Give him a call and let him know if you change your mind."

Confused, she looked at him, looked at the card. A dusty breeze tossed her hair up, then let it down again.

"Oh, that's right, you're broker than I am," he said as he reached into his pocket. He took out his wallet and unearthed a well-folded hundred-dollar bill. "That'll at least get you to a phone. You can call your bank and have them wire you funds to get home."

She couldn't tell if he was serious or kidding. Even as half of her wished she could run away from him, the other half was scared silly. She licked her dry lips.

"There you go," he taunted.

Her eyes narrowed again. The idiot was either punishing her for being grouchy or trying to teach her a lesson. Of all the nerve! She was testifying for *him*. *She* was doing *him* the favor. *She* got nothing for this, but grief. *He* kept forgetting that. And maybe it was time to teach him a lesson.

"Fine," she said, and jumped out of the car. She slammed the door and marched away, feet pounding on the dusty shoulder. A minute later, she ran back.

"The only way you get into this car is if you're willing to play the game my way."

"Who said anything about wanting to get in the car?" she asked flippantly. "I want my things."

She reached into the back seat section and got her purse and her brown paper bag of goodies, things they'd retrieved from the cabin once the authorities had come and gone.

He rolled his gum to his front teeth and chewed slowly, almost as if he wished he were twisting her skin instead of soft rubber. She grabbed her things, pulled them out and slammed the door again.

Bag under her arm, purse bobbing at her hip, she jogged to the side of the road and stuck out her thumb. Michael tapped his fingers against the steering wheel. Traffic was light and the temperature was above ninety. He'd give her about fifteen minutes and if she didn't get back into the car, he was driving into town to wait for her to come to her senses. He wasn't sizzling in the sun all day while she acted like an idiot.

As he sat there impatiently, a blue Taurus pulled up beside Linda, and she started to toss her bag into the open window. Stupefied, Michael whipped open his door and ran over.

At the Taurus, he had the foresight to flash his badge.

"Don't you know it's illegal to pick up a hitchhiker?" he asked the male driver, who looked about eighteen. "And this is one of the reasons why," he added as he tucked Linda under his arm, holding her by the waist like a sack of potatoes. Her legs were dangling and her hair hung like a waterfall, but he needed his other hand and arm to carry her purse and bag.

"Let me go!" she yelped, beating on his leg.

"She's the nation's second-most-wanted woman," Michael said, hoisting her purse strap over his shoulder. "Went on a shoplifting spree in Nevada that would curl your hair."

"Stop this!" Linda demanded, then bit his thigh. "Let me go!"

"I'm willing to forget that I saw you pick up a hitchhiker. I'm also willing to forget aiding and abetting a criminal. But I suggest you just drive away before I change my mind."

He slammed the door and grabbed her brown paper bag. Linda bit him so hard, he could swear she drew blood. "You little idiot!" he bellowed, carrying her to the car, her feet dangling, her head bobbing. "You are bound and determined to get yourself killed.'' With that he bounced her to her feet.

"No!" she shouted, raising herself on her tiptoes so she could put her face in his. "I was getting away from you."

"Well, you're stuck with me!" he roared, opening the door and shoving her inside. He threw her purse and bag onto her lap, then kicked her door closed with enough force that the entire car shook. "And if you ever pull a stunt like that again, I swear, I'll have you jailed."

She swallowed, trying to be casual about settling back in her seat as he stormed around the front of the car, but it was useless. Her limbs were stiff, her stomach was fluttering, and her eyebrows wouldn't come down into a normal position.

She'd never seen him this way. She'd pushed and prodded and poked until he was mad, but never, ever had he lost that aura of control. Even when he'd suggested she leave the car, she suspected he knew she'd be back. That's why she'd been bold enough to accept a ride with a stranger. But right now, at this minute, he looked as though he could kill her himself and save John Santos the trouble.

He screeched the car to a stop in front of the house with the sign that said "Rooms" and didn't even pause before shoving open his car door. He was around to her side before her feet hit the pavement, and if it wasn't for the fact that there were two people walking down the street, she knew he'd have picked her up and carried her again. As it was, he had her wrist in a death grip and was pulling her in such a way she was sure her arm would come out of its shoulder socket if she didn't keep up with him.

Inside the ornately furnished living room-lobby, Linda handed him his hundred-dollar bill, and he didn't even look at her when he snatched it from her hand.

More than a little ashamed of herself, she bit the inside of her lip. It really wasn't fair. With the constant strain of running for her life wearing them down, they were always sniping at each other. She was scared silly most of the time or argumentative just to dull the edge of boredom. And, he was probably bored, too. They were both nice people, and had they met anywhere else under different circumstances, she suspected they'd be friends.

Friends?

What a laugh? They'd never be friends. If they'd met under different circumstances, she knew he would have ignored her because there was an attraction, a playing-with-fire kind of temptation that burned between them, and ignoring her, staying away from her, would have been his way of dealing with it. She didn't even try to kid herself into thinking the attraction wouldn't be there if they weren't running for their lives. She knew better. She saw the way he looked at her when she first rolled out of bed in the morning; and every time he opened the first button of his shirt, be that in the morning, while driving or getting ready for his shower, she got a primitive urge to run her fingers over every inch of him. What she felt for Michael she'd never felt for anyone, not even David. His size, his shape, his scent, seemed to pull her. Call her. And every day it grew stronger and stronger.

Admitting that, she could quit pretending they argued because of boredom and fear. The sparks that continually ignited between them resulted after sleeping fully clothed in a stuffy little bedroom. They came from his being on the floor and her being alone in the bed. They came because he was a very attractive man who thought she was a very attractive woman; and they could insult each other from here to Timbuktu to try to take the sweetness out of the attraction, but Linda suspected that only made it all the more appealing.

He pulled her away from the little counter, and she smiled briefly at the white-haired lady who waved in response. When they got to the long stairway, he ushered her in front of him but held onto her wrist. She said nothing, just kept thinking about forbidden fruit. At the door of their room, she waited silently while he unlocked it. He too remained quiet.

But when he closed the door behind them, he spun on her. "If you know what's best for you," he said through clenched teeth, "you won't utter a sound for the next twelve hours."

She wet her lips.

He took a step closer, then another, his chest heaving with contained anger. "I've never in my life met a more unappreciative—" He took another step. Linda stayed frozen at the foot of the four-poster bed. "Uncontrollable—" He took the step that put him directly in front of her, and Linda swallowed. "Irresponsible—"

She jumped to her tiptoes and threw her arms around his neck, pressing her lips to his. If all this pent-up anger was the result of mutual attraction, if all their sniping and complaining and yelling at each other could be controlled through the easing of sexual tension, then she'd do it—and gladly, if she was being honest.

Michael grabbed her biceps, intending to push her away, but Linda tightened her hold on his neck and stabbed the tip of her tongue against his closed lips, hoping for a little cooperation. He tried to push her away again, but she flattened herself against him as she traced the line of his closed mouth.

Then his hand went to the back of her neck to hold her head, while his other hand moved down her spine, seeking, caressing, and he kissed her, draining every ounce of the pent-up frustration out of both of them.

But he didn't draw away and she didn't want him to. Even as he kissed her, he began to unbutton her blouse and she started on the buttons of his shirt. He smoothed his fingers under the fabric, and it seemed to fall away of its own will as his fingertips touched her warm flesh.

She simply indulged herself in exploring his hair-covered chest under the stiff material of his cotton shirt. His hands roamed, quickly, restlessly. Her hands explored, discovered. And their mouths stayed fused, tongues mating lustily, as he stripped off her bra and rolled her nipples between his thumbs and forefingers. Her knees buckled and he caught her before she collapsed, then carried her to the bed.

In a twisting tangle of arms and legs, they removed each other's clothes and used them to make little mountains on the floor. Her skin, never quite this sensitive, came alive under his fingers, and the desire in her was so great she realized that the pulsing need had begun days ago, maybe even weeks ago. His hair-covered thighs and chest scratched against her smooth legs and plump breasts as he kissed her, touched her, smoothed his hands and legs and mouth over every inch of her.

But she matched him, fire for fire. Her fingers and lips probed and suckled; her toes and feet rubbed and discovered; her legs, her thighs, her arms, her hands, everything that could move touched him, wanted him, until he rolled her to her back, head cushioned by a lumpy pillow, and entered her.

Her head fell back as every inch of her body arched to accept him. His mere entry caused her to climax and that set off the same reaction in him. They weren't silent or gentle, and when the end came, the quietness of the room, the town, settled over them like a cloak. Even with Michael Rosen's bulk collapsed over her like a limp blanket, she could have fallen into a peaceful, satisfied sleep.

He saw her eyes drift shut and rolled away from her. He wasn't going to let her get away with feigning sleep. "You knew that would happen, didn't you?"

She didn't open her eyes. "Yes."

"Well, then I suppose you're pretty proud of yourself," he said as he threw his feet to the floor and started to stand.

She caught his hand, rolling to her elbow. "No," she said, and looked him right in the eye. "Actually I'm grateful."

"Well, I'm not." He shook off her hand and grabbed his jeans. He stepped into them and walked to the open window. A soft, fluffy breeze danced in and tangoed with the lacy sheers beneath the starched curtains.

"I am," she said, and he turned to see her lying calmly and casually, naked on top of a flowery comforter.

Purely for the purposes of self-preservation, he turned away and looked out at the sleepy little town, which could have come straight out of a TV commercial.

"Boy, there's just no pleasing some people. Two minutes ago, you were telling me I was unappreciative. So, I tell you I'm grateful and you turn away," Linda said.

"You have the most unpredictable, warped sense of humor of any woman I know."

"I have an unpredictable, warped sense of everything. Come back to bed, let me show you."

"Will you stop!" he bellowed, spinning away from the window and her hopeful smile. "This isn't right! It doesn't work!"

"It worked for me," she said and her smiling lips became downright seductive.

He groaned. "I care about you. Really, really care about you." He made the admission as though it were a sin.

"So?"

"So, it throws everything off sync—"

"Everything's been off sync with us right from the very beginning." She stopped talking and gave him a big-eyed look that melted his heart. "I'm scared. Really scared. Always scared. Santos doesn't play by any rules I know, and it looks like he confuses you, too. Let's stay here," she begged, scrambling to her knees so she could bound off the bed. She put her arms around him from behind, and the feeling of her soft skin sliding against his hypersensitive flesh sent fresh tingles of arousal through him. "Let's pretend the rest of the world doesn't exist."

Intending to scold her, he turned around and got himself securely folded in the bear hug of a woman who had a disarming ability to charm the birds out of the trees. And she knew it. Even as he felt the initial stirrings of arousal again, he said, "You must be pretty proud of yourself."

She blinked up at him. "I already told you I wasn't."

"Well, you should be. You now know the second reason I can't tell you anything, and you got it out of me without an argument."

"Yeah," she agreed, grinning. "But not without a heated confrontation."

He groaned. She rose to her tiptoes and kissed him. He let her nip and nibble and stroke her tongue against his lips until he thought he'd explode from the pure physical pleasure of being pursued. Then he carried her to the bed again and they stayed there until morning, sleeping only long enough to revive their strength for the next time they made love.

Chapter Eight

"All right, you two, rise and shine. This is a bed-and-breakfast, not a bed-and-lunch."

Michael sat up so quickly he pulled the sheet away from Linda's naked breasts, and she immediately snatched the edge and covered herself.

"I poked my head in at seven to roust you, but you're tired, I could see that, and I let you sleep."

Linda stared at the tiny white-haired woman puttering around their room. She'd set a tray on the round table by the window and was now busily tugging on the old-fashioned window shade, attempting to activate the spring mechanism that would reroll the shade of plastic and let light into the room. Embarrassed, Linda slid the worn sheet to her collarbone and glanced at Michael, wondering how in heaven's name he was going to get them out of this one. He ran both hands over his face and shook his head, trying to wake himself.

Then he took a deep breath and said, "Mrs. Johnson, a man's bedroom is supposed to be private."

"It was," she said, highlighting the *was*. "But it's morning and I gotta do the laundry, and I shoulda had the dishes done already. So I figured that as long as I brought coffee—" she pointed at the tray "—you wouldn't mind if I woke you. You've been in that bed since three o'clock yesterday afternoon," she reminded, then busied herself with the cups on the tray. "Not that it's any of my business, mind you, but considering what you could and did do last night, you still got at least six hours sleep and six is enough."

Linda couldn't help it, she giggled, and when she did so Michael pivoted to face her. She could see he'd wanted to say something, probably scold her, but when he looked at her, something very strange happened. His lips parted, but no words came out, and Linda couldn't have spoken if her life depended on it. For a full thirty seconds they just stared at one another, seeing each other as different people. Seeing the person they'd made love with in the dark. Knowing everything was different.

Michael quickly looked away. "We can take it from here, Mrs. Johnson. We're sorry we slept late—"

"Oh, shoot," she interrupted him. "It really doesn't matter. I know how you city folks are. You work yourself to death, then your doctor tells you you need to get away for a while and you just drive until you find some quiet little town like Greensboro, and by that time you're so exhausted you'd sleep around the clock if I'd let you, but I don't, because that's no good for you, either." She turned and walked to the door. "By the way, we don't have any tourist attractions. No public transportation. No moviè house." She stopped and smiled. "But maybe you two aren't looking for outside entertainment."

"Actually, Mrs. Johnson, our marriage counselor sent us away to try to resolve our marital problems," Michael said, surprising Linda so much she stared at him. She knew they were pretending to be married, but wouldn't a happily married couple attract less attention?

"Well, this is as good a place as any to do that," Mrs. Johnson decided proudly. "You got a good solid bed and a nice quiet town. Shoot, I'll even let you alone if you promise to at least have breakfast with me."

Michael smiled. "It's a deal."

She nodded once. "Good. Then I'll see you tomorrow morning."

When the door closed behind the innkeeper, Linda casually slid the cover to her neck and said, "That was clever."

Michael got out of bed. Totally unconcerned about his nakedness, he walked to the tapestry chair where his jeans lay. Linda looked at his back, his arms, his rock-hard thighs, and remembered touching them, tasting them.

"She wanted an explanation and I couldn't very well tell her we were running from the mob. Besides, she looks like the type who'd be sympathetic to a couple having marital troubles." He stepped into his jeans. "So, kid, we've now got our cake and can eat it too."

When he called her *kid*, Linda's chest tightened. After some of the things they'd done the night before, he shouldn't think of her as a kid anymore. "What do you mean?" she asked quietly.

"Well, I'd bet my britches that old biddy will guard our privacy like a mother hen," he said, walking to the table where the small metal coffeepot awaited. "So, if we want, if we keep a low profile, we could probably stay here for a while."

Linda's mouth dropped open in happy surprise. "You mean it?"

He handed her a small china cup filled with warm coffee. "We'll think about it."

The tone was back. That hard, authoritative tone that reminded her that they weren't really lovers, they weren't even friends. He was the guy protecting her from the mob, and something akin to boredom for him and desperation for her had driven them to become lovers. And they definitely weren't going to talk about it, and it absolutely wasn't going to happen again. "Okay," she said, nodding.

"Your clothes are still in the car," he said before he took a long drink of his coffee. "I'll get them for you, but first I want to take a quick look around. I won't be long, so you just stay in bed while I'm gone. Then we won't have to worry about somebody accidentally seeing you, until I'm sure it won't matter."

Not quite able to meet his eyes, she nodded.

He said, "Good." Then he dressed in silence and left the room.

Linda flopped back onto her pillow. What a mess! What a mistake! Not making love. Oh, no. That was a memory she'd cherish for the rest of her life. The mistake, the stupid idiotic mistake she'd made was falling in love. She was married for years to a man she greatly admired, trusted and cared about, but she never loved him. Once or twice she tried, but it just never happened. In fact, she was beginning to think she was immune. And now, after only a couple of weeks, she was in love. Head over heels in love with a man who didn't love her, because he couldn't love her. Once she testified, she was supposed to disappear. A smart man wouldn't fall in love with a woman who wouldn't be around to live a normal life with him. And Michael was definitely a smart man.

So what was she going to do? What were they going to do? How was he going to let her down easy when they had three or four more weeks together before the case would come to trial? Could she survive it if he became a cold, distant stranger again?

She rolled over and huddled under the comforter, even though it was warm enough that she wouldn't need it. She felt as if she were the only person on the planet, the last survivor after a nuclear war. There wasn't a clock ticking or a muffled voice or even the sound of a car on the street. All there was was silence. Like the silence of her bedroom when her mother had passed out and her dad had left because he wouldn't hang around to watch his wife kill herself with liquor, or his daughter die of loneliness....

But the joke was on him, Linda thought triumphantly, because she hadn't died. The alcohol might have killed her mother, but the loneliness never really got Linda. Oh, it tried, but it never got her. If anything, it made her stronger, smarter, able to deal with things in an objective, totally unemotional way. After all, had she taken any of it personally, it would have been that her dad didn't care, not that her mother drank. Her mother was sick...her dad was the fool. A tiny blond child begged him for help, begged him to stay....

One night...please, daddy, just one night...

But he left and she stared at the door, knowing she was on her own, knowing she wasn't a child anymore, even though she was only six....

Linda turned, staring at the swirled plaster ceiling. In the stillness of the room, she could have heard a mouse breathe.

And then she felt it. The strange premonition, the warmth of thoughts not her own as they traveled through her blood and told her things without words, without sounds. There were just quick impressions and warmth. Warmth she could have enjoyed, until she realized it was meant to be a comfort of sorts because it was the bearer of bad news.

She now understood why fate had chosen her to witness Bob Bingham's murder. She already knew life wasn't a fairy tale, and she wouldn't be disappointed by the fact that her life was about to be snatched away from her again. And it was. She knew that it was. She harbored no illusions about the rest of her destiny, about the price she'd pay to bring John Santos to justice. Her future wasn't just bleak, it was empty. The balance of her life would be spent moving from town to town, afraid to trust and too cautious to love.

She bit her lip, closed her eyes and swallowed hard. She never actually thought she was the kind who'd get a house in the country, three kids and a dog, but when she left David, there'd been a hope, a tiny shaft of light at the end of the tunnel because she could at least try to make a normal life for herself. But John Santos had snuffed out that light just as surely as he'd killed Bob Bingham, and now she was back to being alone again. Only this time it was forever.

She wanted to cry but tears wouldn't come. She was warm, she was dry, in another twenty minutes she'd be fed. And she was in love. Really and truly in love. Falling in love with Michael Rosen might not be a permanent thing, it might not even be a smart thing, but she now realized it was a gift. A present from the gods for accepting her mission. And because she understood the rules, the limits, she knew she could take more, he could give more, and they could still walk away when the time came.

Now all she had to do was convince Michael.

She rolled out of bed and crawled to the chair, not just because her jeans, T-shirt and purse were on the floor beside it, but because she took Michael's warnings seriously, and she stayed below window level so no one would see her. Seated beside the spindly leg of an antique chair, she slid into her jeans and pulled on her shirt. Then she crawled to the door, poked her head out to see if the coast was clear and dragged her long-handled purse with her to the bathroom. After taking a birth control pill, she stripped for a shower.

Even as the clock had been ticking away on her ninety-day no-fault divorce, her friends had talked her into getting birth control pills just in case David suggested a reconciliation. Neither she nor David had requested an attempt to save their marriage, but she'd gotten the pills anyway and now she was glad she had. No matter what it took, she was getting her few weeks of loving, and this way there'd be no consequences, no complications.

In the medicine cabinet was a fresh tube of toothpaste and a new trial-sized bottle of mouthwash, so even though Linda didn't have her toothbrush, she cleaned her teeth. She brushed her hair, then sort of tousled it again so it wouldn't look obvious that she'd fixed herself up. Then she dug into her purse until she found her little rollette of cologne, and she smoothed it over her pulse points before sliding into her clothes and crawling down the hall again.

In the bedroom she was careful to replace her clothes and purse just as they'd been when Michael left the room. There was a television on a stand at the foot of the bed and it even had remote control, but Linda let that alone, too. He'd said to stay in bed, and she was going to make it look as though she'd followed his instructions to the letter, not so much for the sake of peaceful coexistence, but because staying naked in bed worked to her advantage.

When Michael opened the door, she was under the covers, staring at the ceiling. He tossed the duffel bag onto the bed beside her, stepped into their room and closed the door. For a full thirty seconds he stood with his hands behind his back, still clasped around the doorknob. Finally he said, "I didn't just leave because I wanted to check out the area. I needed some time alone to think."

She suspected as much, but didn't say anything.

"I'm not exactly sure how we got into this situation and, to be perfectly honest, I'm not sure we can get out of it."

He was talking about the entire scope of things, not just the fact that they'd slept together. She knew that, because insurmountable problems had been the catalyst that threw them into bed, and he was trained to deal with cause and effect, not just effect. They might have known that this wasn't going to be easy, but neither could have predicted it would end up being so hard, either. They were battling more than just John Santos. They had conflicting personalities, motion sickness and boredom to contend with, not to mention limited funds, limited modes of transportation and a limited number of places they could dine or rest. There were times when Linda felt it would have been easier to just stay in one place and dare John Santos to kill her without getting caught.

"So I told myself that if you disobeyed me, if you weren't in bed when I got back, I was going to tie you up and gag you. I wasn't even going to loosen the gag until after you were on the witness stand. In fact, I wasn't going to untie you, either, which meant I'd have to carry you to the witness stand. But I figured that might be a good idea because then you'd look like an unwilling witness, and the Santos people might let you alone after the trial."

If another person had said that to her, she probably would have laughed, thinking he was making a joke, but with Michael the more ridiculous the idea, the more the probability he was serious.

"Oh."

"Then I told myself that if you were still in bed, I could take it as a good sign, a sign that we were doing the right thing even though it seems risky.'' It was then that he looked at her. He held her attention in such a way that she couldn't move, couldn't breathe. "And then I told myself that would mean I should just pull back the covers and join you."

She wet her lips. "I stayed in bed the entire time. I didn't even sit up."

"Then why does the room smell like a moonlit night in August?"

"I haven't the slightest idea."

"You're the only woman I know who can lie with a straight face, without getting red and without looking away."

"It's a gift . . . come back to bed."

He shook his head very slowly and looked at the floor. "I'm not sure about this."

"I am."

"It means we have to change our plans. . . ."

"I don't see how. At the few hotels we've stayed, we've posed as husband and wife. This is just the first time we've actually acted as husband and wife, and judging by Mrs. Johnson's reaction, I think it worked."

She could see by his facial expression that she'd found an angle he'd missed, so she pressed on. "Come on, Michael, we've been ignoring this for weeks, and because of that we've bickered like two elks trying out their new antlers. We have enough to worry about with John Santos alone, not to mention motion sickness and lack of money. So why don't we just give in to the attraction, then together we'll try to figure out what to do about John Santos and money."

"Money's not a problem anymore. I put a call in to my dad, but he's out to lunch. I gave him our number. He should call us back very shortly."

She gasped. He'd never done that before. They'd taken the man's money and used his credit cards, but he'd never known their exact location. "You told your dad where we were?"

"Don't worry. My dad's the best friend we have right now."

"I hope you're right."

"I know I'm right. So the only thing we have to worry about now is John Santos and the hundreds of people who work for him."

"And we just forget about the rest?"

"What rest?"

"This..." she said, pointing out that she was naked and they'd shared a bed.

"Well...Linda, I..."

"Come back to bed," she coaxed again, this time she stretched under the covers, watching his eyes as they followed the movement of her limbs beneath the flowery comforter. She caught his gaze and held it. Trying to look more serious than provocative, more mature than her years, like a woman who knows exactly what she's doing, she whispered, "Please?"

He didn't say a word. He just began to unbutton his shirt as he walked to the bed again. She grabbed the duffel bag and threw it to the floor, and he sat on the vacated space to remove his shoes. He stood and took off his shirt, then his jeans, and, mesmerized, Linda continued to watch. His body wasn't glorious or magnificent or perfect, but it was male. Wonderfully male.

Naked now, he bent, grabbed the comforter and peeled it away from her. With another man she might have been scared or inhibited, but not with Michael. Never with Michael. This wasn't sex in the dark, it was lovemaking. Two adults expressing emotion with their bodies, and she loved him enough that his way wasn't embarrassing, it was right.

"I DON'T KNOW, Simon, maybe we're going about this all wrong."

Simon looked up from his breakfast. John, Jr. hadn't touched his eggs or his toast. Even his juice glass was full. Tilting the legs of his high-backed white wicker chair, he sat stretched out with his eyes closed, letting the morning sun caress his face and warm his limbs.

"What do you mean?"

"Predictability," John said simply, straightening in his seat. "Rosen's a smart enough man that he could keep our femme fatale on the road for the next several weeks. As a moving target, the possibility that we'd find her is slim. My father," he went on, leaning forward as he picked up a fork and began tracing the edge of his plate, "would spend a lot of money and expend every favor owed him looking for Linda Miller. And there's the possibility that he wouldn't find her. And that's the game Michael Rosen's planning to play...been planning to play for what? Eight? Ten years?"

Not fully comprehending, Simon nodded anyway.

"Therein lies the crux of the problem," John, Jr. said, leaning back in his seat again. The patio was warmed by the sun and adorned by lavish possessions, comfort to the highest degree. "Rosen's been at this for years. He probably planned the hiding places. He probably has cash reserves. Contacts. Helpers." He laughed dryly. "That cabin should have clued us in that we'd only joined a game Rosen's been playing for years."

"You're losing me, Mr. Santos. I don't see how this ties in. We suspected all along that he'd be prepared."

John, Jr. patted Simon's hand. "He's fighting my father, Simon, because I'm acting like my father. And he's beating us."

Pleasantly surprised by John's insight, Simon nodded in agreement. Had this been the senior Santos, that last negative comment would have been Simon's cue to loudly and strongly disagree, because to a certain extent it was his responsibility to keep up John, Sr.'s morale. With this Santos, he could be honest.

With his elbows on the table, John, Jr. steepled his fingers and tapped his chin. "Take the Amanda-Lynn situation," he analyzed as Simon reached for a cigarette. "We never harmed a hair on that child's head...bought her two bears and a tricycle...and heaven knows what else she picked up at the mall." He grinned at Simon and Simon shrugged, failing in his efforts to control his own grin.

"And yet," John went on, "her grandfather cooperated fully. Perhaps it's time to stop the predictable violence."

Simon took a long, slow drag on his cigarette. "You make it sound like an experiment."

John thought about that. "I suppose it is."

"At risk," Simon reminded, rolling the ash end of his cigarette along the edge of a crystal bowl, "is your father's life."

"You're suggesting then that we stay with the tried-and-true methods?" John asked.

"No. You sound like you're unsure. I thought it best to play devil's advocate, remind you of the risks."

"Ah, but the benefits, Simon," John, Jr. said as he rose and began to pace.

"You'd never get an argument from me when you're proposing nonviolent coercion," Simon agreed, and John, Jr. chuckled as he leaned against a waist-high railing and inhaled the fragrance of summer. The pond, the flower gardens, ripening fruit.

Simon rolled the ash from his cigarette again. "But, keep an ace up your sleeve."

Smiling proudly, John faced Simon. "Okay, how's this? First we infiltrate the DA's office. Hmm . . ." He paused, bobbing his head as he thought. "Let's buy an assistant, preferably the one assigned to Dad's case. Using a balance of ineptitude from the prosecutor, coupled with a sharp-as-a-tack defense on our part to discredit Ms. Miller, we create reasonable doubt. She was drinking that night. I read it in the statement. That's a very strong point in our favor."

"I know," Simon agreed, nodding as he crushed his cigarette in the crystal bowl. "And reasonable doubt is all we need." He picked up his coffee cup. "Now, your backup?"

"My guess is, Ms. Miller won't testify on day one. The defense will be building a case, therefore, she'll be the climax."

"Okay." Simon nodded again.

"After the first day of testimony, I think we'll know what our money's purchased at the DA's office." He stopped again and waited for Simon's nod of agreement before continuing. "So, if things aren't going in our favor, we'll kill the witness as she's leaving the courtroom."

For a minute Simon said nothing. Then he looked up at his new boss who was again waiting for a sign of approval. He really couldn't give it. Not when the stakes were so high. "How?" he asked quietly, trying to keep the skepticism out of his voice.

"I think," John, Jr. said, smiling triumphantly, "we'll invite Amanda-Lynn to my home for another visit . . . an extended visit. Undoubtedly her grandfather will be at the trial because he was one of the officers at the scene. If I don't like the way things are going, I'm going to shake my head. From there on out it will be up to him.''

"And if he doesn't cooperate?''

"He will. He knows the rules now.''

THE TRILLING SOUND of the phone awakened Linda, and she twisted away from Michael to reach for it, but he beat her. Sighing, she lay down again, using his chest for a pillow and allowing her fingers and hands to roam familiarly under the worn and faded sheet.

She couldn't believe they'd stayed in the same place for two weeks. Even more unbelievable, she and Michael had achieved more than a state of harmony, they'd found utopia, nirvana...something. And she almost wished they could stay like this forever...isolated from the rest of the world.

She sighed again and stretched her supple flesh against every available inch of his rock-solid body, almost purring with contentment. He was speaking in hushed tones, but she'd tuned him out because most of the calls he received had nothing to do with her, and, laughably, three-quarters were from his father, who was calling to get Michael's input on the family business.

Michael recradled the receiver, pillowed his head and slowly, methodically, stroked her shoulder. Her eyes drifted closed and sleep beckoned again, but Michael cleared his throat.

"The proceedings start next Monday. Because the case is so cut-and-dry, they estimate you'll probably testify Tuesday.''

Her eyelids sprang up. It was over.

Chapter Nine

"How about a walk in the woods?"

Linda flicked off the television set as Michael entered their room, returning from his morning jog, which was his excuse to use a pay phone to check in with his superiors. They could take calls in, but couldn't make calls out because there'd be a record of those somewhere.

"A real walk? Outside?" It was Saturday and they were leaving Sunday morning, a short enough time that she never expected he'd gift her with a trip outside. Not when they were this close.

"Yeah," Michael said, and started to laugh. "Lord, you'd think you'd been confined for two years instead of two weeks."

"Sometimes it feels like I was born and raised in this room. Almost as if I didn't have another life..."

He silently shushed her with a finger over his lips, then motioned with his arm for her to hurry up. Not really understanding, she frowned.

"Let's hurry and maybe we can catch the deer feeding," he said, nodding toward the door, another indication that she should hurry.

When they were outside walking to their rental car, Michael said, "I can't explain fully right now, but we're going to the woods to talk. That television repairman Lydia so freely let into our room yesterday didn't check out. So we can't talk in our room, and I don't want you to say anything important in the car either, because he may have bugged our car, too. Make small talk so they don't realize we're onto them, but don't say anything of consequence.''

She nodded in agreement, but her knees turned to jelly. Nobody had to tell her he was taking precautions because their room or their car had been bugged. What puzzled her was why they were going to the woods. Why didn't they just move on? Run? If someone had caught up with them, why weren't they running?

In the car they talked about the weather. It was a beautiful sunny day, and though they took the eastern road out of town, Michael mentioned the west. He talked about street signs and a little grocery store that weren't anywhere around, but Linda guessed they were on the other side of town and he was deliberately trying to make someone think they were headed in the other direction. In fact, he might have even been tricking them into believing they were leaving for good, because he didn't turn off the ignition, he left the car engine running. He silently told her not to open her door, pulled her along the seat and had her disembark from his side. Then he closed the door so quietly it didn't even squeak, and he had to check to be sure it was secured.

"What was that all about?" she asked as soon as they were ten feet from the car. He motioned for her to be silent again and shook his head, and they maintained that vigil for another twenty feet.

When they were in the foliage, he said, "A member of the DA's staff was hit by a car yesterday afternoon. She died this morning."

"Oh, no."

"She was conscious long enough to explain that she'd been approached by Santos's staff but refused to help them. She said she hadn't mentioned their offer to the DA, because they threatened her son's life and she agreed to keep quiet. Stupidly she'd thought that was the end of it, but the Santos people don't operate that way. Since she wouldn't do their dirty work, they made her the messenger."

"I don't understand," Linda said, shaking her head.

"It's really very simple. They approached her, she refused to help and they let her walk away, fully expecting that she'd tell the DA she'd been approached. Then they killed her, so that the next person they approach will know he either helps or dies."

"Oh, no."

"That's not the worst of it. Santos's attorney is pushing to speed up the trial. He's accepting certain testimony in deposition form to save time and get right to the heart of the prosecution's case. The DA feels he must have something that will discredit your testimony. And he also thinks you'll take the stand Monday, not Tuesday as everybody expected. So you'll have to be there from day one."

"Great," Linda muttered, grabbing a tall weed and yanking it from the ground. "In other words, everything we've gone through in the past few weeks could have been for nothing."

"Not necessarily. Santos's attorney could be bluffing to scare us or just trying to hold his own with the press."

They walked a little farther along the dirt path. Linda continued to pull at the weeds; Michael sighed.

"Linda, they want me to ask you a couple of questions. To really sew this up, we have to somehow connect Santos and Bingham, and so far the DA's only come up with a witness who can place them in the same room, but no reason for why they'd be in the same room. Now, I know you're as loyal as the day is long, but if we want to convict Santos, you're going to have to break personal confidences. Your statement says you'd never seen or heard of Santos before, but you must know something."

"I don't. I swear."

"Well, just talk then. Tell me everything you know about Bob Bingham, and then I'll relay it to the DA and he can sort it out."

She ran her hand through her hair. "You should be talking to Molly Benson. She's worked for the Binghams for ten years. I only worked for Mr. Bingham...oh, nine, maybe ten months. And to be honest, he knew more about me than I knew about him. About six months after I started working for him, I discovered I was pregnant, I ran into my marital problems and he started counseling me, helping me. And it was only then that we became friends." She stopped and sighed. "Frankly, I was so wrapped up with my troubles I never noticed that it was a one-sided relationship."

"He never mentioned anything that would make you think he had mob connections?"

"No! Heavens, no."

"How about his kids? Any drug addicts? Any gamblers?"

She thought for a second. "I only met four of his six kids. They were nice, well-adjusted people...all in their thirties, all married, all normal."

"Did Mr. Bingham ever give you any reason to believe he gambled?"

She laughed. "Are you kidding? He opposed legislation to legalize gambling. He sponsored the drunk-driving bills. If anything, Bob Bingham was the conservative's conservative.''

"Darn."

They crested the hill they were climbing and came to an open field. "I'm sorry."

Looking out over the horizon, Michael said, "Don't worry about it. It's certainly not your fault."

"Then why do I feel it is?"

Michael took her hand and kissed the knuckles. "That's one of the occupational hazards of dealing with the mob."

"I wasn't dealing with the mob."

"Precisely," Michael said, and turned her in the direction of their car again. "The less involved you are when you accidentally bump into them, the more guilty you feel when your efforts fail and you can't put them behind bars."

She stopped then. Because Michael had her hand, he stopped, too. "That's not a lawman talking."

He started walking again. "No, it's not."

She stopped again. "What did you see?"

"Enough."

"Not enough to get you killed. Not enough to make you run for your life." She tugged her hand free of his. "Dammit, Michael! Why am I running for my life, when you didn't have to?"

He took a long breath. "They didn't see me watching them, and I didn't go to the police."

"You what?" she gasped.

He shook his head. "I didn't go to the police. I was sixteen and . . . look, it's a long story."

"I want to hear it," she said simply. They were lovers, they were friends, but they weren't confidants. Just as with her ex-husband, she'd never achieved that level of intimacy she so desperately craved. And despite the fact that she knew he had to get back to the DA, the information she'd supplied him wasn't as important as her desperate hunger. The clock was ticking away and their time together was running out. She didn't want to settle for being lovers or even chums. She wanted that last step. She wanted the intimacy of sharing secrets. It would be like having a part of him no one else would ever get. "We don't move until I hear it."

He looked at her, really looked at her. Then he glanced down the hill at their car, which was idling beside the quiet road. "I suppose if anybody would understand, it would be you." He stretched forward, looking past the trees at the long ribbon of road that led to the main highway. It, too, was deserted. "Let's sit."

Linda lowered herself to a mound of dirt, and Michael chose to lay in the grass below her. He ripped a green blade from the ground and then broke it into tiny pieces, letting each piece fall as he tore it away. "My father had a very good friend who ran a small chain of grocery stores in Cleveland. Every summer this man would send his son to work with my father, and my father would send me to work with him."

Fascinated, Linda watched him as he spoke. He was stretched out on the grass, leaning on one elbow, seemingly concentrating on the grass he was mutilating. His tone of voice changed subtly when he said the word *father*, but after living with him for the past several weeks, hearing his phone conversations with his father and knowing they could spend hours chatting about nothing, she'd come to realize he and his father were bound tightly and nothing could ever separate them. It was a union so wonderful in Linda's eyes that she didn't think anything should be allowed to separate them.

"The theory was that Jason and I would sort of apprentice in the other set of stores and then come back and share our knowledge with our fathers." He paused to chuckle. "Twenty years ago communications weren't what they are today."

"No, they weren't," she agreed, leaning forward so she could rest her elbow on her knee and watch him as he spoke. She wanted to see the expression in his eyes, hear every inflection in his voice, so she'd have them to remember on cold winter nights. In the grass, telling something he'd never told before, he looked younger, approachable, and she wished more than ever that they would have had a chance to really share their lives.

"Anyway, we did that every summer. That's how my father and his friend exchanged their ideas. I guess you could say that was their way of networking."

"They should have had a newsletter."

Michael sniffed a laugh. "I agree totally. Because they used me instead of a newsletter, I met the infamous John Santos. A pleasure I will always regret."

"You met him? Like 'shook hands' met him?" Linda asked curiously.

Michael sighed. "No, I phrased that wrong. I watched him drip acid on Peter Smith's hands until he signed the papers to sell his grocery store chain."

Linda gasped. "You're kidding!"

"No," Michael said quietly. "His wife, Maria, found me peeking at them from behind a tall cooler, and she very subtly motioned for me to get in the back room...and I slipped away."

Michael stopped again. He didn't speak for so long that Linda almost crawled from her perch to see why. Finally, very quietly he said, "Santos left and Maria packed my bags and shooed me home. But by the time the train got me to Johnstown, both Pete and Maria were dead. The store that housed their main office burned to the ground, and they just happened to be the only two people in it at the time.''

"And you never went to the police?'' Linda asked, so confused she just stared at him.

"No. Dad and I returned to Cleveland, ostensibly to put Jason in the hands of his aunt. Once we had Jason squared away, we went to an attorney—a family friend—and told him the story. He listened and promised to see what he could do, but sent us back home without a visit to the police because he said the situation was touchy and that I was in danger. We didn't hear from him again until six weeks later when he said that the fire marshal ruled out arson as the cause of the fire. No arson. No murder. The attorney then said that Jason had received a fair and equitable sum for the stores and that there really wasn't any evidence to prosecute Santos for what he'd done to Pete's hands with the acid. But the real bottom line was that the DA's office wouldn't even entertain the possibility that Santos had murdered the Smiths.''

"Maybe he didn't?''

"Oh, he did,'' Michael said. "I knew it then...in my gut,'' he said, pointing at his stomach. "And now my intellect tells me that he's guilty because that's how he operates. He got the signatures, then got himself off the premises, then got rid of them. After studying him for ten years, I realize that even though the Smiths signed their stores away, he still had to kill them because he couldn't risk that they'd renege on the sale or go to the police. So, in a certain sense, I'm only alive today because it took John Santos two hours to get across town. I always felt it was something like fate or destiny that I watched him in action and got away.''

"So that you could eventually stop him?"

"No. You never really stop a man like Santos. He's an organization, a power," Michael said, then sighed. "I think I saw what I did, to save my dad's life."

Linda shook her head. "You lost me again."

In the distance a car horn destroyed their peace. Michael rolled to his feet and held out his hand to help Linda stand. "It's like this," he said, and pulled her to her feet. "My dad's a mystery freak. He reads them day and night. And because of that, he's suspicious of everybody, everything. So, six months after Pete and Maria died, three of their stores were leveled to make way for a highway. Even if I hadn't seen John Santos dripping acid on Pete's hand, my dad would have known somebody killed him to get his properties. Because I was there, we knew who did it. We couldn't prove it and, as our attorney pointed out, the only thing I had was my word against theirs, but at least we knew. If I wouldn't have seen, my dad would have tracked Santos down from the names on the bill of sale, then he would have confronted him and Santos probably would have just shot him and dumped him in the river because he doesn't like loose ends."

With Michael leading the way, they started walking down a hill, taking slow, cautious steps so they wouldn't fall.

"Sometimes I wonder about Mr. Bingham," Linda quietly admitted. "Why he had to die. What he'd done or wouldn't do that got him killed. I can't picture him as a criminal, because he was my friend. Yet, I can't see him as an innocent, either. I've been around the block too many times to be so naive. There's a part of me that screams for an answer, because we won't really know if justice is justice unless we get the whole story."

"Murder is murder, Linda. Nobody deserves to be killed. Even if Bingham was Santos's right-hand man and he stole fifty million dollars from him, Santos still had no right to kill him."

"Honestly, Michael, I cannot imagine him doing business with the mob. And as for blackmail, I don't know what it would be."

She heard the crunch of feet smashing twigs two seconds before she heard a strange voice say, "My guess is that Santos lent the man money...."

Linda gasped and jumped. Michael dropped her hand and she dropped to the ground, huddling ineffectively against an anticipated round of bullets.

"Dad!"

She rolled to her back, almost hysterical with relief. Her heart was beating a thousand times a minute, and it felt as if it were going to explode right out of her chest, but she was safe. Again. Still, one of these days her luck was going to run out and she knew it.

Michael bounded across the ten feet that separated him from the intruder and hugged the old man he'd just called dad. Linda licked her lips, then blew her breath out in a long sigh. Nice guy or not, savior or not, that man had scared three years off her already-too-short life.

"Linda, come here! Come here!"

"I'm coming," she said, pushing herself off the damp ground. She brushed her rear before she walked over.

"Oh, shame on you, Michael. You didn't tell me she was so pretty."

"Linda, this is my dad, Matthew Rosen. Dad, this is Linda."

"She's a mite short, don't you think...."

"Will you stop," Michael said, good-naturedly slapping his father's back. Linda couldn't help but stare at them. From his thinning gray hair, his well-lined face, his slumped shoulders, Linda could tell Michael's dad was a good seventy years old, yet he acted like a school chum or brother to his son, who treated him the same.

"Did you bring my package?"

Matthew Rosen patted the breast pocket of his plaid shirt, a shirt that could have been Michael's were it larger. "Got it right here. What are you going to do with three thousand dollars anyway?"

"First, I'm going to buy my witness a new dress to testify in," Michael said, looping one arm around Linda's shoulders and one arm around his father's shoulders. He began to lead them down the hill again. "Then, I'm going to let her spend Sunday night at a nice hotel instead of a fleabag—"

"Mrs. Johnson doesn't run a fleabag," Linda protested, but Michael went on as if he didn't hear her.

"Then, I'm going to make sure I have enough cash on hand in case we have to make a quick getaway."

Both Matthew and Linda stopped and stared at Michael.

"I thought this was an in-the-bag case?"

Michael took a deep breath. "Dad, it's not. They never are. Remember Ramona Raymond?"

"All too vividly." Matthew's voice was sadly hushed.

"Well, I'm not going to let that happen to Linda."

"Michael," Linda began, kind of confused, kind of pleased, mostly scared . . . again.

None of it mattered, because Matthew touched Michael's arm and took his attention. "You're my only son, heir to my business. There were days I would have sold . . . but it's a legacy. . . ."

Michael stopped him by raising one finger, but he didn't say a word.

For several minutes Matthew Rosen merely studied his son, and Linda could tell they were communicating, perhaps by remembering past agreements, choices made when they were both clearheaded and calm. It would be like Michael to plan for a disaster, an emergency, and expect everyone to follow the plan to the letter when the time came. Even if it meant Matthew had to let his son disappear with a witness.

Linda looked at Matthew, realizing he was facing the loss of his son. His only son. The son for whom he'd built a business.

She reached for his hand. "I'll protect him," she said.

"She really will," Michael agreed. Laughing, he shook his head and started down the hill toward the car.

Linda turned to Matthew. "You don't have to worry. You're going to get him back in one big, grumpy, stubborn piece," she added, desperately trying to communicate to him that no matter what happened, she wouldn't let Michael make the ultimate sacrifice. She was in this alone and she wasn't taking anybody with her. Not even if they thought they wanted to go.

Matthew frowned at her as he studied her the same way he had been studying his son only a few seconds before, then when the meaning of her words began to sink in, he smiled weakly. Obviously he didn't realize Linda could be just as stubborn, just as crafty, as Michael.

"Trust me," she said, smiling cryptically. She couldn't assure him verbally, because Michael was still within hearing distance.

But he caught her meaning and he chuckled. "Oh, so the two of you have been having a good time then," he said, and started down the hill a few feet behind Michael, but he

turned around and held out his hand to help Linda negotiate the slope.

She took it. She'd taken his money, used his credit cards
and accepted his help, but she wasn't going to take his son.
He knew that now.

Chapter Ten

He knew she was happy when they got off Route 83 and took the sloping turn that brought them to Second Street. He didn't even have to look at her or hear her speak, because he was sensitive to her now, sensitive in a way he'd never been before. Not with anybody. Not Sam, not his dad, not anybody.

"Scared?"

She took a deep breath. "Petrified."

"I'll be right beside you," he said, and knew he'd comforted her. He knew what to say and how to say it, just as well as he knew she liked having her back kissed or that she preferred making love in the morning. Just as he knew she didn't want him to say anything more. But then again, he didn't need to.

The heels of her shoes made a sharp staccato sound on the floors of the federal courthouse, but rather than the sound annoying him as it usually did, Michael found that he rather liked it. He liked the way she looked in the sleek red suit. He loved the way she smelled...the way the bathroom in their suite smelled after she'd showered. Where other women had always been a nuisance to be borne, this one's feminine habits and hygiene had a strange seducing effect on him. And for a man with seven sisters, that was something of a miracle.

He pushed open one of the double doors to the court-room and, out of politeness, allowed Linda to precede him, then wished he hadn't. One-third of the audience for the trial belonged to the FBI. One-third was the unbarred press. And the last third was the Santos crowd. Twenty big, meaty guys who sized her up, decided how to elimi-nate her and saw themselves spending their reward, all in one sideways glance. Michael took Linda's elbow to steady her, but she quietly, calmly extricated herself.

He held back a smile. She was protecting him. It wasn't going to work, but it was still cute. That crowd on the left was going to take one look at them and realize a personal relationship had developed between the witness and her protector; and he'd warned Linda of the potential prob-lems that would cause. But she said she had to be here. Right here. Right in this room for the whole trial, because she wanted to know how Bob Bingham was connected to this pond scum. And he understood that. He wanted to know, too. And they both realized he'd always been in a certain amount of danger pursuing this crowd, a little more danger didn't really make that much difference, but he still thought it was sweet that she'd try to fool an unfoolable force to protect him. And he still wished he could have convinced her to relax in the judge's chambers and wait for her turn to testify, instead of exposing herself the way she was.

They took seats directly behind the prosecuting attorney and his ample staff. Four men dressed in navy blue suits filed in and sat beside them, two on Linda's left and two on Michael's right. Already in place, seated in the rows behind the one reserved for the witness and her body-guard, were twenty-six tall clean-shaven men who didn't move a muscle or utter a sound. The whole room was quiet, almost morguelike. Then they brought in John Santos, Sr., hands cuffed behind his back, and after one collective indrawn breath, everyone began to chatter.

"All rise for Judge Urwin Jones."

The room rustled with the noise of a hundred people standing, and then the proceedings began. In a technical, unemotional, rather boring speech, the prosecutor opened his case. The defense refused the opportunity for an opening statement; and the prosecutor took the floor again.

Though Linda sat on the edge of her seat, Michael paid little attention to the actual testimony designed to convict John Santos of murdering Bob Bingham. He looked around, instead, wondering why the defense waived their opening statement, wondering why they hadn't asked for a change of venue, and wondering if either one or both of those things meant Linda was in danger. He glanced at the senior Santos and frowned because the man was calm and quiet as a stone.

Fidgeting beside the defendant was his son, the mastermind behind every bullet Michael and Linda had dodged. Though constantly moving, Johnny wasn't nervous. He looked supremely satisfied. Happy. Bubbly. Bouncy. That was it, bouncy, like a kid on Christmas eve. Michael began to sweat. Santos was waiting for somebody or something. And for all anybody could guess about this bloodthirsty family, the whole room could be in danger.

He checked his rows of bodyguards against the number of Santos's men in the courtroom and decided even the Santos organization wasn't stupid enough to precipitate a shoot-out in a federal courtroom. Which meant they'd bribed a witness or kidnapped the mother, father, husband or child of someone on the prosecutor's staff. Slowly, carefully, he began to examine the emotions of every person seated at the table in front of him.

SIMON WATCHED John, Jr. shove his hands into his pockets and close his eyes. The strain of the responsibility of carrying his father's life in his hands was wearing on him, making him jittery, jumpy, foolish. Never—not even now with his life in jeopardy—did John, Sr. show any sign of emotion. John, Jr., however, was very different from his father and in some ways that was very, very good and in others it was very, very bad.

Simon didn't like the fact that John, Jr. hadn't told his father the plan. Security at the prison had been drum tight, but they had ways—there were always ways—to get the information behind the prison walls. But, John, Jr. wanted to keep the secret. He wanted it to appear as though all was lost, because he wanted the impact of that eleventh-hour save. And, strange as it sounded, John, Sr. sat calm as you please even though he was facing the death penalty, while John, Jr. squirmed in his seat although he knew his plan was foolproof. That in and of itself made Simon worry, but he held his thoughts back. This was John, Jr.'s show. He was putting it on for his father as a sort of ritualistic display of worth. When this was over, John, Jr. would have proven he could run the business; and, by the look of his color and the shallowness of his breath, John, Sr. would happily hand over control and then move to Bimini to recuperate from the ordeal of doing nothing while his fate rested in the hands of a son who hadn't been able to prove himself in the thirty or so years before this.

"It was obvious she'd been drinking," George Downing admitted, and for that, John, Jr. sat up and began to listen. Simon watched the younger man closely. It pleased John, Jr. greatly to see George run a finger under his collar. A display of nervousness such as that showed a reluctance to reveal the information and gave it more worth than it should have. John smiled. The corner of Simon's mouth kicked upward, too.

"Yet, you didn't cite her."

"Objection."

"Overruled. Counselor, I'm assuming this has a point."

"It does, Your Honor."

"Proceed."

"Why didn't you cite her?"

"She was scared silly," George said.

"Is that procedure?"

"It's discretion. I couldn't tell if she'd been drinking so much she was acting strange or if she was so scared she was acting drunk."

A titter of laughter ran through the room. The judge pounded his gavel.

"Would you care to explain?"

"Well, she wasn't really a threat. I'd only stopped her because . . . well, because she was driving slow. Not because she was driving weird. So, when I realized she'd been drinking, I didn't want her to drive. I suggested we take her home in the cruiser. She wouldn't hear of it, and before I could force the issue, she told me that her office was around the corner and she'd call someone. We followed. She pointed to a Lincoln and told us her boss was there and would take her home. I warned her we'd be back to check. When we made a circle around the building, we did see a light in one of the back offices, but by the time we got back to Front Street—to where we dropped Ms. Miller—she was running down the street."

"Are you sure you didn't decide to let her off scot-free once you realized she worked for Senator Bingham?"

"What?"

"Answer the question. Did you cut her a break because her boss was Senator Bingham?"

He thought a minute then smiled. "No. She never told us who her boss was. I remember after we caught her running away from the house, she mumbled something about Senator Bingham, but I was already running toward the building because she'd said 'murdered.' Anyway, I remember stepping into the only office that was lighted and seeing the senator in his chair and thinking, 'Shoot, that boss she kept referring to was Senator Bob Bingham, not just some average Joe.'"

"But she had been drinking?"

"Well, yes," George answered slowly, the quick reversal leaving him confused.

"And you testified before that when you caught her, she didn't realize who you were. In fact, she didn't even know you were a policeman. She thought you were one of the men who'd killed her boss, one of the men who were supposedly chasing her."

"Yes."

"Would you say then, that she'd have to have been a little drunker than you'd originally assumed?"

"I don't understand."

"You testified that you spoke with her for at least five minutes, yet she didn't know who you were when you caught her running down the street."

"She was scared."

"Oh, come on now, Officer Downing. She was scared of you when you stopped her for her driving. Then she was scared again when you found her on the street. That excuse is beginning to wear thin."

"Objection! Defense is badgering the witness."

"Sustained. Confine your questions to facts, not speculations, Mr. Taylor."

"Yes, Your Honor." Frank Taylor stuffed his hands into his trouser pockets. "Let's try another tack," he began, and Simon took a deep breath and glanced at his watch.

"You've testified that she was hysterical. You've testified that she could have been drinking. Yet, she positively identified one man who was in the room, and only one man, and you believed her."

George laughed. "That's because he was the one who stuck the knife in the senator's chest."

"So you say," Frank Taylor said, then walked to the defense table. "No further questions."

"SHE HAD A MIND like a steel trap." When Simon heard that, he tapped on Frank Taylor's shoulder. As he leaned forward in his seat, he could hear the uneven sound of John, Sr.'s breathing.

"I hated her," Molly Benson said with a laugh. "But I loved her, too, because I never had to remember anything. She had systems enough that she could remember her files and mine." Molly was fortyish, round and jolly. She'd already testified that she worked for Bingham and Bingham only because she desperately needed money, and she'd already testified that Linda Miller was one of those people who'd help you out, " . . . like when your kids were sick and you needed to leave early or if you had to spend two hours on the phone with the gas company because they'd overcharged you." Now she was confirming that Linda had a mind like a steel trap, which made Linda's license plate identification good.

"Call for a recess," Simon whispered. "Mr. Santos looks like he could use the rest."

Frank Taylor did as he was told, and the judge, after glancing at John Santos, agreed a fifteen-minute break seemed in order.

"Give Mr. Washington the signal, then go explain the situation to your father," Simon said to John, Jr. as the rest of the people in the room rose to their feet. "This is too much of a strain."

"No," John said, and Simon noticed that he was shaking uncontrollably. The real battle had begun. The crucial moves were about to be made. And the general was breaking down under fire. "The signal's not enough. I want to make sure Mr. Washington understands exactly what we want him to do."

"I'll come with you," Simon decided, not because he agreed but because he wasn't sure John, Jr. could walk the whole way to the hall without collapsing.

John took a deep breath. "Yes, I think you should." He walked to the center aisle and took another deep breath. "Simon, could I trouble you for a cigarette?"

Simon immediately reached into his coat pocket. "Everything's going to be fine," he said, but he really didn't mean it, just said it automatically. He was thinking quickly, concisely, going over everything in his mind because he felt personally responsible for the fact that John, Jr.'s plan was failing, and, albeit in the background, he'd have to pull the plan together before it fell apart completely. He wasn't sure how or where or when, but he'd have to do something.

"Mr. Washington," John, Jr. said, sighting his quarry. "Perhaps we should take a walk."

"No," Bill said, spinning to face John, Jr. He motioned toward the end of the hall, then pivoted away again. Simon and John, Jr. began walking toward the door, and when they got there they discovered it was the stairwell. Bill joined them three minutes later.

"My niece taught Amanda how to do a somersault today," John said, taking the last drag on his cigarette. He blew the smoke into the air. "She's adorable. If you fail in your efforts to eliminate Linda Miller today, I think perhaps I'll keep her. It's a simple, simple thing for me to get a fake birth certificate and even have it incorporated into the records.... Always wanted a little girl, and I adore this one."

"You..." Bill spat, grabbing John by the collar. Simon quickly, easily removed his hands.

"Just do your job, Mr. Washington," John said, dusting off his sleeve. "And I promise..." He looked directly at Bill Washington with a sincerity that couldn't be faked. "Amanda will be returned to you and her family. She'll be yours to love and kiss and cuddle. You'll go to her graduation...."

"I'll go to jail."

Simon motioned for John to precede him into the hall. As John stepped through the door, Simon turned to Bill Washington. "Not if there aren't any witnesses." He straightened Bill's collar. "Get rid of Rosen, then get rid of the girl. Actually, it should be very simple for a smart guy like you."

MOLLY BENSON TOOK the stand again. "Mrs. Benson, had you ever seen the defendant before?"

"Oh, yes!"

"You're positive."

"Absolutely."

"Will you please tell the court when it was you saw Mr. Santos."

"Well, it was April...April tenth. I remember because I had to stay late."

"You don't generally stay late?"

"Are you kidding? I never stay late."

"But you were at the office on April tenth. Why?"

"Polly Bingham, Mr. Bingham's niece, had a brief due at Commonwealth Court. She was waiting for new law...there was a case under consideration that would have an effect on her case, so she didn't do her brief until the court issued its decision. And if it wasn't for the fact that she buys my kids each a Christmas gift, I wouldn't have stayed, but she does that, so..." Molly trailed off and shrugged.

"Okay, so you stayed late April tenth and what happened?"

"I finished typing Polly's brief and she said she'd take care of distribution. She was going to hand-carry the thing."

"That night?"

"Oh, no!" Molly shook her head. "It was past nine. She was going to take it to the courthouse on her way to work the next day."

"So, she left you there, at the office. Why didn't she wait to make sure you got to your car safely?"

"Well, she was meeting a friend for a drink and I shooed her out the door."

"Then what happened?"

"I nearly had a heart attack because that old house is scary at night. It's dark and creaky."

"But you said Mr. Bingham and the defendant were in the house with you."

"I didn't know that. I was upstairs, with the word processing equipment."

"And that's why you didn't know you had company."

"Right."

"And that's why they didn't know they had company, either?"

"Yes."

"Okay, so you thought you were alone in the house. How did you find out you weren't?"

"Well, because I was scared, I went barreling down the steps, taking two at a time. When I got to the bottom, I saw the spill of light in the hall and I stopped dead in my tracks because I knew I had to go back down that whole darn hall to turn it off. On my way back I heard Mr. Bingham yelping that it wasn't his fault the mother had a miscarriage, and then I heard the other voice say that wasn't his problem, either."

"What do you think they were talking about?"

"Objection!" Frank Taylor bellowed, bouncing out of his seat. "Calls for speculation on the part of the witness."

"Your Honor, we can let the witness paraphrase the conversation she overheard or she can repeat it verbatim," the prosecutor said, spreading his hands in appeal. "Your choice."

"Let her repeat it verbatim."

"Molly, you heard the man," Jim Reynolds said, this time tossing his hands in defeat.

Molly complied, and for the next few minutes she recounted the shouting match between John Santos and Bob Bingham.

"So, what you're saying then is that Bob Bingham had promised John Santos a baby?"

"Oh, yeah. No doubt about it."

"To sell?"

"Objection . . ."

"Sustained. Counselor," the Judge cautioned.

"Your Honor, I'm trying . . ."

"I don't know what it was for," Molly stated, ignoring everyone. "All I know is John Santos had a home for this baby, but there was no baby and he was mad."

Linda tugged on Michael's arm. "They're talking about me," she said, looking at him with round, frightened blue eyes.

"What?"

"The day... April tenth, one week after my miscarriage. The senator had found a home for my baby. I hadn't signed anything, but he felt... I know he did it because I was so scared about getting divorced and having a baby.... He was selling my baby!

"Oh, my God," she said, and pulled her hands through her hair. "He was going to sell my baby to someone in the mob."

"You don't know that," Michael said, even though they both did. He wanted to put his arms around her and comfort her, but he couldn't, and he felt useless, impotent, stupid. "Just calm down, okay?" he whispered hopefully.

"I can't. I just can't. I can't think. I can't sit here anymore."

She started shaking, and Michael leaned forward to tap the prosecutor and request another recess, this one only long enough to ensconce Linda in the judge's chambers, but as Michael moved forward he caught sight of John Santos, Sr. looking back at Linda. His breathing was very heavy and his eyes had narrowed into little beads. He'd known all along that Linda was the mother who'd miscarried his merchandise, and he was defying her with his eyes. Daring her to make the trial a circus.

Linda didn't disappoint him. She leaped from her seat and started up the aisle. "You were going to sell my baby!"

Four men caught her and restrained her from lunging for Santos's neck. He seemed surprised that she'd put actions to her words and, somewhat stunned, he rose, along with his counsel and several assistants and the entire row behind them.

"You monster!" Linda screamed, kicking and clawing. Michael reached her just in time to catch a heel in his knee.

Santos began to back away, but he only took two steps before he clutched his chest. "John, Simon," he gasped, grabbing the table with his gnarled fingers. He fell to the chair. "She killed me. I knew she'd kill me." With that, he dropped to the floor, looking like a big stuffed doll with lead in its knees. Gasping, people crowded around him, and amid the noise and confusion a call went out for a doctor. Then an ambulance.

Wide-eyed, Linda quieted in her captors' arms.

"Let's go," Michael commanded, freeing Linda and grabbing her arm. He wasn't waiting around to see how this turned out. All guns and knives should have been spotted by the metal detectors outside the courtroom doors, but Michael wasn't taking any chances. Not with this crowd. "We're gonna make a run for it."

"Tom and I'll go with you," a deep voice said quietly behind Michael.

Michael nodded, and the two volunteering agents raced from the courtroom and toward the elevators with Linda and Michael on their heels.

Frantic, Bill caught them in the hall before they reached their destination.

"There's no time to wait for an elevator," he said. "Let's use the stairs."

Chapter Eleven

At the stairwell, Bill turned to the two FBI agents who'd escorted them from the courtroom. "You two go down on the elevator. Make sure there's no one waiting for us on the first floor."

Michael's only thought was appreciation for the old man's foresight, then he felt the barrel of a gun being shoved into his back.

"Just stop where you are."

They were on the five-by-five square landing and just about to begin their descent. The scream of an ambulance siren pierced the air, and chaotic noise literally poured from the courtroom. There was a crowd not more than twenty feet away, yet he and Linda might as well have been in the desert. Santos's men were guarding Santos. The FBI was guarding Santos's men. The press wasn't about to miss a minute of it. And Bill held a gun to his back.

"Put the gun away, Bill." That was automatic. The first thing that popped into his head. And the stupidest thing he'd said in years.

Bill looked sad, apologetic. "They've got my grand-daughter." He turned to Linda. "I'm really sorry."

Linda clutched Michael's arm, and he could tell she was trying to think of something to say, if only to stall for time, but she was stunned. Betrayal came in every size, shape and form when you were dealing with the mob. One right after another, she was discovering her friends were actually enemies.

"You're really sorry?" she said, just staring at him in a kind of stupefied disbelief. "What a laugh! Don't you dare say that. Don't you dare even try to get me—"

The instant Bill's attention was diverted, Michael drove his elbow deep into Bill's solar plexus, collapsing him in a heap. His gun flew until it hit a concrete wall, discharging on impact, and Michael fell to the floor, dragging Linda with him. Bill charged at them like a crazed animal.

"Damn," Michael grunted, rolling out of the way. He grabbed Linda and boosted her up. "Go!" he commanded. "Run!"

She didn't waste a second and neither did Bill. As she scrambled down the steps, Bill lunged after her. He caught her jacket and she instinctively shrugged out of it. He roared again, sounding like a pained animal, and Michael rolled to his feet, catapulting himself at Bill as Bill clawed for Linda's clothes, causing her to lose her balance and fall, thumping down the next three steps.

Michael came to life then in a way he never had before. In that second, he understood everything about love, about true selflessness, as both he and Bill Washington battled for the same purpose. To protect their own.

Bill, a grandfather, lunged for Linda because that was the only way he could save his granddaughter. Blind with emotion, Michael growled low in his throat as he charged his opponent from behind. They scuffled, still hearing the clatter of the gun as it preceded them down the stairs. Bill managed to get his footing again, but Michael was operating on instinct and adrenaline. Breathing like a wild creature, he leaped from his crouched position on the landing. He got a good hold on Bill's throat, but Bill struggled out of his grip and tossed Michael against a wall, then charged toward him. Instinctively Michael kicked high and hard, issuing an energy-producing yell that reverberated through the stairwell. His foot made contact with Bill's chest and sent the older man flying backward. He bent over the banister, screaming as his spine seemed to arch to its limit. Arms flailing, he struggled fruitlessly for balance, then, almost in slow motion, he gave in to the force of gravity, and, headfirst, he disappeared. Then Michael heard Linda scream.

He took a deep breath and scrambled down the steps. The soles of his shoes could have been made of cement such was the noise he made in the echoing chamber. When he reached Linda, she was huddled against the wall, her blue eyes round and wild. Every breath she drew shivered through her whole body. He didn't say a word, just picked her up and continued running down the steps. As they approached the first floor, Michael spotted Bill's body in front of the door. He took another breath and swallowed hard.

"Close your eyes, okay?"

Biting her lip, Linda nodded. She looped her arms around his neck and closed her eyes as she nestled into his chest. At the bottom of the steps, Michael had to kick Bill's body out of the way to open the door. As though sensing what was happening, her arms tightened around his neck and she began to cry, at first very softly, then harder and harder until the sound of her sobbing echoed around him, around them, and followed them into the lobby.

There were people waiting to help them. He ignored them and strode to the glass doors. Using his hip, he pushed open the door, then jogged down the steps. He didn't stop running until he reached his car.

They drove to the hotel in a silence punctuated only by the soft sounds of Linda's sobs. Michael pulled the car into the parking lot, turned off the engine and tossed his head back with a heavy sigh. He knew exactly what she was thinking, and there was nothing he could say to comfort her.

He opened his car door and slid out, rounding the hood to get to Linda's door. She sat quietly, her hands folded on her lap, her shuddering sobs the only indication that she was alive. Even after Michael sprang her door, she didn't move. Michael didn't say a word. He just reached in, sliding one arm around her shoulders and one arm under her thighs to lift her out. He closed the car door with his foot and carried her to their room.

She clung to his neck while he fumbled with the key. When they were inside, he slid her to the floor and held her face in his big hands. "I know this sounds really inept, but I'm sorry."

She rose to her tiptoes, sliding her arms around his neck. "Oh, Michael, I'm so scared. There's absolutely no one on my side."

"There's me," he reminded in a hopeful whisper.

She pulled away from him, her arms slipping from his neck and down his chest. When she smiled, she put faith and hope into the dictionary again. "I know."

She lifted her face for a kiss, and he took it. What he felt, how he felt, had been changed drastically over the course of the morning. They'd both narrowly escaped death, and he fought to save them, to save her, not because it was his job, but because the thought of life without her was unthinkable.

The kiss grew, deepened. Outside, the world went on as though nothing unusual had happened that day. The sound of a truck's air brakes mingled into the confusion of a group of happy conventioneers as they waited for the parking lot attendant to bring their car to the hotel entrance. Down the hall a door closed.

Michael skimmed his fingers along the satin smoothness of her cheek. Her soft tears dampened his fingertips, and he took them with him as he outlined the curve of her jaw, let his fingers trail the column of her throat and trace the contour of her collarbone. She was the smallest, softest, sweetest woman in the world, and it didn't seem fair that she'd be persecuted so ruthlessly. His hands gripped her shoulders and then skimmed her biceps, and he felt himself falling victim to the magic again. Only this time there was no regret. This time there was no macho disgust at being under the control of a small, soft, silent creature who rendered him helpless with a sigh. He finally realized she needed him, perhaps not physically, but definitely emotionally. And for Michael, making love found its definition.

He slipped his hands to the collar of her blouse and easily undid the bow. The top two buttons fell out of confinement, and he skimmed his fingers along her smooth, warm skin. She pulled her mouth away from his.

"I should get a bath, maybe take a nap."

"Uh-uh. You should just relax and let me make love to you." He took her elbows and pulled her up to his height again so he could nibble her lips.

"I don't really feel like making love...."

"Uh-uh," he said again, smiling against her lips. "You don't have to feel like anything. You don't have to do anything...except relax." He kissed her again, feeling for the first time not the physical presence of one mouth against another, but rather the trust and vulnerability involved in a simple kiss. He'd had women before...he'd had this woman before...but he'd never had her trust, he'd merely satisfied her need. Now, as morning turned into afternoon, he experienced the pure pleasure of sex becoming love.

He undid her blouse, his hands big and awkward, his fingers thick and masculine against the tiny pearl buttons. When her chest was bare, he traced a blue vein, realizing what he'd once thought to be a mere colored line was actually the vessel of her life's blood. It was marvelous, a miracle.

He looked up from his task and found her watching him curiously, her head tilted to the right and her brow furrowed. Holding her gaze, he drew the blouse from her skirt, then rolled it from her shoulders and let it fall to the floor. She wore a full slip, the kind with soft, feminine lace that sat against her bosom and tempted a man beyond his reason. But in her eyes he could see the question, the doubt. *Do you really love me?*

Still keeping eye contact, he ran his fingers under the warm lace to caress the flesh that warmed it. He didn't stop or pause. In one fluid movement, he skimmed one breast and dipped into the crevice, then traced her second melon-sweet mound. He reached the thin silk ribbon strap that bound back to bodice just as she closed her eyes, soaking in the warmth of his touch, then he raised his second hand and slowly, sensuously, slid the straps from her shoulders, gliding his fingers across her bare skin, following the thin ribbons as they fell over her arms.

He watched as they tumbled lower and the lacy bodice fell in lazy folds, stopped only by the swell of her hips. For a while, maybe a minute, maybe three, he stared at her, lost in a twilight zone of human experience. He felt as though

he were seeing her for the first time, even though he wasn't.
But there were things, feelings, flashes of fantasy from
youth where you try to imagine what love's going to be like
and come up with a version of perfection you never
achieve. He was finding it, feeling it, living it.

The zipper of her red skirt was at the base of her back,
and he reached for it, undid it and let the garment drift
away. Her slip slithered after it. Without a thought, he slid
his hands under the elastic of her panty hose and drew
them down. When they reached her feet, she lifted one,
then the other and her panty hose were gone, too. As he
straightened from the floor, she met his eyes. She hooked
her thumbs under the band of her white bikinis and slowly,
gracefully, slid them off, then stepped out of them.

She was beautiful. No matter what, no matter where or
why or how, she was beautiful. He took one step and she
matched it. His hands dropped to her shoulders, and he
feathered his lips across hers as the blood pumped through
his veins and a litany of praises danced through his head.
Even as he kissed her, touched her face, breathed her scent,
she began to undress him. He felt the warmth of her hands
lingering, caressing while they did their jobs. And their
warmth, their softness, their fragile femininity drove him
over the edge of reason, made him hungrier than he'd ever
been before.

Thoughts of love and tenderness escaped him as the demons of need begged him to ravage, to take what he
wanted quickly, greedily, but she lulled him with soft
stroking and quiet words that drew him to the bed, and he
fell with her to the pillows, feeling as though he were
floating. When they kissed, it was slowly, sweetly, as if
they had all the time in the world. Her fingers danced over
his belly. He touched and pressed, lost in her softness, the
essence of her sensuality, of her femininity. Lost in the

thought that as he made love to her, she made love to him. Lost to need. Lost to greed. Lost to the beauty of the total vulnerability that was love.

IN THE TWILIGHT, with her hair sun dried and her nose sunburned, she looked like a child. It could have been because she was short and petite. It could have been because her hair was feathery, baby fine. It could have been because she was building a sand castle, looking as if she didn't have a care in the world.

Or it could have been because she was vulnerable, and Michael knew it. He'd sensed it, seen it, lived it. Yet since the day of the trial, she hadn't talked about it. They made love, but it wasn't the same as that one experience, that twenty minutes frozen in the annals of Michael's mind where two people really did become one.

They'd run again. This time to the Rosen family's summer retreat off the coast of South Carolina. He hadn't left word with anyone. He'd just taken her away, because she needed the rest. He hadn't thought beyond that. Not even to consider that John Santos very definitely knew of this island, just as Michael knew the Santos family summered in Vermont.

But today he was thinking of all those things. He'd acted instinctively, animalistically, maybe even ritualistically. He was, for all practical intents and purposes, protecting his mate. And that's why his brain was clicking again. Two weeks was a long, long time to stay in any one place. Maybe not to a normal person, but to a person on the run it's an eternity. So, it was time to move again. To take her somewhere else. To protect her. It was very cut-and-dry, very simple, because she was his—not just his responsibility, his, period—and he never thought any further than that.

Michael leaned back on his elbows, watching her through narrowed eyes. She played in the sand on the very edge of the water, which occasionally lapped up over her feet or her thighs, depending on how she was sitting. Even in the twilight he could see the strips of white skin exposed when she reached or stretched out of her bikini bottoms. He was amazed at how dark her skin got in only two weeks. Then he remembered that she was outside every day, all day long. She swam, boated, played in the sand so that every hour of every day was full, busy, happy. And she didn't mind if he sat in this little cove with its shading of small trees and foliage around him. Just as long as he didn't demand that she stop her playtime, and as long as she could see him, then Michael didn't have to be with her.

He understood her fear. Understood why she was bottling everything up inside. Denying it was one way of dealing with it. But it wasn't the one that would keep her alive. He'd have to keep her alive.

The branches above his head rustled, and Michael leaned his head back in a reflexive action. The bush was still, almost lifeless. Deciding he was getting edgy from sitting alone, he hoisted himself from his sandy bed and jogged to Linda.

"Can I help?"

She looked up and smiled. "I was just about to kick it down."

He grinned. "I'm very good at that. Just ask my sisters."

"Well, you see, that's just the point here," she said, standing and dusting off her hands. "A person doesn't mind a little help building, but when it comes to the kicking, they want that pleasure themselves."

He crossed his arms on his chest. "Suit yourself."

"Oh, now don't pout."

"I'm not pouting," he said, then sighed with disgust. "You're teasing me, right?"

"Yeah," she admitted with a grimace. "I can't help it sometimes, you know? You're such a straitlaced, serious..." She let her sentence trail away and gave her sand house one good kick. "There," she said, then skipped around the uneven mounds of sand so she could take his arm. "What's on the menu for tonight?"

"I was thinking about a restaurant."

She pretended to consider that. "They have menus."

He looped an arm around her neck. "Yes, they do. Very good menus. In fact, I think restaurants invented menus." When he reached his little cove, he fell to the sand and dragged her with him. "But first, we talk."

She gave him a blank look. "Talk?"

"You know, you and me and words passing between us. You're upset, I know, but—"

"I'm not upset." She flung her arms wide. "Who could be upset here?"

"You're avoiding—"

"Nothing. I'm avoiding nothing. I've just become a realist. For me it's one day at a time and I know that now." When she took a deep breath, Michael knew she was getting angry. "For all practical intents and purposes, I have learned to play the game...just like you always told me I should."

She jumped up and would have run away, but he grabbed her bikini bottom and hauled her to the ground again. When she was stable, he drew her into his arms. "It sounds suspiciously like you're blaming me for your troubles again."

She took a deep breath. "I'm trying really hard not to, but it's sort of impossible to separate you and trouble." She pulled out of his embrace. "There are times when I see you as two people. One's a pushy, bossy guy who needs a favor and the other's my lover.''

He gripped her shoulders. "I understand that."

She blinked up at him. "Do you?"

"I'd have to be pretty stupid not to. And though I've had my thick moments, I'm not totally..."

"Without your good points," she said, then bounced up and gave him a smacking kiss. "You have lots and lots and lots of good points," she said, tracing her hands down his sides, tickling him. The combination of her pecklike kisses and tickling tumbled him backward, and she happily sprawled atop him. "And then there's other good points," she said, skimming her hand along the elastic of his swimming trunks. Her fingers lingered in the thick growth of hair on his lower belly, then skimmed and tickled until she found him.

"I think I'm being propositioned," he said, and punctuated that thought with a lusty kiss that elicited a sigh of pleasure from her. Mingled with the sound of her sigh was the rustle of the bush, and Michael instantly tensed, grabbing her shoulders and rolling her off his chest.

"What—"

He pressed his finger over her lips and made a low "Shh" sound, then somebody coughed, and both Linda and Michael looked above them.

"Sorry."

"Good Lord, O'Malley! Are you trying to scare the last thirty-five years off my life?"

The tall, muscular man dressed in wild, flowered shorts and a sleeveless T-shirt descended the sandy incline with his arms extended as if he were surfing, not walking. "What the heck are you talking about?" O'Malley countered, laughing. "I thought I was about to be treated to a scene from *Lady Chatterley's Lover*. I thought a rustle and a discreet cough were definitely in order. I take it this is our endangered species," he added, pointing at Linda.

"No," Michael said, sighing with disgust at the phraseology. "This is our witness."

"Don't need a witness anymore," O'Malley said, and pointed up the small hill. "Let's go see Bunker."

Michael offered his hand to Linda to help her stand. She took it and gave him one of those confused big-blue-eyed looks of hers. Were it not for the fact that he was trying to protect her, he could have given the same look back. Instead, he asked as calmly as he could, "Bunker?"

"Yeah, let's go, okay?"

Again O'Malley pointed up the hill, and Michael got the same feeling he imagined men felt when they were walking the last corridor to the electric chair. Linda dusted the sand from her bikini briefs and took a deep breath. Michael took her hand. She gave him a curious look and he gave her a reassuring smile, squeezing her hand for good measure. But she shook her head, glanced pointedly at his hand holding hers and raised an eyebrow. Michael smiled wryly. After the episode in the cove, a little hand-holding wasn't out of line.

They reached the house, and O'Malley waited while Michael opened the sliding glass door and allowed Linda to precede him. Once Linda was inside, O'Malley motioned Michael in, then slid the door closed. Michael and Linda exchanged a look, and this time Michael didn't bother to hide his concern. Something was terribly wrong.

"Helped myself to a drink. Hope you don't mind."

Linda gasped and spun around. Michael stayed quiet for a minute as he studied Fred Bunker, a quiet, subdued little man of about fifty who liked cigars and a glass of good Scotch. He couldn't picture the balding chief without either one in his hand. "No, I don't mind."

"You missed the party," he said, and ambled into the room, down the three steps that took him from the dining room into the comfortably furnished sitting room. Linda seemed to shrink away from him, taking refuge on a tall-backed wicker chair with a fat rose-colored cushion and several matching throw pillows. She took one of the pillows in her arms and hugged it, staring at the little man over its edge.

"The senior Santos had a heart attack and died." Bunker smiled slowly and plopped to a seat on the plump-cushioned couch. "I'd say that's justice at its finest."

It seemed to take a minute for Linda to digest this, but once she had, she was on her feet. "I'm free?"

Michael spun on her, ready to respond. Bunker beat him to it. "Not quite."

"What do you mean, not quite? This isn't a sixty-forty proposition here," she said, angry, though Michael wasn't quite sure why. "We're talking about my life. The way it looks to me, I either get to go back to my life, my apartment, my friends . . . or I don't! Which is it?"

"You're never out of it," Michael said, grabbing her arm because it looked as if she were going to take all sixty-four of her inches and challenge the man across the room. "I told you before, Linda, you're in for life."

"That you are," Bunker chortled, then relit his haggard cigar. "But you got some real problems. As I started to say, Rosen, you and your little friend here missed the party. Not only did the senior Santos meet his maker, but Johnny, Jr. flipped out for everybody. It was a show and a half."

Michael rolled his eyes. "I'll bet."

"I wouldn't take this so lightly if I were you," Bunker said, turning serious suddenly. He scratched his index finger across the tip of his nose, stalling, it seemed. "And we do have a problem. We can't just drop her into the middle of Idaho and hope for the best, like we'd planned. The way I see this, we're going to have to do a little plastic surgery." He pulled his lower lip between his teeth and studied Linda. "I think we could change her looks and..." He stopped to study her again. "And because she's so young, we could get away with losing her in the school system."

Linda pivoted to face Michael. "What is he talking about?"

"You knew all along you couldn't go back to your old life. You knew we'd have to hide you eventually. What they're proposing is that we change your looks with plastic surgery. Then we give you a new identity and send you to college."

"You spend a semester or two at, say, oh, Omaha University or some such out-of-the-way place, then we change your name and transfer you to another college. I think in your case we'd have to do that about six times. Six colleges, six names, same major."

"I don't..." Linda interrupted, but she stopped, obviously thinking. "Does that work?" she asked, steeped in a kind of confusion.

Bunker smiled. "You bet. You're young enough that we could really put you into that system and nobody'd find you. Your name might change, we might dye your hair and give you different-colored contacts, but your transcripts would follow you, so you'd end up with an education to boot. By the time you had all your credits, Santos would have forgotten you... or lost your trail."

Confusion gave way to pleasant surprise right before Michael's eyes. He watched her lips go from a frown to a smile and her big-eyed fear turn into a happy sparkle. "That's good. That's really good!"

"And it works," Bunker stated.

"Sometimes."

Bunker gave Michael a disgusted look. Linda frowned again.

"Come on, Bunker," Michael said, pacing to the sliding glass door. "You're making it sound easy."

"It's better than being shot at," Bunker said.

"Yeah," Linda agreed, staring at Michael now as if he were the crazy one.

"There are loopholes in this," Michael said, spinning to face both of them. "Number one, you're going to have to start over again, not once or twice, but six times."

"It's still better than being shot at."

"Or hunted . . ."

"Yeah, or hunted," Linda said, still staring at Michael.

"Okay, not only do you move around, but consider what happens when you move around. You leave your possessions behind . . . and your new friends. You can't give your new friends your next new name or your new address, you just lose them and they lose you. Period. Finis. If you keep contact with even one person along the way, you jeopardize the whole thing."

"I can handle that."

"She can handle that."

"What about different school administrations, different school customs, different textbooks?"

"Michael, you're making mountains out of a bunch of molehills."

"Yeah, Rosen," Bunker interjected. "Listen to yourself. You're telling her about the problems she's gonna be having adjusting to different textbooks, I'm saving her from bullets, bombs, banana-brains." His eyes narrowed as he stared at Michael. "You have a better plan, don't you?"

Slowly, taking a deep breath, Michael turned to the sliding glass door again. O'Malley was standing in the sand, trying to look natural and looking as out of place as an igloo. "I think," Michael said quietly, "we should kill her."

Mouth and eyes wide open, Linda spun to face him. "What?"

Bunker was cool as a cucumber. "It'll never work." He walked to the glass coffee table and used a coaster as an ashtray. "Come on, Rosen, do you think the mob will really believe she's been killed? Conveniently, just after John Santos, Jr. has vowed to follow her to the ends of the earth and snuff her little light out, she dies in an auto accident and the mob's gonna buy it? You're nuts."

"We could make it look like the mob did it."

Bunker chuckled. "Oh, that's great. What should we do, sign the left fender of the car, 'This car destroyed by John Santos, Jr.'...and he'll buy it...Rosen...." He stopped and sighed, then ran a hand over his mouth. "I know what you want. I know what you're trying to do. If we could make her death believable, then she'd be safe. It'd be over for her, for us...for the taxpayers. But think, we can't kill her now. It's too convenient, coincidental, and Santos won't buy it. He won't stop looking for her. And we won't have accomplished anything except wasting money."

"Okay, then we'll wait awhile. We'll ship her to school for a few weeks then run her car over an embankment."

Bunker sighed again. "Unless we do it before we hide her, it won't have the same effect. Think, Rosen. Once we drop her into the system, we won't be killing Linda Miller anymore, we'll be killing Jane Jones who may or may not be Linda Miller, and Santos won't buy that, either. And if we don't do something now, either hide her or kill her, they're going to find her."

Michael tapped his fingers on the cool glass. "The trick to the death scenario is to make it believable."

Bunker sighed with disgust. "I know that. I'm the master, remember? There isn't a variation to that theme I don't know. Trust me, Rosen, there's no way we can make it believable this time. If there was, I would have thought of it."

For the first time in ten minutes, Michael smiled and turned away from watching O'Malley. "Not necessarily."

Bunker sighed again and plopped to his spot on the couch. "Okay, Mr. Cocky, you've obviously thought of the way out of the no-win situation. So, stop gloating and tell us. What is this wonderful plan of yours that will make John Santos believe beyond a shadow of a doubt that Linda Miller really is dead."

"I'm going to die with her."

For a full minute silence reigned, then Bunker bounded from the couch. "No! Absolutely no!" Before anyone drew a second breath, he was across the room and facing Michael. A short bald man versus a very tall, very persistent one. "Have you thought about the repercussions to this? Just being in the same car with her," Bunker said, pointing at Linda with his vile little cigar, "puts you in the line of duty. Your family can file for worker's compensation, life insurance, wrongful death. There'll be lawsuits out the kazoo, and insurance companies all over the country will be checking this out."

"You could take care of that," Michael reminded coolly. "But if you don't kill her and you can't hide her, the American public pays six, eight, even ten times the insurance company debt in plastic surgery alone."

Bunker growled, "You're making me mad," and stormed away.

Michael crossed his arms on his chest. "It makes sense. That's why you're mad."

"It makes sense," Bunker agreed, though he didn't want to. "But I'd have to get clearance—"

"Wait a minute...." Linda came to life, slowly rising from the wicker chair, looking confused and slightly angry. "It's my future we're discussing, right?"

"Yeah," Bunker said, blowing smoke toward the ceiling.

"Well, then, do I get a choice?"

Bunker looked at Michael. Michael looked at Linda. Linda wet her lips. "Do I get a choice?"

"Yeah," Bunker said, once again using the coaster for an ashtray. "You get a choice—something of a choice anyway. For instance, if you can't stand bugs, we won't force you to live in Florida. Or if you can't stand cold, we won't force you to live in Alaska."

Linda wet her lips again. "Then I want to go alone."

Michael spun to face her. "But we can't do the death scenario if you go alone! Nobody'll believe it unless an innocent bystander dies, too."

"Well, I'm not going to let an innocent bystander get involved."

"You have to!"

"I don't! I don't have to do anything!" Linda shouted right back at him. "If I really wanted to—and sometimes I do—I could walk out that door, and you wouldn't find me and neither would Santos."

"I think we played this out in Nebraska," Michael reminded coolly, "and it didn't work."

"It didn't work because I wasn't ready. If I were ready—"

"Ah, Ms. Miller," Bunker interrupted quietly. He was a professional now. Coolheaded and calm while those around him were losing their heads. "This is my job and the country's obligation. I can do—no, I will do whatever you want. In fact, I'll leave now and give you some time to think about this. But I want to know for sure in twenty-four hours." He picked up his hat and turned to go.

"I don't need twenty-four hours," Linda began, but Michael stopped her by shaking his head. She obeyed reluctantly.

"Don't forget O'Malley," Michael said, motioning to the door with his head.

Bunker chuckled. "I'd like to forget O'Malley." He walked to the sliding glass door. "I'll be back tomorrow night about eight. Okay?"

Linda nodded. Michael said, "Fine."

The sliding glass door rumbled closed, and Michael gripped Linda's shoulders. She wouldn't look at him. "I know you're confused," he said, tilting her chin until she was forced to look at him. "And I figured out why," he added in a whisper.

"No," she said, pleading with her eyes. "I think you're the one who's confused."

"Linda, listen to me," he said, sliding his hands down her arms. "I want to do this for you. . . ."

She shook her head viciously. "Don't! You don't know what you're saying. You can't give up everything for me. Your family, the family business, your job . . . your house . . . your father. It's more than you think."

"Listen to me! I love you! I'm trying to tell you that my life won't be the same without you." She looked away and he shook her lightly. "What am I going to do without you? This isn't a question of what to do with you anymore. It's a question of what I'll do with me, too." He softened his voice again until it was a strained whisper. "I can't live without you."

With a show of force that surprised Michael, she pushed out of his arms. She turned away from him and then pivoted around again, her lower lip between her teeth. It took a minute before she said, "I can't live with you."

That statement sank in by degrees. Finally he said, "What?"

"I can't live with you." She moved to the couch and blew her breath out in a big gust. "I can't say that I love you, and if I don't love you—" She spread her hands helplessly.

"You do love me, you just don't realize it yet," Michael said, walking behind her and sliding his hands around her waist. "You need time."

"We don't have time," Linda reminded, once again moving out of his reach. "I don't love you," she said, and sighed deeply. "I'm not sure I can love you—"

He grabbed her arm and spun her around. "How can you say that? How can you stand there and tell me you don't love me! We've eaten, drunk, slept together... made love. You're the first woman I've ever made love to—" Stupefied, he dropped his hands.

She turned away again, swallowed, took a deep breath, then faced him again. "It wasn't the same for me."

The room got so quiet, the roll of a penny on the floor would have sounded like thunder. For a full thirty seconds they just stared at each other, then Michael quietly said, "Well, that certainly puts me in my place, doesn't it?"

"Michael, I . . ."

"No, don't," he said, waving his hand to stop her. "The last thing I want right now is pity or platitudes. I made a mistake, that's all. I thought you loved me and you'd want me—'' He cleared his throat. ''Never mind.'' He walked to the long bar, looked at the open bottle of Scotch, then shook his head. ''I'm going out.''

Linda whispered, ''Okay.'' And when the door closed behind him, she sank to the couch, shaking. Giant sobs came from her belly, and she let them out as she beat on a fat pillow.

''That wasn't just noble, Ms. Miller,'' Bunker said, entering through the sliding glass door again. ''That was the right thing to do.'' He puffed his cigar twice. ''Grab your stuff. I don't think you should see him again.''

Chapter Twelve

"Three surgeries in a year. Amazing."

"And six universities and six different names," Simon added, pacing to the window behind John, Jr.'s desk. Instead of adjusting to his father's death and ultimately basking in the glory of his new position of authority, John, Jr. got more and more determined to find Linda Miller. And the more determined he got, the more bizarre his techniques.

"I can certainly see why it took us so long to find her."

Simon merely smiled. He'd known Linda Miller's whereabouts every day of the past year, he'd just kept that information to himself. But at this point, Simon considered Linda Miller's life a small price to pay to keep John, Jr. from becoming a carbon copy of his demented father.

John, Jr. flipped through the pages and glanced up again as Simon took the seat in front of his desk. "All these surgeries were done in California. Expensive."

Simon shrugged.

"And don't you think the government's been unusually honorable?"

This time Simon frowned. "I don't understand."

John, Jr. leaned back in his chair. "I find it odd that they're so persistent. In most cases they change a witness's identity, dump them in some forsaken corner of the world and then forget them." He leaned forward and tapped the manila folder once. "Read this, Simon. They're virtually baby-sitting this kid."

"You haven't exactly been discreet in your efforts to find her. They probably felt they had to be thorough and cautious."

"Poppycock," John said, and rose from his seat. "It's Rosen. I'd bet my bottom dollar it's Rosen."

"That could be why he hasn't left the service yet."

John turned toward the window. "That has to be it." He faced Simon again. "Although his story of not wanting to work with his sisters is a very convincing one."

Simon chuckled knowingly. He'd dated Michael's sister, Caro, for two months. The purpose of the escapade was to gather information about her brother, but the end result was that Simon vowed he'd never marry. Caro was tiny and beautiful and ran the Rosen Corporation like General MacArthur ran the army. He didn't blame Michael Rosen one damned bit for not wanting to go home. Caro wasn't the type to share command, and Michael Rosen wasn't the type to take orders.

"Maybe it's a combination of things," Simon said after his moment of thought. "You know how I feel about Caro Rosen. And you know that I don't think Michael Rosen's lying when he says just the thought of working with his sister gives him hives. But that's what makes this cover so beautiful. He's creating a lie around the truth."

"And so because neither you nor I would work for Caro Rosen, we can honestly believe Michael Rosen wouldn't, either?"

"Precisely. And in the meantime, Rosen monitors his witness as she travels around the country." Simon paused, then speculated, "In fact, it's possible that he's bankrolling some of this."

Hands shoved into the pockets of his charcoal-gray slacks, John, Jr. arched his brows and whistled. "That makes wonderful sense. At least it makes much better sense than believing the government suddenly got a conscience." He walked from the window to his desk, then turned and walked to the bookcase. "You know what, Simon?" he asked, his voice deceptively calm, considering the unholy gleam in his eyes and the thin line of his mouth. "I'm sick of that man. When push comes to shove, that's the guilty party. That's the one who killed my father. Not Linda Miller. If Rosen hadn't been so good at keeping her alive, my father would have never seen the inside of a courtroom and he'd be alive today."

Simon nodded slowly. "I think we've always known it. We just didn't want to see the forest for the trees. But—"

"I'm sick of the forest and I'm sick of the trees!" John yelled, sweeping his hand across his desk and scattering papers to the floor. "I'm killing him. FBI or not. I'm getting him. And he's going to know who and he's going to know why."

"You're just going to march into his apartment and shoot him, right?" Simon said sarcastically.

John, Jr. smiled. "Give me credit for being a little more sophisticated. A little more creative—"

"I'll be giving you cigarettes in the state pen, if you don't get the chair," Simon reminded, getting angry. "Do you think his apartment isn't monitored? Do you think his car isn't wired for security? Come on, John. He's off-limits. You kill him or even try and you'll get caught. We've always known it. It's why we never tried before this. It's why your father couldn't touch him. He's so up-front about who he's pursuing that even if his lover shot him in a fit of passion, you'd get blamed. If nothing else, they'd try to prove she was on your payroll.''

"I said I'd get him and I will," John said, casually gathering his papers from the floor. He was calm. Too calm. Simon didn't like it. Not one bit. "So the only question left is what."

"What what?" Simon asked, sighing.

John, Jr. rose from the floor. "What do we do with Linda Miller? Now that I've got her, what do I do with her?"

There were two tiny taps on the office door, and both Simon and John turned to see Amanda poking her head into the office. Because a year had passed, her hair was to her waist now. She wore a peach robe and slippers that looked like stuffed elephants. "It's bedtime. Nini said say good-night. Okay?"

"Of course, it's okay, pumpkin. Isn't it, Simon?"

"Absolutely."

Amanda grinned and darted into the room. Her elephant slippers made a definite thump and Simon smiled.

"How's my favorite girl today?" Simon asked as she jumped on John, Jr.'s lap.

"Good," she said, smiling sheepishly as she snuggled into John, Jr.'s neck.

"Amanda had a very busy day with Nini," John announced, referring to his mother the same way Amanda did, since she'd never quite been able to call her any of the traditional grandmother names. "They went to Pittsburgh to do their Christmas shopping."

"Ooooo," Simon said, then chuckled because this child had reduced two grown men to blithering idiots. Ever since the decision was made to keep her, Simon and John had been oohing and aahing and prone to baby talk. The funny part was, they hadn't minded.

"Story, Dad?" Amanda asked the man she had been told was her father. Despite the fact that she couldn't see John's mother as her grandmother, she easily allowed John Santos to assume the role of her father. A transition that solved a good many problems and saved Simon a lot of sleepless nights.

John, Jr. sighed. "Dad has a problem, sweetheart." He kissed her hair, then pressed the intercom button on the phone. "Josephine, would you please do me a favor and read my daughter a story tonight?"

"Yes, of course, Mr. Santos."

He disconnected the call and Simon smiled. "You're very lucky your cook loves children."

John, Jr. smiled wryly. "Don't I know it." He kissed Amanda's forehead and bounced her to the floor. "Go find Aunt Jo," he said, then kissed her again.

"Yes, Dad," she said, hugged him and ran around the massive desk to Simon. "Night, Uncle Simon," she said.

"Good night, pumpkin," he said, hugging her tightly. She bounced out of his arms, ran to the door and yanked it open. After sliding behind it, she peeked around one more time and waved and then closed the door behind her.

"Best move this company ever made, keeping that child."

"You'd never get an argument from me on that, John."

"I've got to get her a mother, though." He sighed heavily and once again leaned back in his chair. This time he closed his eyes. "Not only is single-parenting hard, but she has a very vivid recall of a blond woman...."

"Her real mother?"

John sighed again. "Yes. She mourns her loss just as strongly as if her mother really had died."

"That's what she believes."

"That's why it hurts her so much, she does believe it."

Simon shrugged. "Well, then, that's good."

"When she hurts, Simon, I hurt." He rose and began to pace again. "The way I have this figured, she'll mourn her mother's loss forever unless we get her a replacement."

"Uh-huh," Simon agreed. "That's logical."

John walked to the bookcase. "The only problem is I would have to marry the woman to make her Amanda's stepmother."

"Not necessarily. Hire a governess."

"The child needs the security of the commitment. Don't you understand what I'm driving at here?"

"So marry," Simon said, then shrugged. "Virginia Taylor's been angling to marry you for years."

John turned from the bookcase and fixed Simon with a killer glare. "I wouldn't let that woman within a hundred feet of my child."

Simon spread his hands helplessly. "Just a suggestion." He paused, considering, then said, "You're worth millions, you should be able to find a suitable wife in about a month."

"You mean buy a wife."

"So what? You find a woman who loves kids, somebody who's taken with Amanda, and if need be, you proposition her. You pay your cook, your driver...for heaven's sake, John, you even support your mother. Why not pay your wife?"

"It's tacky."

"Just think about it," Simon suggested, knowing that was the only solution. John, Jr. wanted a mother-wife now. So he'd get one. Hire one. Buy one. Despite his protests, that was how he did everything else. This would be no different.

"So do we settle the Linda Miller thing tonight, or do we sleep on it?"

John, Jr. walked to his desk. He picked up the photo and studied it for a minute. "No matter what they do to her, she looks the same to me."

"They changed her eyes. They changed her nose. Her jawline is totally different," Simon said, laughing. "She could have walked up to me on the street and introduced herself and I wouldn't have known her."

"No. No," John said, waving his hand. "I'm talking about...I don't know, something. Look at her. Look into her eyes," he said, tossing the picture across the desk. Simon took it. "She's so—I don't know, sweet or something."

Simon took a close look at the picture and realized what John said was true. She had that wholesome girl-next-door look. "I think it's her skin tone," he said, then laughed. "We sound like an Ivory soap commercial."

John took the picture again. "It's her eyes. Her eyeballs," he said, pointing at his own. "Something they can't change. The way she looks at people—" He stopped, pacing away from the desk again. "You know, Simon, in the courtroom, she kept looking at me and I couldn't help looking back at her."

Simon shrugged. "She's very pretty. You're very handsome. No big deal."

"No. No. It was more than that. The way she looked at me was like she knew me and couldn't believe I'd ever done anything bad. Never mind. That makes no sense."

"It makes sense," Simon disagreed. He was fighting for Linda Miller's life again. He could sense it. The right word, or the wrong word, meant life or death. "From my investigations, I gathered that she was just one of those naturally naive people who loves everybody—thinks the best of everybody."

"You don't like the fact that I'm persecuting her, do you?"

"I don't like to see anyone persecuted."

"What would you have me do? I mean, if you were me, would you let your father's death go unchallenged?"

Trick question. Simon knew that, but answered anyway. "I thought you were going after Rosen?"

"I am, but she has to make amends, too."

"Consider it amends that she's given up her friends, her family."

"She had no family."

"Maybe that's another reason to feel sorry for her."

John sighed heavily and took his seat. "In a way I do." He picked up Amanda's picture. "We're all casualties. Dad. Me—I'm different, don't shrug your shoulders and pretend you haven't noticed. I know you have. Dad's dead. I've changed. Amanda's lost her family. You're getting gray hair and Linda Miller's now—" He shuffled through the papers in the folder. "Linda Miller's now Linnea Graham. Not one of us is the person we were two years ago. We're all casualties."

There was no denying it. Simon didn't.

"One big happy family," John said, and leaned back in his seat, closing his eyes. "Caught in something that we can't control. We're all losers who can't stop the game because there's no way out. We're all in this for life." As John, Jr. said the words, Simon watched his face change. He watched his lips curve into a smile and his eyes light with laughter as he sat up again. "Ms. Miller lost her baby," he began, counting off his points on his fingers. "Amanda lost her mom. I gained a daughter and need a wife...." He trailed off, smiling, shaking his head. "I think we've just found our answer."

"But John—"

"Let's go get her. Maybe we can convince her to change her name one last time."

LINNEA GRAHAM PUSHED open the door of the enclosed stairway of her apartment building. Immediately dry cold air stung her face, but she kept going. This was very important to her. The highlight of her week.

She never realized the significance of rituals and traditions until she didn't have any. Christmas, Thanksgiving, Easter were just like any other day of the year unless you celebrated them. So, too, Sunday was just like any other day of the week unless you made it special. And that's why she was going out into the cold, across the street and through the park.

She paused at the intersection and looked for traffic. A slow-moving car approached and she unconsciously paced back. The closer it got, the slower it seemed to move, and the beginnings of panic germinated under the first layer of her skin. She took a deep breath, the car passed her, continuing its journey along the icy street, and Linnea casually looked for traffic again before venturing across the pavement to the park.

She wouldn't think about what had just happened, because there were no less than ten scares like that in any given day, but even that was good. There was a time when there were fifty scares like that a day, so she knew she was improving. She didn't look over her shoulder quite as much. She didn't question the motives of anyone and everyone who shopped in the same store she did, or shared the same street, or happened to have a similar schedule. As far as Linnea was concerned, she was doing very well.

Along the edge of the park the streetlights gave the impression of afternoon, but there were dark patches everywhere. Trees blocked the light; in some places there simply was no lamp for light; and in still other places shadows of buildings hung. Nonetheless, she entered the park, skirting a mound of snow to get to the sidewalk. She huddled her coat collar around her neck, then watched her breath curl around her as she slowly released it. She wasn't scared. She wasn't. And it was only because of exercises like this one that she was regaining her confidence and rejoining the land of the living.

The cold wind skimmed the pavement in front of her, and Linnea skidded on the glossy sheen it created. The trees were black-barked and leafless. The benches held little piles of snow deposited by the wind and then carved and shaped by the next hour's wind. Some places, the snow caught starlight or moonlight and reflected it back as crystal sparkles. In other places the snow was just as dark and lifeless as the section of the park in which it sat. Wire trash bins were empty because no one had ventured out since Friday, trash day. The only sign of life was the wind. A low-moaning, dry-ice wind that numbed your cheeks and paralyzed your lungs. Still she walked on.

Think of this as aerobics, she told herself. After all, her heart rate had increased and her blood was moving, just as she was moving. It was either that or freeze. So she was getting a workout, as well as exorcising her demons. This time next year she'd laugh about having to teach herself to step outside her door. This time next year, she might even have friends. In fact, that was her next goal. She'd subtly investigate a person or two, and if she liked and trusted them, she'd let them into her life. Then there'd be no need for pretend letters to Michael, because she'd be able to talk to a real person again. There'd be no more walking across cold parks to make herself feel as if she'd actually mailed her fake letter, even though she knew she couldn't. And there'd be no more staring at his telephone number, the private number she'd conned from his father's secretary, because her life would become normal again. All she had to do was make it through this one year.

Her favorite trash bin came into view. Like the others, it was empty save for snow and sticky garbage that had frozen to the wire bottom. The bushes clustered around it were bare. The trees on either side of the pavement were bare. And there was a bare circle around the bin itself, caused by the way the wind whipped around it... but, it was the end. The last bin before the street. She'd walked the length of the park. Safely... again. Things were really looking up.

She unfolded her arms and brought Michael's letter out from her armpit. She wanted to hold it to her face and sob bitterly, but she drew a shuddering breath and positioned her hands on either side of the envelope. This was always the hardest part. If she could bring herself to tear the letter in half, then she could tear it into shreds, and throwing it away was a breeze. But this, this first tear was so hard, because the envelope really did have his address on it and there really was a letter inside and she really did miss him... meant every word that was in that letter....

Rip.

She stacked the halves and pulled again, tearing the two pieces into four. She stacked those pieces and ripped them again. And again. And again. Then she released them. The shredded white paper fell to the bottom of the bin like so many snowflakes. She watched them break up and scatter. Then the wind danced through them, and some of them eloped with it, drifting off into the cold, silent night.

She took a deep breath, and the dry frigid air burned her nostrils, then her lungs. When she released her breath, it was a white cloud of moisture. She stared at the tiny pieces of her letter shivering at the bottom of the trash barrel, and as she watched them, the wind howled louder and harder than before. It pasted her jeans against her legs and bit her cheeks, and she realized her skin was as cold as the air. If she stayed out much longer, she'd be setting herself up for a case of frostbite. She turned, but heard a noise and spun back again.

The wind, she told herself, and almost pivoted away, but the same out-of-place rustle stopped her again.

That's not the wind.

You're paranoid. Just turn slowly and walk home.

She swallowed. She wanted to run, but couldn't because exertion in his kind of cold wasn't possible. If somebody was out there, even a mad rapist who didn't know John Santos existed, she was a perfect target. Cold, tired, emotionally drained.

Will you stop! Just turn around.

Put one foot in front of the other.

And go. Slowly, steadily get yourself home.

She started off slowly, but gradually her pace increased. The insides of her thighs were beginning to burn, and she told herself she was moving more quickly because she needed to get warm. The wind howled. A cloud rolled over the moon and darkened the world. A cold chill raced across her shoulders and tumbled down her spine and she swallowed. That wasn't from the cold. It was one of her instinctive early-warning signals of trouble. She told herself to ignore it and hurried on, slipping and sliding through the darkness. She almost wept when she reached the protective shield of a streetlight, and she did cry when she skidded across a patch of ice and fell. She scrambled to her feet without incident, but the hair on the back of her neck was standing on edge now and she knew why. They were there. Her apartment was just across the street and they were there. They knew where she lived. They knew who she was.

She commanded herself to run and barreled right into the waiting arms of a man who was two heads taller than she and padded with enough clothing that she felt as if she had hit a mattress.

She whirled, her feet slipped on the ice, and instantly she hit the pavement. Her teeth rattled in her mouth, and she felt the skin of her knuckles cracking from the cold. "Damn you," she said through a shiver of pain and cold and fear, then she tasted blood. "Damn you!"

She rolled to see her assailant towering over her, laughing. "I got her, Dick," he yelled, then bent to pick her up.

She bucked her head under his chin and rolled away, scrambling to get on all fours so she could right herself. Shivering, dragging cold air into her burning lungs, she darted toward the street. From the corner of her eye, she saw another man lunge at her from behind the bushes. The next thing she knew, she hit the pavement again. Every brittle bone in her body cracked as she hit the frozen cement with a thump. Knowing she didn't have time to count the damage, she rolled again, but before she could get away, her attacker crouched beside her and took her numb shoulders in his thick-gloved hands.

She kicked him where she knew it would do the most damage, and his yelp was lost in a howl of the wind. But she could see his lips as he cursed at her. She kicked him again, then butted her head into his belly and knocked him flat onto his back as she scrambled to her feet.

She ran across the street without looking for traffic. When she reached the apartment building, she yanked open the stairway door, ran up the steps then fumbled for her keys and unlocked her door. She got it open, fell inside and kept on running, knowing the lock would kick in automatically when the door slammed closed. Breathing so hard her chest hurt, she stumbled to her phone. She took only the time to peel off her gloves before she began punching out Michael's private number. This was the one she had memorized, and she didn't have time to look for Bunker's.

She heard the stairway door open.

The phone rang once.

"Please, please, please," she chanted, shivering, jumping from one foot to the other.

The phone rang again.

The heavy thump of footsteps sounded on her stairs.

She heard the click, click, click on Michael's phone as the answering machine began to take the call. And her heart stopped. He wasn't home!

Her attacker began to take slow, measured steps down the hall.

"Oh, dammit," she moaned, dragging air into her lungs at a rate close to hyperventilation, but the low, clear tone of Michael's voice, his rich baritone mumbling a request that she leave a number, had the strangest effect on her. Even without conscious thought, her breathing slowed to normal. Tears pooled in her eyes and for a second she stood mesmerized, just listening. She hadn't realized how very, very much she missed him until she got close enough to hear his voice, yet not close enough to talk to him.

Then she heard a thump in the hall as if her hunter were dragging his leg or using a cane. She took a deep breath. Her apartment door was locked and unless he had an ax he probably couldn't get in, but knowing the Santos people as she now did, she couldn't take that chance. Her shaking fingers reached to disconnect the call, but Michael broke into his recorded message and answered the phone in the last second before her finger made contact.

"Hello."

"Michael! Michael! Oh, thank God!" Shaking, she sat on the chair beside her phone table. Her apartment was still dark, she hadn't stopped to turn on a light, so she flicked the switch on the old-fashioned floor lamp, then put her hand on her galloping heart and took a deep breath. "They found me. I don't know how, but I can't think of anybody else who'd chase me through the park."

"Linda! Linnea! Linnea!"

"Michael, I can hear their footsteps in the hall," she said, calmed by the security of his voice. "You have to tell me what to do. Can I call the police? Or should I just sit here and wait for your people?" she asked, then looked up and froze.

"Okay, here's what you do," Michael said. "You call the police right now and tell them someone's prowling through your building. They'll check it out and that'll be enough to keep our friends away. Then you just sit tight and I'll come for you, okay?...Linnea? Linda..."

John Santos put his hand over the mouthpiece and smiled at her. "Tell him okay. Just say, okay."

She wet her lips as he put the phone receiver to her ear again. Then he pulled a small gun from the pocket of his overcoat and pointed it at her forehead.

She took a deep breath. "Okay, Michael," she said quietly.

"Call the police, then just sit tight and wait for me...got it?"

John Santos pushed the cold barrel of the gun against her skin. She wet her lips again. "Okay."

Chapter Thirteen

"It's such a pleasure to finally meet you," he said, and began unbuttoning his overcoat. She noticed that he didn't take off his gloves and knew it was because he didn't want to leave fingerprints.

"Well, the feeling's not mutual," she snapped, braver now that he'd pocketed his gun. It didn't matter if she was nice to him or insulted him to high heaven, the end result would be the same either way, and she wasn't going to give him the satisfaction of hearing her beg for her life.

He clicked his tongue. "Testy tonight." He threw his overcoat across the back of the flowered couch, then took a deep breath. "How about some coffee? We've got a long night ahead of us."

"If you want coffee, there's the kitchen," she said, crossing her arms on her chest.

"All right," he said, then smiled. "We'll play it your way. I'll make the coffee because I agree with you. Women have been an enslaved race for too long. Society's ignored your potential. But I don't, I won't."

She had a sneaking suspicion he was leading to a point, but she wasn't going to puzzle it out. The second he disappeared into the kitchen, she was bolting for the door.

"Do you have a coffee maker or do you use instant?"

"I have a coffee maker," she said slowly, carefully. She had to admit he wasn't as creepy as his father, but he was strange. Clean-cut and sophisticated, yet a cold-blooded killer. She couldn't, wouldn't, forget that.

"Fine," he said, then smiled again before he turned to walk into the kitchen.

She gave him thirty seconds, then sprang from her seat and ran to the door, thanking God that she hadn't taken off her winter coat and boots and that she hadn't locked the dead bolt. She grabbed the knob, whipped open the door and faced two tall, burly men standing on either side of her doorway like sentries.

"Close the door, Linda," John called from the kitchen. "Not only is it cold, but I'd prefer you stay away from that element of my staff."

Oh, Lord! She took a deep breath and began retracing her steps to her chair. When John Santos returned from the kitchen, drying his hands on one of her dish towels, she licked her dry lips. "Come," he said, jerking his head in the direction of the kitchen. "We have a good bit to discuss while we wait for Mr. Rosen."

She didn't even think of arguing, just rose and began walking toward her kitchen.

"Dispose of the coat and boots," he suggested, smiling again.

She sighed, but she did as she was told.

"Don't hang them," John commanded when she turned toward her closet. "I hope there's no weapon in there, but even if there is, I shouldn't have to remind you it's three against one."

She shook her head.

He smiled again. "Common sense. I think that's the thing I like about you the best. I'm thirty-six and I've dated a lot of women," he told her as he motioned her into the kitchen. "But do you know why I've never married?"

She shook her head again.

"Even though I genuinely believe women are the smarter sex, most of them lack common sense."

"It's not fair to make a generalization like that."

"I'm not really a fair man." He pulled a chair away from the table for her and she sat.

"Now, where is Mr. Rosen?" he asked as he reached into her cupboard for cups. After he closed the door, he took the dish towel and wiped the silver handle until it shone.

"I don't know."

"Oh, please. I watched you from the bathroom. You didn't even have to look up his number, you simply dialed. We know he's on his way, but I'd like to know how long it's going to take him to get here. So, where is he?"

She didn't say anything, just looked at her hands and he sighed. "Linda, I don't want to hurt you." The way he said *hurt*, raised gooseflesh on her arms, and she envisioned all kinds of tortures, but he surprised her and said, "So, the devil with Rosen. When he gets here he gets here. We have other things to discuss until he does."

Puzzled, she glanced up.

"Oh, we're waiting for him," Santos said, leaning against the counter as he crossed his arms over his chest. "You see, you may get to live, but he absolutely, positively, definitely cannot."

"What?" she gasped.

"We're going to kill your little friend tonight, and if you're a good girl I won't make you watch."

"You can't kill him! He hasn't—"

Santos laughed with evil delight. "He's in my way and I kill anybody who gets in my way," he reminded slowly but plainly, transforming into a being closer to his father than the sophisticate of a few minutes before. "There's a saying, 'Better the devil you know, than the devil you don't know.' Are you familiar with it?"

She stared at him, refusing to answer on principle, but oddly curious.

"Well, that's why my father kept Michael Rosen alive. He knew him, he knew how to handle him, how to fight him. Now, with my father gone, the business is different. More respectable."

"Oh, have drug dealing and prostitution been eliminated from your repertoire?"

Shaking his head, he laughed. "Such a kidder." The coffee maker groaned its final release, and he turned and took the pot by its handle. As he poured the steaming black liquid into burlap-brown mugs, he said, "I've also admired your sense of humor. Once, I believe it was in Toledo, you said something to him in bed—"

"You listened? You—"

"To every word in every town that we found you." He handed her a cup and she glared at him. "Oh, now, don't be dismayed. We're very good, but Mr. Rosen's usually better. We only caught you in two towns, and both times he craftily threw us off the track with pillow talk." He traced the crew-neck collar of her green sweater. "Most of the time, you never said a word. Making love seems to put you right to sleep."

She jerked away from him and threw him a foul look, but he only laughed. "Cream?"

"No. I drink my coffee black."

"I mean for me," he said, and walked to the refrigerator. "No cream, huh? Well, milk'll do." He pulled out the carton and returned to the table. This time he sat. "As I was saying, the business is different, more sophisticated, but not without a few structural deficiencies. This year I plan to clean house, and that may cause some hard feelings . . . or perhaps it may inspire fear.''

Curious again, she tilted her head and watched him as he reached for the sugar bowl.

''Mr. Rosen's name is a household word in my organization, and anyone who gets angry with me could find him—easily. Add what he knows to what an insider could tell him, and not only will my business be destroyed, but I'd most certainly go to jail.''

''I thought you dealt with traitors the old-fashioned way, you killed them.''

''We have to find them first.''

''Oh, so you really want to get rid of Michael because he's smarter than you are and if you clean house and somebody deserts, Michael's the only person who could hide them.''

''Don't speculate,'' John said, holding up a cautionary finger. ''The less you know—''

''Oh, cut the bull. You're only telling me to shut up because you don't want to hear the truth.''

He rubbed his fingers over his eyes. ''I'd forgotten what a sharp little tongue you have.'' He sighed and picked up his mug. But he didn't sip his coffee yet. ''Linda,'' he said, then pressed his lips together. ''I'm going to offer you a proposition. I know you're not going to like it, but you see, the alternative for you is death. Whether you like it or not, whether you admit it or not, I am holding all the cards.''

She didn't answer, just looked down at her own steaming coffee.

''Now, I realize that you don't want to betray Mr. Rosen, and I'm going to respect that by not forcing you to tell me where he is. So, that's actually an even bargain.''

She glanced up.

"Right?" he asked.

She reluctantly nodded.

"So, that gives Mr. Rosen something of a head start. He knows we're here with you, at least he knows we're in your building, but we don't know when he's coming. In fact, he could be bringing fifty agents with him. Or he could have called the bureau, and agents could be surrounding the building right now, with Mr. Rosen scheduled to arrive for cleanup. We don't know and we're sitting ducks. So, wouldn't you agree, that I'm spotting him points, giving him a fair chance?"

Once again, she nodded reluctantly, if only for the sake of getting him to move on. She didn't for one minute believe that he didn't have the deck stacked in his favor.

"So, now we bargain. I give Rosen the fair chance. In return, it would benefit me greatly if you'd tell me the name of Mr. Rosen's helper."

"He didn't have—"

"He had to have someone on the outside who bankrolled a good bit of your journey. There were times when it seemed as though you'd disappeared from the face of the earth. There were no credit card slips. There were no hotel bills. There were no reimbursement sheets turned in to the bureau. You could have stayed on the road, sleeping in your car, and I believe you did do that sometimes. But I think you stayed hidden because Mr. Rosen used another person's credit cards. You see, paying with cash makes you stand out in the crowd. And fake credit cards give themselves away, not to the hotel manager or gas station attendant, but to the people who compile your bill. So we'd have spotted a fake credit card or cards. Yet we never did. We only found you when someone actually saw you. So we know he had a helper. We know this helper let him use his cards and we know this helper wasn't within the bureau."

"No. You're wrong."

"Okay, I won't ask you to name names, just confirm our theory. Once we know that there was an outside individual who assisted Mr. Rosen, then we'll know how to combat that technique the next time around. If you tell us, we won't go searching for this person. We just want to be able to fight that technique the next time around."

She didn't believe him. She didn't know why or how, but she didn't believe him. But even if she confirmed his theory it wouldn't matter, because it wasn't a person, it was a company that had hidden them. Their credit card slips were lost in the expense sheets of not one, but ten buyers for Rosen Foods. In fact, confirming this theory would throw them off the track again. "If I confirm Michael had a helper—"

"Ms. Miller, you just did." He snapped his fingers. "Simon."

The word hadn't really passed his lips before she heard the sound of her closet door being opened. In the next minute a man entered her kitchen. She recognized him as the man seated beside John Santos, Jr. at the trial.

Protesting for the sake of realism, she sprang from her seat. "I didn't—"

"You did," John Santos said, turning to the solemn-faced man behind him. "Pool our people, get a name. Track their progress across the country and find a credit card with expenses that match that zigzag pattern of theirs. When you find that man, woman or child, shoot them."

"Yes, sir," Simon said, then pivoted and walked into her living room and began punching numbers on the phone.

She quickly turned her head so he wouldn't see from her expression how pleased she was that she had them barking up the wrong tree. With the way she and Michael went up and down and all around the country, even the busiest traveling salesman wouldn't have matched their trail. Santos and his people would be tied up for the next year looking for somebody they'd never find. And while he did that, the credits for Rosen Foods would sink deeper and deeper into the corporate pool.

Santos misinterpreted her action when she turned away from him. "I'm sorry I had to trick you, but I know you don't know the name, and I had to let you think you were bargaining. Otherwise, you wouldn't have told me anything at all." He sipped his coffee, then said, "Rosen wouldn't be stupid enough to let you see the credit card he used, and he certainly wouldn't tell you the name, because if you knew it, that would put you in danger.... You see, Linda," Santos said, then smiled. "I know you don't believe this, but he loves you. He really does. He's worse than me when it comes to disliking women, so the way he took care of you..." He paused, thinking. He sipped his coffee, then took her hand. "It didn't surprise me that he'd sleep with you. A man doesn't need to love a woman to sleep with her. But he risked his family when he took you to South Carolina. In a certain sense he chose your safety over theirs."

He was telling her things, giving her clues as to how he'd always stayed one step ahead of or one step behind Michael, depending on whether he was pursuing or being pursued. And if she could keep him talking, and then stay alive, she could pass all this information on, and maybe they could put this Santos out of commission, too. "But there was no one on the island. And if there would have been—"

"No, you don't understand. He never uses his family— never involves his family in his work. They're a separate entity, and thus protected because he keeps them ignorant and out of the way. Taking you to a family retreat opened the doors to limitless problems, accidental encounters being the most significant. He certainly didn't call his family and say, 'Stay away, I've got a witness at the cottage,' because then they're not ignorant anymore. So, somebody could have popped in and discovered you anyway. Even worse, we went through the house with a fine-tooth comb, looking for clues of where they'd sent you. We were there for two days, and again a family member could have stumbled onto us and we most definitely would have killed them. But everyone was lucky all the way around. No one barged in on your tryst. No one found us looking for clues. And the Rosen family continues to live under a blanket of blissful ignorance.''

''If you knew where we were, why didn't you just come and get me?''

''On the day after I vowed I'd kill you, in front of a courtroom full of witnesses?'' Santos laughed. ''Even if you had fallen off a boat in the middle of a storm, I would have taken the blame.''

''You could have hidden our bodies and no one would have known we were dead. They would have thought we were still running.''

''No,'' he said, and laughed again. ''I might have been able to kill you and get away with it, but not if I'd killed Rosen. He was checking in with somebody and that somebody would have pinned me to the wall.''

''If all that's true, what's different about this?'' Linda asked. ''Your goose is cooked now, too!''

''Really, Linnea Graham? If your car goes over a cliff, do you think the local authorities will alert the FBI?''

His reminder was like a pin in a balloon. Swift and sure, it hit its mark, and she deflated and dismally shook her head.

"And as far as Rosen is concerned, I'd be a suspect, but I wouldn't be the only suspect. And they'd have to prove I killed him."

"But if you kill him here—" she said, knowing she was buying time, knowing she was fighting for Michael's life "—and I die, somebody from the FBI's going to put two and two together."

He laughed lightly. "How stupid you must think I am! I don't want to kill you, remember? I'm giving you a chance to live."

He walked to the counter again and poured himself another cup of coffee. Simon entered the kitchen. "I'm taking Art and Dick and we're heading for Nevada. Let me take her, too," he said nodding in Linda's direction.

"No, no," Santos said, chuckling. "I'll need her when Rosen gets here. Besides, she and I haven't completed our business." He turned from the counter. "Has her car been taken care of?"

Simon smiled. "We did the brakes."

"That'll do it," Santos said, then faced Linda. "Now we deal. Simon?" he said, and motioned for his man to leave. Simon chuckled, shaking his head, and turned to go.

"Ms. Miller—"

Santos palmed his coffee mug, suddenly nervous, and Linda looked at him curiously as the light began to dawn for her.

He'd sent his men away. There could be others, but she didn't think so, because Santos probably suspected Michael would come alone if only to keep things low-key. He'd fly here expecting to find an entourage of criminals, and when he didn't, he'd think the police had scared them away and he'd skip right up the steps to Linda's apartment and John Santos's trap. Santos needed Linda here and alive to force Michael into a position of obedience because he didn't merely want to shoot him. He wanted revenge. He wanted a slow, painful revenge. He wanted Michael to know who was killing him and why. He wanted the ceremony. Just like his father. Or maybe for his father.

"This is so awkward. And I honestly never dreamed I'd be doing this." He stopped and sighed. "Linda, I have a child. A lovely four-year-old who needs a mother."

"You want me to be a nanny?"

He opened his mouth and looked as though he would contradict her, but he took a deep breath and said, "Well, yes and no."

"That's all?" she asked, even though she knew it was because that was enough to keep her under his watchful eye. The one he really wanted to punish was Michael, and she'd handed him to Santos on a silver platter.

MICHAEL ROLLED his rental car to a halt across the street from the building where he knew Linnea Graham lived. Reflexively he looked up and saw a second-story light was lit, then he glanced around, checking for his people, but he didn't see any. There wasn't a car on the street, a jogger in the park or a bum huddled in a doorway. It was the dead of winter and the dead of night, but neither was an excuse for not doing your job. And if he found those guys sipping coffee in the building lobby, he'd . . .

He pushed open his car door, cringing against the damnable cold and told himself not to get excited or jump to conclusions. The plan had been for everyone to sit tight. One agent was to make contact to be certain she wasn't in any immediate danger. That same agent would stay with her to protect her while the others guarded her building until Michael arrived on the scene. Michael would then call the cleanup crew. As her lover and her protector, his first thought had been for her safety, and he'd seen to it that she was in no danger, but nobody was supposed to move her until Michael gave the order. Still, there was always the possibility that someone got the instructions wrong, and instead of holding her they'd already shipped her out; perhaps the agents had gone with her, and the cleanup crew was using the light to pack what she needed and dispose of the things she didn't. And if that was the case, there was going to be hell to pay.

It galled him that Bunker got control and kept control, but Michael didn't feel he had the right to interfere. After all, Linda had made a choice and he respected it. She was young, beautiful and smart. She didn't need an old FBI agent mooning after her, pining for her. But tonight—tonight, she'd called him. When the chips were down, she'd called him. It wasn't an accident, it wasn't fear, it was instinct. Because she needed him.

Before pulling open her apartment building door, Michael looked around one more time. If that was the cleanup crew upstairs, there'd be a van on the street or in the alley. There'd be men trooping down the stairs with boxes and bags and suitcases and such. It would be quiet, but it would be busy, yet there wasn't a soul around him.

He took his hand off the doorknob and sucked in his breath. His lungs nearly collapsed from the frigid air, and he expelled it quickly, glancing around again. The other possibility he'd neglected to ponder was that Santos's men had taken care of his agents before they'd secured the area. If Linda never got to call the police, then Santos wouldn't have been chased away and Michael's unsuspecting four men could have arrived on the scene, only to find Santos's men were waiting for them. And if that was the case, the cleanup crew would still be in the local office, waiting for a call. They were not the people in that apartment.

Swallowing, he shoved his gloved hands into his trouser pockets and walked to the corner of the building. He glanced down the alley. There was no van, just a long, empty corridor, a steel fire escape that screeched in the wind, and one big trash bin. Even the stray cats were in for the night.

If the cleanup crew was done, the apartment light would be off. If the cleanup crew was still here, then there'd be a van around somewhere. And if the cleanup crew hadn't gotten here yet, then there should be agents jogging, huddling and otherwise occupying themselves while they watched this building, but they weren't around, either.

Quick as lightning, he jumped into the alley and flattened himself against the brick wall. It looked as if the entire plan had fallen apart in the three hours it took him to get here, and though he couldn't be sure, he couldn't be stupid, either. He took a deep breath and considered the two alternatives. If the Santos group was waiting for him, it was in the lobby of the apartment building. They could be expecting him to just sashay up the walk and open that apartment building door, and when he did, he'd be riddled with bullets. That was the good option. Because if they weren't waiting for him, if he opened that apartment building door and found no one, if he jogged up those steps without being shot, if he got to her apartment, opened her door and wasn't confronted, then what he'd find would be the mutilated body of the only woman he'd ever loved.

He licked his dry lips, tasting fear, tasting hate. He couldn't think of a reason to leave the light on if they'd already killed her, but then again nothing any Santos did would surprise him. And if they'd killed her...

He took a deep breath to calm himself and estimated that he'd been on the scene for about five minutes. If they were waiting for him, they might already know he was here. And if they knew he was here, they would have killed him, no questions asked, because they knew who he was and they wouldn't give him the opportunity to defend himself. So, since he hadn't been shot at, they obviously hadn't spotted him yet, which meant no one was in the alley. He eyed the screeching fire escape, thinking, then glanced around again. If he was going, it would have to be now.

He jumped up the first two steps, and the wind absorbed the noise of his footfalls. Even with his heavy bulk weighing it down, the aging stairway rattled and shook in the strong gusts, but Michael took it as good fortune, because the same wind that was freezing his fingers through insulated gloves was also protecting him, camouflaging his noise, and once again he took the steps two at a time, until he reached the lighted window. He flattened himself facedown on the landing right next to the snow-covered sill, knowing his black jacket and jeans would blend into the background darkness and his movements sounded enough like the wind that they wouldn't draw attention, either. He closed his eyes and took three deep breaths, preparing himself for the worst, the sight of Linda dead in her kitchen chair, then licked his lips and prayed for the first time in years.

When he opened his eyes, he lifted his face and peered in. A brown-haired, thin-nosed Linda was seated on a wooden chair, but she was talking. Her eyes, those undisguisable baby blues of hers, were narrowed, and every time her new nose wrinkled, she stabbed her finger at the air in front of her. Michael breathed a king-sized sigh of relief but didn't relax, because the man she was pointing at, arguing with and in general tormenting was none other than John Santos himself.

He drew another gulp of air and slid, inch by inch to the window. He belly-crawled all the way, brushed the snow from the sill and examined the wood. It was an old frame, but it seemed to be in good repair. If it wasn't locked, he should be able to open it. That is, if he could get a good grip on it without standing.

He couldn't.

Disgusted, he crawled beside the window so he could sit where he wouldn't be seen. Half of him wanted to kick in the glass and then jump through the window like Superman, the other half knew that was a stupid plan. He put his elbow on his knee and his forehead on his fist and gritted his teeth. Like it or not, he was going to have to get Linda's attention.

He rolled to his belly again and was just about to tap on the glass when she saw him. Her eyes widened dramatically, but she quickly looked away so Santos wouldn't follow her line of vision. She took a breath and peeked at Michael again, glanced at Santos again, then jumped off her seat and began shouting.

"You're an idiot," she stormed, running to a part of the room that Michael couldn't see. "Scum. Do you hear? Scum! There's no way..."

Michael knew what Linda was doing. She'd gotten herself and her captor out of the way, at the same time that she took Santos's attention long enough that Michael could break the window and jump in. Smart kid.

He rolled again, angled his feet and kicked in the glass. It crashed and tingled and made all kinds of noise, leaving only one nasty jagged piece that Michael would have to avoid. He took another second to reposition himself, then jumped into her kitchen.

"Rosen! I should have known."

Linda had apparently been pummeling his chest, because Santos had a hold of her wrists as if he'd been trying to stop her. When he saw Michael, he released her one arm, spun her around and twisted her other arm behind her back. Even as Michael went for his gun, Santos brought one out of his jacket pocket and shoved it at Linda's temple.

Michael froze, feeling stupid and inept.

Linda, however, had played out this scenario a hundred times in her head. She thought of all the stupid plans she'd made, she thought of the things she'd yelled to television victims in similar situations, she thought of how one false move would make this maniac shoot her, and she realized she didn't care if he shot her. If she could get his attention long enough that Michael grabbed the advantage, then even if Santos shot her, Michael would get away. She decided to faint, and she let her body get limp and heavy, even as she rolled her eyes back in her head and moaned lightly.

Santos lost his grip on her arm and she hit the floor, but she heard a shot and screamed instinctively as her eyelids sprang up again.

"Damn you!" Santos hissed, blood oozing between his fingers.

Even as Santos fell to the floor beside her, Michael ran to her, pulled her to her feet and began running to the door.

"He's bleeding pretty badly, but he's only wounded," Michael shouted. "So go!"

"Why?" she asked, turning. "He's out cold."

Michael turned, too, and when he realized she was right, Santos was out cold, he marched over, crouched beside him and began checking for a pulse.

Both fell silent, then Linda said, "Is he dead?"

"No. The wound's only superficial. He must have fainted. Probably when he saw the blood," Michael said, then took the revolver from Santos's hand. He ran his hands over specific areas of Santos's body, obviously looking for another weapon. Then he rose and dusted off his hands before he pulled a set of handcuffs out of his jacket. "My guess is he'll be out for a while," he added as he stooped again. He rolled Santos to his stomach and pulled his hands behind his back. "I'm going to call an ambulance."

The cold winter wind invited itself in through the broken kitchen window, and it wrapped itself around Linda, chilling her as much as the sight of a motionless John Santos. Hugging herself, she waited as Michael spoke with the dispatcher for the ambulance, but after he disconnected that call, he began dialing again, and from his conversation, she knew he'd called a group of agents who were waiting somewhere close by. He explained what had happened, why they hadn't gotten the call to come sooner, and told them to hurry because Santos needed medical care and an ambulance had already been called. Then he reminded them that it would be smart to have at least two agents accompany Santos to the hospital just in case somebody tried to stop the ambulance. Before he hung up, he told his people to be careful because he hadn't secured the area.

"They'll be here in about three minutes," Michael said, holding her coat that he retrieved from the back of the couch where John Santos had told her to set it because he wouldn't let her open the closet. "Then we have to go."

She took her coat from his hands and slid into it. "I guess I better get my boots, too."

"It would help," Michael said, smiling.

Disoriented and tired, she walked out into her entrance hall where her boots stood beside the door. When she looked at her boots, the boots John Santos forced her to remove as another precaution against her attempting escape, it hit her that Michael didn't realize John Santos was alone. "You know, he had about four people with him, but the one guy came in and announced that they were all on their way to Vegas."

"So, you think there's nobody else around?" Michael asked curiously.

"I know there's nobody else around," she said.

"I don't know, Linda, I still think—"

She sighed. "He wanted privacy. So he sent his men away."

Michael frowned. "Privacy? I don't understand."

"Not only did he want to kill you personally, but he..." She cleared her throat. "There were certain things he wanted to talk to me about."

He leaned on the doorjamb. "Like what?"

She sighed. "He asked me to marry him."

Michael burst out laughing. "That would have been cute."

"No, I'm serious. He has a four-year-old daughter and he sort of wanted a nanny, but he wanted a nanny that would be more like a mother..." She trailed off, sighing again. "It would have been a nightmare."

Michael shook his head. "Linda, John Santos doesn't have any kids. He's never been married."

"That's funny," she said, and pulled on her boot. "He showed me a picture of this cute little girl. And he told story after story. Amanda's got the most beautiful red hair in the world. Amanda's smart as a whip. You'll love her. Amanda loves stories. *Winnie-the-Pooh* is her favorite right now. Amanda's got thirty bears."

"Linda, the man does not have any kids. How could he?"

She pulled on her second boot. "I don't know how, but he has a daughter and her name is Amanda. He specifically called her his daughter...wait," Linda said, sighing with impatience at her own stupidity. "You can see for yourself. There's a picture in his pocket."

Michael rolled Santos again and searched his suit pockets. Even as he pulled a handful of assorted items from Santos's breast pocket, the wallet-sized photo tumbled out of his vest. Michael scooped it off the floor and hardly glanced at it before he drew a sharp breath. "Oh, my Lord! This isn't John Santos's kid. Linda, this is Bill Washington's granddaughter."

"Let me see that."

Before she could take the picture from his hand, Michael rose. "Linda, I've looked at this picture six hundred times. I'd know Bill Washington's granddaughter anywhere. Even if they dyed her hair purple. Did he tell you where he has her?"

"Yeah, at his house in Harrisburg. But—"

She stopped talking because Michael wasn't listening. He ran into the living room and grabbed the phone. "This is Rosen. Ship about six men to John Santos's house in Harrisburg. He's got Bill Washington's granddaughter...." He paused. "Of course, I'm sure. Just get going. Now! Santos has been shot and he's out cold. But if you wait, the word will get out to his people and they'll move her! So go!"

He hung up the phone and turned to her again. "I can't believe this. Do you realize that once they positively identify Amanda as Bill Washington's granddaughter, Santos is as good as convicted. Which is really good news for us, because now we're out of it. If he's convicted of kidnapping, he'll get a stiff enough sentence that we won't have to testify about any of this." He moved his arm in a semi-circle to indicate the messy room.

"Yeah. That's good."

In the silence that followed, the wind rolled in through the broken window, causing Linda to shiver. Still hugging herself, she sat on one of the chairs by the kitchen table, and Michael sat on the radiator by the sink.

"We thought for sure that kid was dead."

She glanced at Michael. "No, she's alive and well and he loves her very much. I can't count the number of times he called her adorable."

"The fact that she's adorable probably saved her life."

He shook his head, sort of smirking, and Linda said, "What?"

"It's funny. That one slip. That one sliver of humanity is what's going to put him behind bars. We tried for years and years and years to put him away for all the corrupt things he did, and his one and only humane act is what's going to send him to prison. Isn't life ironic."

"Yeah. It is."

There was a two-minute silence, then someone yelled. "Rosen, it's Pete!"

"It's clear, Pete," Michael answered, and rose from his seat on the radiator to answer the door.

"Ambulance get here yet?" Pete asked as he holstered his gun.

"Not yet," Michael answered, leading the man into the kitchen where Santos still lay unconscious.

Pete stopped to look at Santos's wound. "You hardly scratched him. Musta fainted because of the shock," Pete said, and rose again.

"Look, we're going," Michael said, and reached for Linda's hand. "Neither one of us wants to be around when he comes to."

"Yeah, yeah, okay," Pete said, waving a hand. "Just check in with Bunker when you put down roots."

"Got it," Michael said, and began hurrying Linda out the door. They ran the length of the hall and down the steps, then burst out the front door. When they reached the sidewalk, they didn't look before they crossed the street, they just kept running, but when they got to a midsize black car and Michael opened the door on the driver's side, Linda stopped him.

"I have a really great idea."

"Not now!" Michael thundered, and tried to shove her into the car.

"No, listen," she said, bracing her hands on the door frame so he couldn't push her inside. "You're in bigger trouble than me." Because he quit pushing her, she turned to face him. "They've decided they're cleaning house."

"Could you tell me this later? When we're in a warm room, when we don't have to worry about Santos's men returning?"

"No, listen," Linda said again. This time she grabbed his hand. "You are in more trouble, because John Santos wants to clean house and the first person he's getting rid of is you. So you have to hide out as much as I do now."

He sighed. "That's nice to hear."

"Well, actually, it's not as bad as it seems. I have a plan." She said, squeezing his hand. "What if we make it look like we decided to take my car, not yours?"

"Your car?"

"It's in the lot behind the building. Santos cut the brake lines or something so I couldn't escape.... So, if they think we took it, we could roll it over a hill and they'd think they killed us."

"The death scenario..." He sighed. "I don't know, Linda."

She hit his arm. "You dope! We don't have a choice."

"Oh, I agree with that part. It's just that you heard them say they'd cut your brake lines. Aren't they going to think we're pretty stupid—"

"Or scared? They could think I was too scared to remember the brakes were cut on the car."

He sighed again.

She punched his arm again. "Darn it! Listen to reason."

"Okay, but here's how we do it. You drive my car, I'll take the one with the bad brakes. I'll get it over a hill while you sit with your feet under a heater. Is that understood?"

She nodded.

"Okay, where can we roll this over a hill so it'll look like an accident?"

"We're in luck. Not three miles out of town we can roll that car over an embankment, but the best part of it is, there's a nasty curve in the road. We can make it look like we slid on the ice and couldn't negotiate the curve, so we went over the hill."

"We'll have to call—"

She grabbed his forearm and stopped him. "Not Bunker."

"No, not Bunker," he said quickly, instinctively, then he seemed to catch himself. He looked at her oddly, as if he were looking at her for the first time, or maybe as if he were looking at a stranger he didn't trust.

The expression on his face was a manifestation of the realization that they weren't the same people they were a year ago. The Linda Miller he loved and trusted didn't exist anymore. Even if she could pick up where they left off last year, he couldn't. "We don't exactly have time to ponder this,'' she said, huddling into her coat, feeling a cold that had nothing to do with the weather.

He nodded and ducked her head before he pushed her into his rental car. ''Wait for me to get your car from behind the building, then head for that place with the curve and the embankment. We'll figure the rest out later.''

Chapter Fourteen

A cloud moved across the moon, and the wind was an angry god now. Without brakes, Michael didn't drive over fifteen miles an hour, so Linda reached their destination more quickly than he did. She sat warming her hands while she waited for him, watching his headlights in the darkness of the long strip of road before the curve.

It had taken Linda only a minute of the ten-minute ride to figure out what she was going to do. All plans and promises made a year ago would be canceled. She hadn't saved his life to trap him in a relationship he no longer wanted. She angled her toes closer to the warm air blowing out of the vent as Michael whipped open the passenger-side door of his rental car and jumped in.

"Before we do this, I've got to ask you something."

"Shoot," she said, rubbing her hands together as she shivered inside her jacket. She hoped, for both their sakes, that they wouldn't actually talk about parting. And as she waited for him to ask his question, she decided that when the conversation went in the direction of what-do-we-do-next, she'd simply talk about her plans in the singular, then inquire about his. That would not only avoid a scene, but it would get him off an uncomfortable hook.

"What did you mean when you said you didn't want Bunker involved in this?"

She took a deep breath. "Just that. If there's a way around it, I don't think we should tell him."

"Why? Did something happen? Did he do something?"

"Are you going to run off on some macho tirade if he did? If you're only asking because you want to sock him in the mouth, then you're going to be disappointed."

He sighed. "No." He tapped his fingers on the armrest. "What happened?"

"Actually, nothing. And everything. I never felt safe. Never. Not once. I constantly told myself it was old fears resurfacing, or that I was just a chicken, or that it was natural to be scared, but I'd get these horrible feelings all the time. And I'd see guys watching me from behind newspapers every time I found a new home and there'd be odd phone calls...."

"What kind of phone calls?"

"The telephone would ring and no one would be there, or I'd be asked to participate in a survey that made no sense...just odd things. Now, why did you say something about Bunker?"

"Because..." He stopped, tapped his fingers on the armrest again and then sighed. "Because he wouldn't tell me anything. It was admitted, acknowledged, understood that I was the Santos expert, yet he never once asked me for advice about where to hide you."

"Are you sure you weren't just being oversensitive?" she asked, hiding a smile.

"He didn't have to take my advice, Linda. And I could have given him three or four different places to hide you, and there was no reason he'd have to tell me which one he chose, but he never asked me anything. And in September..." He paused again, sighed again and tapped the armrest again. "He bought a Porsche."

"Not exactly the affordable car of the normal FBI agent?"

"He said his mother's sister died and left him a small fortune. Turns out his mother's sister did die, in a rest home, penniless."

She gasped. "You investigated your boss?"

"And he wasn't even smart enough to realize I would, or maybe he didn't care if I did because he's been doing things, saying things to make me look... Not crazy, just too emotionally involved, and no one pays a whole lot of attention when I question the things he says or does. Anyway, he bought a Porsche, made up a lie and didn't cover his tracks. But he probably thought he didn't have to, because you were safe. There wasn't any reason for anyone but me to suspect him of anything. He is—was—the best and you were living, breathing proof of that. Until tonight."

He sighed. "He's not a bad cop. In fact, my guess is he wasn't dealing with Santos at all. Otherwise, he wouldn't have gotten involved. No, I'd say whoever was paying Bunker never expected to use the information. They had no intention of killing you, and Bunker must have known that, and that's why he freely—"

"Sold the information to one of Santos's employees," she said dismally, once again realizing there was no one, not one soul involved in her life who couldn't be bought.

"Probably Simon. Not-So-Simple Simon we call him."

"The guy in the closet," she muttered, then bit her lip. She was going to have to save herself, protect herself, and she realized that learning to play the game entailed more than doing what she was told. She was going to have to get as smart as Michael about Santos and his people, because this time tomorrow she'd be on her own.

"He's underworld through and through," Michael said, "but he's got a soft spot for women and a real hang-up about violence. In the bureau, we used to guess he worked for Santos because he wanted to reform him."

"Yeah," Linda said, thinking back, remembering the two minutes or so she watched him after he popped out of her closet and as he looked talking on her phone. "Santos himself is kind of crazed... strange... odd... but this Simon was like a walking notebook or something."

"He's always been the Santos right-hand man. Administrative assistant of sorts because he's an organized, thorough person. And he doesn't steal their thunder by using violence. He goes the distance through normal channels and if he fails he asks for help from one of the family. Then lets them do the dirty work because they enjoy it. But he won't watch, doesn't even listen to the gory details. That's why he wasn't in Bob Bingham's office. Anyway, my guess is Santos assigned Simon to be in charge of the search for you, and Simon, knowing how far he can push his boss, bribed Bunker by promising to keep the information out of Santos's hands. So Bunker must have figured it wouldn't matter if he sold the information, they weren't going to use it."

"Until now, because they're cleaning house, changing because John, Jr. wants to run a different business than his father did." She bit her lip. "Michael, it's you they want."

He sighed. "I always knew it would come down to this someday."

Looking down at her hands she said, "I'm sorry."

He shrugged. "It's certainly not your fault. This has been a long time coming."

"Yeah, I guess," she said, and part of her was comforted because logically she knew he was right. "So now what do we do?" she asked softly, dreading his answer but realizing it was time to make a break. A good, clean break wouldn't hurt so much.

"Now, we roll your car over that hill and then shove my glove into the gas tank, light it and run like hell."

She waited for him to continue, but he didn't say anything else. "That's it?" she asked, confused. "Don't we have to call somebody and tell them what we're doing? Who's going to... how will we..."

He rubbed his hand over his face. "We'll definitely have to involve somebody. At the very least, we've got to get birth certificates, drivers' licenses and a credit history." He stopped and sighed. "But whoever we call has to be somebody we can really trust. This is going to have to be a clandestine kind of thing, something we do almost by ourselves. It's a pretty sure bet Bunker's on Santos's payroll, and even if he's not, I'm not willing to take the chance of trusting him one last time to find out if he is or isn't. We'll have to find another person, somebody else who's on the inside, take this person into our confidence, tell them our suspicions about Bunker, and hope he believes me enough to risk his job to help me."

"That sounds like a pretty shaky plan. Isn't there another way? Can't we just go over Bunker's head? Go to his superior with our suspicions and ask him for help?"

Thinking, he pressed his lips together. "You have to understand that Bunker's got his own hide to protect now that you're no longer safe. Not only is he going to look suspicious to the bureau, but if we get away, then he's in trouble with the mob."

"So he's going to be snooping—"

"Looking in trash cans, breaking into confidential files, the works. And he is the master. Once he found us—and he would—he'd be able to rig your death in such a way he'd make Santos happy and the Bureau proud. And I'd just happen to die in the line of duty."

"Rats."

"Yeah, rats."

"What about your father? Can we call your father?"

He shook his head. "My family will have to think I died, too. That's what's going to make this death scenario believable. Everybody knows how close I am to my dad. Nobody would ever suspect I'd just pretend to be dead unless I told him. He's always been my fail-safe mechanism and he's always known it. He's never liked it, but he doesn't have much choice, considering the alternatives."

For a minute she sat quietly, remembering the sad look in Matthew Rosen's eyes and finally understanding it. "Then how are we going to rig this?"

"Well, we're going to leave circumstantial evidence. Like, I'll unscrew your license plate and toss it beside the car where it will get discovered, but it won't get burned. Then we'll have to hope they think we were burned to ashes, or maybe hope they don't find the car for a couple of weeks."

She hit his arm, trying to knock some sense into him. "Michael, that's not at all convincing! We'll never be safe! We'll never be free!"

"I know, but it's the best I can do without a support staff and on such short notice."

"Don't you have a friend—somebody else in the bureau who could do all the things we need done? Make calls."

"I have lots of friends, but they're also friends of Bunker's. And he's been discrediting me, making me look overinvolved, overly suspicious. Sort of crazy for the past year. There isn't anybody who'd believe me over him... except...except! Oh, this is perfect!''

"What? What?"

"Well, there's this new agent. He's an accountant. One of those guys you ship in to do an audit to look for discrepancies."

"Oh, great. He sounds like a lot of help."

"No. Listen. He likes me, loves me, thinks I'm some kind of hero." Shaking his head, Michael started to laugh. "He joined the FBI because his life as an accountant was really boring, and then he discovered that the FBI wanted him to do basically the same things he'd been doing for private industry. Anyway, he'd do this, not just because he idolizes me, but because it's the kind of thing he joined up to do. He'd think it was interesting, spylike. And he doesn't trust Bunker either." He snapped his fingers. "I think we've got our man."

Linda just looked at him, twisting her lower lip between her teeth. "Are you sure he'll know what to do?"

"I'll tell him what to do. As soon as we take care of things here, I'll call him and tell him to get his tail out here to oversee the local officials when they file their reports about discovering the car."

"I still don't understand."

"Well, he'll fly out here tonight, have a meeting with the head of the local law enforcement agency, the coroner and probably the fire department. That's depending upon what time he gets here. He's not going to get here on time to actually set things in motion at the scene. But he will get here in time that news of our deaths can hit the local paper by Tuesday's edition."

"It's going to be in the paper?"

"It has to be in the paper. This entire community will have to believe beyond a shadow of a doubt that there were people in the car. So my friend is going to have to get on the phone while the car is still burning so that the hints we drop will be picked up and used. So, take off your earrings and give me that necklace. You know what the best part of all this is?"

She shook her head as she began undoing the clasp of her necklace.

"Because my friend will keep all this a secret, the bureau won't find out about our deaths until Bunker reads about it in the paper, and he'll think Santos did it, because the bureau didn't do it. But because Santos didn't kill us, Simon will call Bunker, thinking the bureau did it to hide us again, and because Bunker's on his payroll, he'll expect Bunker to hand over the information. But Bunker doesn't have any information to hand over. And since Bunker was in charge of the case but he didn't hide you, and he can't find any evidence of bureau involvement, then Bunker, Santos—everybody—will think we slid on the ice, speeding to get away, and rolled over this hill. And we're home free!"

He stopped and gave her that odd look of his again and glanced out the window. "The only problem is, then what do we do once we're free?"

She glanced out the window and licked her lips. Now that the time had come, she couldn't get her mouth to say the words that would take him off the hook of the promises he'd made the last time they faced this situation. Fine white snowflakes had begun to fall.

"Your hair's brown," he said, and she felt his fingers filter through it. It was shoulder length and poker straight, so when he picked it up and let it fall, it fanned before it hit her shoulder again.

She turned to face him and smiled. He was putting off the inevitable, the last goodbye. And she'd join him for a minute or two, to enjoy his company and sort of savor a private minute, but she wasn't going to make this difficult. There was no sense in prolonging the agony. "I see yours is getting a little gray."

"I wouldn't doubt it," he said, then laughed. "Though I don't know why I worried myself gray. From the look of you tonight, I think you could handle just about anything."

"Don't kid yourself," she said, and glanced away again. "What I did tonight was a fifty-fifty gamble. If Santos had expected anything from me, it would have been another silly heroic stunt. So, I did the unexpected, that's all. He fell for it."

"No, you fell, gravity pulled him with you, and I shot him in the shoulder so we'd have time to get away. Another good plan from—"

Her eyes narrowed. "You did that on purpose? You only shot his shoulder because that's what you were aiming for?"

"Yep."

"Michael, that man has vowed to kill you!"

He shrugged. "You never told me that until we were outside. Which takes us back to the beginning. What are we going to do with the rest of our lives?"

She took a deep breath. At least he wouldn't feel guilty when they parted. She'd already proven she could take care of herself, now she'd prove she could support herself too. "Well, in another year I get my degree. I take a few tests and I'm an architect. The only thing I haven't figured out yet is what name to put on my diploma."

"You're that close?" Michael asked, amazed.

"I didn't have much of a social life. I took extra classes every semester. Went to school through the summer." She shrugged. "You know you can get credits by taking tests to see if you already know the information to be taught in the class. I took a few and passed most of them and got the credits without taking the courses."

He whistled. "Well, you're one up on me. When I get out into the cold, cruel world, I'm without a skill—unless, I get a job as a cop in a small town."

"You're going to settle fights between schoolboys and rescue the kittens of cute little girls for the rest of your life?"

"No, I have a different scenario in mind. Linda, come here," he said, and patted the seat beside him.

She swallowed. "No, this is okay."

"At least move out from under the steering wheel." This time he used the tone of voice she hated and loved. The one that said he wasn't taking no for an answer.

Reluctantly she scooted beside him. He put his arm across the back of the seat, and she looked down at her hands.

"Been pretty lonely over the past year, huh?"

She nodded.

"Lonely enough to decide you love me?"

She licked her lips. "I always loved you."

"And I always loved you, too."

"No, you didn't. You felt sorry for me."

"Don't put words into my mouth. I never, ever, said that. I loved you enough to give up my life for you—"

"But you didn't have to." She faced him then. "Don't you see? I didn't want to feel guilty for the rest of my life. I didn't want to feel that you'd made a horrible sacrifice for me."

"But it was okay for you to make that sacrifice for me tonight?"

She looked down at her hands again. "I don't have a family. I never had a family, never had anything to lose. You would have lost everything."

He hooked a finger under her chin and lifted her face until she was looking at him. "I think you have this whole thing backward. I lost everything when I lost you, not the other way around."

"I'm sorry," she whispered, ridiculous hope welling up inside her as what he said sank in by degrees.

"You ought to be," he said, then bent and brushed his lips across hers. His mouth was warm and firm and she melted. Her eyes drifted closed. Real blood began to pump through her veins again. Life didn't seem like a blank page anymore.

"But you will be punished."

She blinked open her eyes and pulled away from him. "I will?"

"That's the totally different scenario I was talking about. You see, the way I have this figured, I'll be a cop to support you while you get your degree and your license. Then, I'll quit working and go to school and you can support me."

"You want *me* to support *you*?"

He punctuated the thought with a quick, smacking kiss. "Precisely," he said, and smiled. "That's give and take. Focused goals. Marriage is supposed to be like that. But you know that, you're the one who wanted to write the book."

Her eyes narrowed. "Are you making fun of me?"

He shrugged. "I don't know. From where I'm sitting, it's pretty silly that a smart woman—especially somebody who thinks they know so much about compromise—could run off in the middle of the night, without a discussion, without even an hour to cool off, without time to think her decision over. Seems to me that person shouldn't brag.''

''You louse! Just for that, I will write a book.''

''Uh-uh-uh, low-key, remember? We can't do anything stupid like become famous movie actors, or rock stars or even published writers. You never know who you'll meet at a book signing.''

''I only said I was going to write the darned book, I never said I was going to get it published.''

''You know, I think you really are getting the hang of this.''

''Honey, not only do I know how to play the game, but I think I can teach you a thing or two, so don't . . .''

He kissed her then, long and hard, as if he'd been starved for the taste of her.

And she wrapped her arms around his neck, breathing in his scent, tasting his mouth, feeling a hundred kinds of happiness she never knew existed.

''Never leave me again,'' he said, then kissed her softly, tenderly.

She pulled her mouth away, but hugged him as though her life depended on it. ''I won't.''

He kissed her one more time, then smiled at her as he pulled his glove from his pocket. He dangled it in front of her nose. ''Got a match?''

Harlequin Intrigue®

Nicole had a second chance... to live.

One moment Nicole was standing in the deli's doorway, smiling at the handsome oceanographer. The next, she reached out to stop the gunman who'd jumped out of the rain-shrouded Manhattan day.

But when Nicole awoke, it was early morning August 30, a full week earlier. Had she been dreaming? Doubt grew stronger as the day unfolded—a day she remembered before it had even begun. Then she again met the oceanograher—David Germaine—and her world shifted on its axis.

David was her desire, her destiny, her only hope of averting disaster. Could this memorable stranger help her reverse fate? Meantime, dark forces gathered....

Don't miss this exciting Harlequin Intrigue coming this July wherever Harlequins are sold.... Watch for #142 *Déjà Vu* by Laura Pender!

HI-142-1

Harlequin Superromance®

A June title
not to be missed....

Superromance author Judith Duncan has created her
most powerfully emotional novel yet, a book about
love too strong to forget and hate too painful to
remember....

Risen from the ashes of her past like a phoenix,
Sydney Foster knew too well the price of wisdom,
especially that gained in the underbelly of the city.
She'd sworn she'd never go back, but in order to
embrace a future with the man she loved, she had to
return to the streets...and settle an old score.

Once in a long while, you read a book that affects you
so strongly, you're never the same again. Harlequin is
proud to present such a book, STREETS OF FIRE by
Judith Duncan (Superromance #407). Her book merits
Harlequin's AWARD OF EXCELLENCE for June 1990,
conferred each month to one specially selected title.

S407-1

Take 4 bestselling love stories FREE

Plus get a FREE surprise gift!

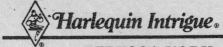

REBECCA YORK

Labeled a "true master of intrigue" by *Rave Reviews*, best-selling author Rebecca York makes her Harlequin Intrigue debut with an exciting suspenseful new series.

It looks like a charming old building near the renovated Baltimore waterfront, but inside 43 Light Street lurks danger . . . and romance.

Let Rebecca York introduce you to:

> *Abby Franklin*—a psychologist who risks everything to save a tough adventurer determined to find the truth about his sister's death. . . .
>
> *Jo O'Malley*—a private detective who finds herself matching wits with a serial killer who makes her his next target. . . .
>
> *Laura Roswell*—a lawyer whose inherited share in a development deal lands her in the middle of a murder. And she's the chief suspect. . . .

These are just a few of the occupants of 43 Light Street you'll meet in Harlequin Intrigue's new ongoing series. Don't miss any of the 43 LIGHT STREET books, beginning with #143 LIFE LINE.

And watch for future LIGHT STREET titles, including #155 SHATTERED VOWS (February 1991) and #167 WHISPERS IN THE NIGHT (August 1991).

HI-143-1